The Senses Bejewelled

The exquisite but cold-hearted Roxelana
pushed Marietta down with the pointed toe of
her shoe then straddled her. Marietta
struggled but was pinned by the weight on
her outstretched hair.

'You wretch!' she cried, trying to twist free.
'Let me up and we will see who is mistress
here.'

Her lips whitened with fury but she could
do nothing save gaze between Roxelana's
parted thighs. The flame-haired woman spread
them wider, affording Marietta an intimate
view of her moist treasure. She seemed to
take a perverse pleasure in displaying herself.

'Like looking, do you?' she jeered. 'Look
well. This jewel is a seat of power. The means
by which a woman can gain control over a
man but, of course, you know that. You have
been well trained for pleasure, have you not?'
With this, she thrust her hips back and forth
in a grossly lewd manner.

Things were obviously going to change in
Kasim's harem ... but Marietta was not
altogether looking forward to the new regime.

The Senses Bejewelled
Cleo Cordell

BLACK LACE

Black Lace books contain sexual fantasies.
In real life, always practise safe sex.

This edition published in 2004 by
Black Lace
Thames Wharf Studios
Rainville Road
London W6 9HA

Originally published 1994

Printed and bound by Mackays of Chatham PLC

ISBN 0 352 32904 1

Chapter One

Marietta wandered amongst the stalls of the souk, examining the goods on display and delighting in the noisy bustling atmosphere.

Hooded black robes swathed her from head to foot. Long black gloves completed the apparel. All that was visible behind her mask of jewelled leather was the glint of her sky-blue eyes. Leyla, her companion, was dressed in similar fashion. The prized favourites of Kasim Dey's harem never went out dressed any other way.

Harem guards accompanying the two women, hovered at a discreet distance. The common folk stared openly at Marietta and Leyla, trying for a glimpse of pale, pampered flesh. Marietta was unaware of the scrutiny. She smiled behind her mask as she thought of Kasim.

He would be back today from a business trip. How had she borne his absence? He had been gone for three weeks. And he would be as hungry for her as she was hungry for him. In the six months since she had risen to her position as favourite he had sought her out almost every night. This was their first real separation.

Her body felt starved for him. Mentally she felt incomplete. What had she been before Kasim? It no longer mattered. Marietta de Nerval, the aristocratic, spoiled, French woman from Martinique was no more. She was simply Marietta, the willing, adoring slave of Kasim.

There was no focus to her days without the regime of discipline which he had imposed. She knew now that she needed a master to impress his will upon her and punish her so deliciously. Only then, could she express the dark sensuality of her nature. Kasim knew her so well, was so cherishing of her most secret desires. Ah, Kasim.

Marietta turned at the light touch on her arm and smiled at Leyla. A flush rose to her cheeks as she recalled their shared pleasure that morning. While sunlight streamed in through the latticed windows she and Leyla had lain in intimate embrace on a low, silken divan. Leyla had sighed and clutched at her hair while she solaced her with lips and tongue, finally bringing her to a peak of pleasure with one of the exquisite toys, especially fashioned for that purpose.

She fancied that she could still taste the sweet, intoxicating musk of Leyla. True, Leyla was sweet as a candied peach and highly skilled in the arts of giving pleasure. But this day Marietta longed for the harder touch, the subtle masculine smell, and the enigmatic presence of Kasim.

'These are beautiful, my treasure,' Leyla said in her soft husky voice. 'Their colour is for you, no?'

Marietta picked up the strand of amber beads which had a heavy clasp of worked silver set with coral. She ran her gloved fingers over their polished roundness. The stall-holder began his banter. Marietta smiled, hardly listening as he held up other ropes of pearls and polished glass set amongst beads of carved silver. She pointed at the amber necklace, beckoning an attendant close to pay for and collect her purchase before she moved on. Two guards stood nearby, arms folded. Others slouched against the liveried carriage, which stood some way from the main souk. Their faces were red as they sweated in the heat.

Marietta thought with longing of the interior of the harem. It was always cool. Perfumes of roses and lilies wafted in through arched windows, which opened onto the gardens. There would be iced sherbet to drink and slaves to wave peacock feather fans, should she wish for a cool breeze.

On her return to the harem she would visit the bath house, the hammam, and prepare herself with special care, have the attendants oil and polish her skin and dress her in scanty garments of fine gold chain and silks. As always her 'golden fleece' as Kasim called her pubic curls, would be left visible. It was the part of her that so fascinated him. Never, he said, had he seen such pale hair, so soft and silky, a perfect foil for her neat little sex.

A shiver of anticipation passed over Marietta as she imagined Kasim's starkly handsome face, his cold dark eyes, that glittered when he was aroused. There was a feeling of weakness in her belly at the very thought of positioning herself as he required. She knew the posture so well now. Kneeling, her thighs wide apart, so that he could see every detail of her secret pink crevice. Her shoulders back so that her breasts were thrust into prominence. She loved to be displayed so submissively, her body on view and open to his every wish.

Perhaps he would spank her lightly, or order her to do him some service, before he thrust into her at last. The thought sent a warm pulsing to her nub of pleasure hidden within its folds of tender flesh.

Lost in erotic imaginings Marietta hardly noticed that she had moved away from the stalls and was

3

approaching one of the narrow dark alleys that bordered the souk on all sides. Leyla turned towards her and waved. She was holding up a sparkling rope of blue glass. Marietta waved back and blew the older woman a kiss.

Only Leyla's sloe-like, dark eyes were visible through her black leather face-mask. The rest of her slender white face with its exotic features was concealed. Marietta imagined the full red mouth curved in a smile. How many times had she kissed that mouth and felt those lips moving over her flesh, teasing and sucking, drawing out subtle gradations of pleasure? Leyla had been strongly drawn to Marietta from the first and she found many ways of expressing her desire and admiration.

The months in the harem had made Marietta's body into a finely honed instrument of pleasure. She needed physical release now, like she needed food. Oh, how wise Kasim was to have seen that desire in her. It was incredible that she had fought him for so long.

The shade within the alley was pleasant. Two guards lounged, one either side of the entrance, leaning against the white-painted bricks. Marietta ignored the smell of urine and rotting food. A skinny dog gulped down a pile of offal. The thin cry of a child came from an open doorway.

Suddenly there was a movement in the shadows. Before Marietta could react something loomed towards her.

A blanket, rough and fusty smelling, was thrown over her head. The leather mask was knocked from her face. Strong arms encircled her body. She was lifted and borne away at speed. Dimly, she was aware of shouts, the sound of fighting. Someone screamed. Leyla? Marietta struggled and kicked, but it was no use. Her breath was squeezed out of her.

Her feet dragged on the cobbles. One of her shoes came loose.

The blanket pressed closely to her face. She could not breathe. Then she was lifted high and flung forwards. Something hard and broad met her stomach, winding her and causing her to cry out. The high pommel of a saddle pressed into her side. Her abductors were mounted. She heard someone curse, then there came a jolt as the horses moved.

She moaned with pain as her stomach ground against the horse's back. The heavy robes and the blanket were stifling. If she was not allowed up soon she would suffocate. A heavy hand on the small of her back steadied her as they swiftly threaded through the narrow streets and alleys, the shod hooves clattering on the pebbles.

Shouts and screams accompanied their passing. She hardly registered that whoever had captured her had a great deal of nerve. They were either very brave or stupid. No one she could think of would dare steal Kasim Dey's most treasured possessions. She gritted her teeth and comforted herself with the thought of what Kasim would do when he found out that she was gone.

He would scour the narrow streets, offer a reward for her and Leyla's return. Those who captured her would pay dearly for the insult. Through the gnawing pain in her stomach, she smiled grimly; whoever you are, you will pay with your life for this outrage, she thought.

Then the terror swept over her and panic sent the darkness to claim her.

Marietta half sat up. It was dark, evening. Her stomach felt as if someone had kicked it. She rubbed her eyes and looked around.

'Marietta! Oh, thank the Gods. I thought you were dead. You were so pale and still.'

5

'Leyla! You are unharmed? But where are we?' Marietta realised only then that her feet were shackled.

She and Leyla lay on the banks of a canal. Both of them were secured to a wooden post set in the ground. The smell of water and mud clogged her nostrils. A number of cloaked figures stood some way off. There was no sign of the horses.

'I heard them talking,' Leyla said. 'We're to travel by barge.'

'But where are they taking us? Who are they?'

Leyla shook her head. 'I know not. But one of them is a woman. She gives the orders. What can they want with us—' She broke off on a sob.

Marietta took Leyla's hand and drew her close. They clutched each other for comfort.

'We're about to find out,' Marietta said shakily, as a tall slender figure walked towards them.

'So, you are conscious,' the figure said, throwing back the hood of its cloak to reveal a female face.

'You!' Leyla said, in a shocked voice.

'Ah, you remember me beautiful Leyla. It was my pleasure to chastise your unwilling flesh. You were so rebellious. So long ago now . . . No matter. This other does not know me, of course. Kasim has never sent her to the stables for punishment. He preferred to keep her all to himself. It is said that he could not even bear her to be displayed on the public punishment block. He rescued her and carried her back to his private apartments. The hand that tames her must be his alone, eh?' Sita's lip curled as she glared at Marietta. 'She must be special indeed.'

Marietta looked up at the hard-faced woman. 'Why do you wish me harm? I do not know you.'

'I am Sita, captain of the female guard. You, I have seen often, walking in the gardens, flaunting your beauty in the bath house. And beautiful you are indeed. You could turn any man's head.'

6

Sita reached out to fling back the folds of Marietta's hooded robe. Marietta's silver-blonde hair tumbled around her shoulders.

Marietta huddled close to Leyla. She was stung by the hatred in Sita's voice. She did not recognise this woman. The female guards were all dressed alike and rarely spoke to the harem inmates. She could not have put a face to any one of them. How could she have stirred Sita to such emotion?

'Stand up!' Sita rapped. 'When the barge arrives you will be taken to the dwelling place of my new employer, Hamed. But first those who helped me to capture you will have their reward. It is not often that common men set eyes on the spoiled and pampered beauties of the harem.'

There was hardly time to register Sita's words. The six men advanced on Marietta and Leyla. Marietta shrank back as she realised what was about to happen.

'No! Please let us be!' Leyla gave a little cry of distress as two men laid hands on her while a third unfastened the shackles from her ankles.

'Over here. By the lantern,' one of them said. 'I want to look at what I'm getting!'

The others grunted with laughter as they dragged Leyla and Marietta into the pool of light. Marietta struggled, but she was no match for the three men who held her.

Sita stood watching, her face severe, her narrow eyes glittering as the men pulled the all-concealing black garments from the women. Underneath Marietta wore only a breast halter of thin silk and wide-legged silk trousers. Leyla wore a low-necked tunic and full skirt.

'Do as you wish, but do not hurt or mark them,' Sita ordered. 'Hamed is paying us well. If his goods are damaged you will lose your ears and tongues as well as your money.'

7

One of the men sniggered. 'Don't worry lady. I intend no harm. I like my women angry but willing!'

The other men laughed as he reached a hand inside Marietta's breast halter. Marietta closed her eyes as the man's hands roved over her body. His touch was rough but not cruel. He tangled his fingers in the waistband of her trousers, then the cool night air met her skin as the thin silk was torn aside. Underneath she was naked.

'Let's see,' one of the other men pushed close.

'You want to see?' the first man said. 'Then look your fill, friend. Let's see what's so special about this one. Then watch how I'm going to pleasure her, the finest of Kasim's harem. Oh, I'll make her buck and squirm. See if I don't. Haven't I got the same equipment as our revered Dey?'

Marietta bit back a cry as she was pushed forward so that she was leaning over a wooden rail. One man grasped her hands and pulled her arms straight out in front of her. Another kicked her legs apart, then secured her ankles to the rail posts.

She was acutely conscious of her semi-nakedness. Her bared buttocks were open to view while the ripped silk of her trousers flapped around her legs. Her breasts hung forward, spilling out of the halter which she still wore. Shame and humiliation flooded her as she felt someone tear the flimsy halter away and massage her breasts with a broad strong hand. Someone else put their hands on her bare buttocks and dragged them open.

They commented on the hair on her pubis. Exclaiming in surprise, it being customary to remove the hair of the sex organs. Marietta cringed from their crude laughter, their mocking voices as they praised her beauty.

'Ah what a prettily shadowed fount of delight. How sweet smelling and rosy-petalled.'

'Which is Kasim's chosen portal, d'you think? This pretty purse or the tight nether-mouth?'

Tears filled Marietta's eyes as she felt their eager fingers examining her. The whole of her flesh valley was stretched and opened. She felt her sex lips part and gape. The tight brown rose of her anus was pulled open slightly. Her teeth clenched on a groan. Although Kasim loved to expose her in this way, to use strokes of a thin leather switch to punish her sex and draw a sweet spiked pleasure from her, she hated the thought that these coarse and common men could use her so crudely.

'So moist and inviting she is. A plump and tender little sex. And that hair. Most unusual in colour and texture.'

Marietta squeezed her eyes shut as her pubic curls were tweaked and tickled, but not before she had seen that Leyla had been made to lie on her back in front of her. Though they held her down, they took care not to hurt her. The sight of her companion's body, so open and vulnerable sent an almost unbearable pang of erotic pleasure through Marietta's body.

The rippled waves of Leyla's black hair formed a pillow for her to lie on. Leyla's full breasts, with the large, wine-red nipples looked so helpless and delicious in the lamplight. Her tunic had been pushed up to lie in folds around her neck and the full skirt was bunched at her waist, leaving her belly and white rounded thighs naked. Her thighs were parted and pressed in towards her chest, so that her full rounded buttocks were upturned. Leyla's sex, denuded of hair and exposed by her position, was examined and praised as Marietta's had been.

Marietta was ashamed at the rush of heat to her groin. Leyla's eyes had been wide, dark pools in a white face. One of the men was pinching Leyla's nipples and running his hands over her voluptuous body. Leyla began to moan, softly at first, then with obvious pleasure. Marietta opened her eyes and saw that one of the men was kneeling between Leyla's widely spread knees. Another kneeled at her far side. He was rubbing at Leyla's mound, his fingers slipping up and down the naked flesh-folds. The second man put his fingers into his mouth to moisten them, then smeared the spittle over his erect cock.

'Watch your friend. It'll make you wet for me,' the man who stood behind Marietta said. 'Just you relax and imagine I'm some rich pasha come to sample the delights of the harem!'

He rubbed himself against her. She felt his shaft, hard and hot as it nudged at her buttocks, sliding up her parted valley.

Marietta wanted to look away, but she could not. The sight of the other man's member now sliding in and out of Leyla's horribly exposed vulva was madly arousing. The first man was rubbing her pubis in circular motions, now and then dipping a finger down to the crevice that clung to his companion's cock-shaft. His thick fingers pinched the moist folds, while his companion groaned and urged him to smear Leyla's moisture up over her straining bud.

'Aren't I good for you?' he leered, thrusting deeply, his buttocks clenching tight.

Leyla had thrown her head back and was working her hips back and forth. There was a sheen of sweat on Leyla's top lip. Her full, red mouth looked like a bruised rose.

Marietta licked her lips, confused by her arousal when fear and panic was souring her stomach. Her sex grew hot and slick as she watched the men servicing Leyla. Inflamed by the same scene, another of the men unfastened his trousers, caressing his cock as he watched his companion thrusting into the helpless woman.

Marietta saw the man's loose foreskin slide back to expose the moist glans. It glistened in the lamplight.

She felt a perverse urge to feel the cock in her mouth. She imagined drawing it deeply into her throat and sucking on the salty swollen tip. Now the third man knelt down next to Leyla. He pressed his penis-tip between her lips. With a little moan of distress Leyla opened her mouth and stretched her lips around the shiny glans.

Marietta squirmed. Her sore stomach grew taut as the man behind her inserted two fingers deep inside her vagina. She could not hold back her response. Sinking down onto his hand, she ground her hot wet flesh against him. If she had not been so starved for a man's touch, she might have resisted. If the men had been more cruel or vicious she could despise them. But they held her with a kind of unwilling reverence as if she was made of the most precious fabric.

The way they held her, used her, reminded her in some indefinable way of Kasim. She wanted to hate what was being done to her, but she could not. It was all so horribly arousing. Even the fear added its own note. Her body, conditioned to accept pleasure and pleasure-pain, seemed to act on its own accord.

The fingers inside her were gentle, knowing. The knuckles rubbed against her pouting flesh-lips, growing wetter with her moisture. She only just contained a cry of disappointment when the hand was withdrawn.

'There now. See, I told you I'd not hurt you,' the man whispered. She felt him nuzzle her neck, kissing the tender spot behind her ear.

As his rigid member slid inside her at last, filling her and thrusting strongly, one of the men fell to his knees and began suckling at her breasts. He grabbed them in both hands, dragging them together, mouthing the swollen nipples, then pinching and rolling until she gasped with the hurting pleasure of it. To her intense shame she worked her hips back and forth as the men took turns at her.

She did not know which one it was but one man waited for her pleasure to build as he took her, holding back until she shuddered and cried out. Then he rode her strongly.

'That's it. There's no shame in giving in to it.'

Sobbing and fighting herself, she reached a climax twice before he drew out of her.

Sita watched in silence. Her narrow, hard face was flushed. She watched as each man took turns in pleasuring himself with both Marietta and Leyla. She smiled thinly at the evidence of Marietta's pleasure; her breathless little moans, the way she thrust her hips to meet each new invasion.

'You can't help it, can you? You're shameless. Disgusting,' she ground out. 'Kasim's pampered pets. He's worked you well, shaped you for pleasure so that you respond to whatever is done to you. It's not natural to feel so much . . . so much enjoyment.'

Marietta heard the notes of envy and frustration in Sita's voice, underlying the scorn. You wish it were you, she thought. She lifted her head and caught Sita's eye. Marietta's eyes burned into the female guard's face. I know you, they said. And Marietta knew too, that Sita understood the gesture perfectly. She had hurt the female guard and she was glad. It was a small victory, but she revelled in the sight of Sita's shuttered face; her lips which resembled a thin white line, the narrow eyes glittering with admiration and dislike.

Marietta was afraid for a moment that Sita would strike her, but she stood her ground. Sita's eyes seemed to bore into Marietta's skin, watching, measuring. She shook with suppressed emotion, but the female guard was far too disciplined to give way to careless action.

When the last man had finished using Marietta,

Sita walked across to where Marietta was slumped forward over the wooden rail. Marietta trembled all over. It seemed that all her muscles were taut and aching. She hung over at the waist, her wide-apart ankles still secured to the rail-posts. Her pale hair had come free from its combs. It spilled forward to brush the grimy cobblestones.

Marietta's fingers plucked at her ripped halter, but it was ruined, useless as a covering. Pressing her hands against the rail she struggled to stand up. Her thighs were smeared with male fluids and her own creamy, inner moisture.

Meshing her hands in Marietta's tangled curls Sita dragged her head back and stared into her tear-stained face. The silver-blonde hair spilled over her arms.

'Still beautiful, even smeared and stinking of sweat and sex,' she said with surprise.

With her free hand she stroked Marietta's sore breasts, then slapped them so they trembled. Marietta gasped at the stinging pain. With restrained violence Sita moved her hands over Marietta's back and between her thighs.

Marietta flinched away as Sita examined her womanhood, but she could not avoid Sita's cold, hard touch. Sita was rougher than the men had been, pinching the swollen lips between finger and thumb until the engorged flesh throbbed and burnt with pain. She rubbed a slick, careless, finger over the flesh-hood covering her pleasure-bud, then pinched it between finger and thumb. Marietta steeled herself not to react, though she could not contain a moan of distress as Sita worked the little flesh-hood forward and back until her abused bud was once again erect. Marietta bit her lip. Her thighs shook with the effort of holding back her pleasure.

Then Sita plunged her fingers deeply into her, twisting and probing

Marietta's flesh convulsed helplessly around the fingers. She tried to pull away, but Sita placed one hand on the small of her back, holding her down as she continued her investigation. Marietta could not contain a sob of outrage. Incredibly, she reached a third climax, even though she fought the melting sensations that flooded her. She hung her head, hating herself for responding to Sita's callous invasion.

A spasm passed over Sita's face. It was almost as if she felt a reflection of Marietta's tremors of release. Then she resumed her usual severe expression. She drew her hand away at last, smiling thinly. Then she bent and kissed Marietta's mouth, probing between her lips with her tongue.

'You taste sweet too,' she whispered. 'Later it will please me to chastise you. Or to have you pleasure me. But I do not relish used goods.'

She turned to the men. 'Clean them up.'

While they ran to carry out her orders, Sita stroked Marietta's hair, gently now. 'You're not hurt are you? Perhaps your pride is, but what of it, eh? I wanted to see if you famed beauties were as hot and well-trained as I'd been told. I was not disappointed. Hamed is sure to be pleased with you. Perhaps now I understand why he wanted you.'

Sita stepped away from Marietta as one of the men swabbed her buttocks and thighs with cold water. The feel of it on her sore and heated flesh was wonderful. Marietta dried her eyes and stood up shakily when she was set free. She pulled the ruined clothes around her.

'Enough,' Sita snapped as the men took care to see that Marietta and Leyla were comfortable. 'No need to fuss over them like old women! Cover them with their cloaks. It is time we left. Here is the barge. Secure them in a cabin and guard the door.'

Marietta and Leyla were bundled aboard the barge

and forced to go below deck. Huddling together in the tiny cabin, tied hand and foot, they watched the dark water slide by. Leyla was weeping with fear and reaction.

'Oh, those coarse men! How dare they! They are pigs, not fit to kiss our feet. And Sita, she enjoyed seeing us humiliated. I hate her!'

'It could have been worse,' Marietta whispered soothingly, though she shuddered as she recalled the feel of Sita's thin, cold fingers inside her body.

'Sita can mean us no real harm, or we'd be dead already. Someone has paid her to abduct us. And she'll guard her investments well. She spoke of one – Hamed?'

Leyla hung her head. 'Just his name makes me tremble. He is Kasim's bitterest enemy. His reputation is fearsome.'

'But who is he? What grudge does he hold against Kasim?'

'Hamed was a pirate. He and Kasim crossed swords more than once. Now Hamed resides in a stronghold and lives on the fruits of his crimes. They say he is very rich, but he has not been seen for many years. Some say he is horribly mutilated.'

'Saints preserve us!' Marietta cried. 'What will become of us?'

It was morning by the time the barge drew into its mooring.

Mist clung to the dark water's surface. A watery sun cast a diffused orange light onto the surroundings, illuminating a sprawl of hovels and a wooden bridge that looked as if it would collapse into the water at any moment. Rearing up in front of the barge was a smooth high wall. Two balconies enclosed in cages of decorative wrought-ironwork bulged out over the canal.

Marietta woke abruptly as Sita came into the cabin.

15

Next to her Leyla woke and stretched, then remembering where they were her face clouded. She strained against her bonds and reached for Marietta's hand, just managing to brush fingertips with her.

'How touching,' Sita said with mock pleasantry. She cut the ropes that bound the two women. 'Hurry now. Hamed's servants await.'

Sita waited while Marietta and Leyla stretched their cramped limbs, then pulled the remnants of their ruined clothes around them. Her narrow eyes flickered over their partly clothed bodies, lingering on Marietta's high breasts and smooth limbs. Marietta kept her back turned to the female guard, but she could feel those pitiless eyes boring into her back. It seemed as if Sita was itching to lay hands on her again, but did not dare. Fastening her hooded garment Marietta stood up.

'Follow me,' Sita ordered.

'We have little choice,' Marietta said tightly, trying to quell the sick feeling in her stomach.

Sita smiled her cold narrow smile and held the door open. Her chin dipped in a mocking little bow. 'You should remember that fact. Hamed is a powerful man and quick to anger. It will serve you well to appear docile.'

Marietta had hardly time to register that Sita might be offering good advice before she and Leyla emerged, blinking into the brightness of the morning. She looked up at the skyline where the bulk of an ancient castle's walls formed a jagged outline. On the muddy banks of the canal a richly-woven carpet had been spread. Two cloaked figures stood waiting. Hoods covered their heads, but by their height Marietta knew that the figures were male. Both were tall and powerfully built.

As Marietta and Leyla drew close, Marietta detected something familiar about one of the figures. It was the way he stood, a certain assurance in his bearing. This man, the taller of the two by half a head, was wearing deep-brown robes. He took a step nearer as Marietta and Leyla paused and came to a halt on the carpet. As he moved the hood slipped back a little to reveal a strand of fair hair. The second figure, wearing embroidered robes of dark blue put out a hand to restrain the taller man.

The hand was large but well-shaped. On the third finger was a gold ring set with a single cabochon ruby.

'The honour is mine,' the owner of the ring said to the man in brown robes.

The voice was deep and rich, infused with an easy air of command. The taller figure paused obediently. He stopped and stood with his head bowed slightly.

Marietta was intrigued. There was a glint of gold thread on the dark-blue robe. As the figure moved towards her she caught sight of the ornate clasp at his throat. He was well-dressed for a servant. She decided that this man must be a highly placed individual. The master of the harem perhaps.

As he approached the figure made a gesture and Marietta and Leyla found pressure exerted on their shoulders so that they sank to their knees. The carpet was soft underneath them. A hand on the back of Marietta's head ensured that she found herself looking at a pair of red, tooled-leather boots.

'Show me,' came the command, delivered in the same rich tones.

The dark robes were pulled from Marietta's shoulders to fall in a heap around her, leaving her clothed only in the scraps of torn and soiled silk. Marietta heard a sharp intake of breath.

The man in the brown robes spoke for the first time. 'What happened to them?' he said. 'Have they been harmed?'

That voice, well modulated and with the trace of

an accent. It seemed familiar. Yet Marietta could not place it.

'Explain. Why are their garments shredded?' the other servant said imperiously, throwing back his hood.

'They were torn in the struggle when we captured them in the souk,' Sita lied smoothly. 'This one fought dearly for her freedom. She is as spirited as an Arab mare.'

Marietta felt the tension in the air. She did not think the well-dressed servant believed Sita. She chanced a covert glance upwards and saw that Sita was perfectly composed.

The servant, now bare-headed, was a man of middle years. His face was handsome, broad and strong-featured. Thick wavy brown hair winged back from his high forehead. There was a smudge of grey at each of his temples. His eyes, brown also, were wide-set. There was a fierceness to those eyes. This was a man who would not countenance disobedience.

Marietta shivered at the way he was looking at Sita. For a moment longer Sita suffered that penetrating gaze, then she flushed and lowered her eyes.

'The men deserved their reward,' she said sullenly.

'They will be paid in full. You too,' the servant said in a voice that dripped ice.

Slowly he circled the two captives. Marietta, head bowed, was conscious of his eyes on her as he walked around her. He lifted a strand of her hair, letting it lie across the palm of his hand and slipping it through his fingers appraisingly.

Then the large manicured hands slid across her shoulders and up the column of her neck. The ruby in his ring brushed against her skin. It was warm from the heat of his skin. A finger, placed under her chin, urged her to lift her head so that she gazed into his face.

18

'Such eyes! Blue as the faience tiles on my chamber walls. And her skin is as pale as a pearl.' The servant turned to the man in dark-brown robes who stood by motionless. 'You did not lie. This one has beauty indeed. She is just as you told me she'd be.'

Marietta was astonished. The servant spoke as if she had been expected. She had supposed her capture to have been random, an act of revenge against an enemy. Now she wondered if she had been singled out. The thought was indeed alarming.

The man in brown robes murmured something in a low voice. Again she felt a flicker of recognition. There was an indefinable – something, about him. She wondered if Leyla also sensed the tightly leashed impatience contained within the watching, silent figure.

Heat rose in Marietta's face as the servant assessed her feature by feature. She tried to keep her gaze steady and not betray her fear. She remained still as he walked around to her back and paused.

At his gentle touch on her waist she almost flinched. Enclosing her waist in both hands, the servant began to squeeze. He gave a satisfied grunt.

'You were corset-trained from a young age?' he addressed Marietta directly for the first time. She felt the vibration of his deep voice like a caress.

She nodded. His hands felt warm and strong on her bare flesh. The pressure of his hands increased until his fingers met. At the instant before the pressure became unpleasant he released her.

'Excellent. Stand please.'

She did as he asked, confused by his polite, almost impersonal manner. This was not as she had expected. The servant knelt down, his deep-blue, embroidered robes pooling around him. The sun struck glints from the gold clasp at his neck. She felt his hand close around one ankle. He lifted her foot and began to examine it minutely.

19

His voice soft and husky now, he spoke as if to himself.

'Ah, yes. A lovely, high-arched foot. And slender too. Excellent. Small neat toes, each one perfect. Nails like shells. Silky skin. What a delight.'

He examined the other foot, stroking softly between her toes, so that she shuddered slightly. His forehead creased with intensity as he rested the sole of her foot in his palm. He paused for a moment and she heard the in-rush of his breath. Recovering swiftly he traced a fingertip along the bluish veins that showed through the soft skin at the side of her foot. After a moment he rubbed at a rough spot on her heel.

'Well now, we must attend to that tiny imperfection at once,' he said as if happy to find something that needed attention.

When he had finished his examination he bent and pressed his lips to Marietta's ankle bone before setting her foot to the ground. She sensed his reluctance to relinquish his hold on her. For a moment longer he stroked her slim calves, fingering the sensitive skin behind her knees. It seemed that he held himself back deliberately from doing any more.

She was confused. This man did not act like a servant. He was altogether too self-assured, even for a harem master. His manner was that of a voluptuary – something not in keeping with the position she had judged him to occupy. It was obvious that he had derived an almost sexual pleasure from handling her feet.

The man took a step back and Marietta composed herself for the intimate examination to come. She closed her eyes, willing herself not to react when he ordered her to lie on her back and spread herself. But it did not happen. He seemed to know what she expected. He gave a short humourless laugh and motioned for her to relax. There was to be none of the crude fingering, the rough handling of her breasts and sex. She felt relief wash over her.

The servant turned his attention to Leyla and went through a similar ritual. Marietta found the whole thing puzzling. What manner of man must this Hamed be to employ such an oddity?

When the cursory examination was finished, the robes were replaced about the women's shoulders. Marietta was aware that the taller figure, wearing dark-brown robes, was still studying her intently. She had felt his gaze on her since the moment she alighted from the barge. Under his close scrutiny she began to feel uncomfortable.

There was an air of menace about him. She could sense it as if it were visible, like smoke rising from a fire. He had watched, in almost total silence, while the other man examined them. Suddenly the thought struck her. Of course, this must be Hamed, cloaked and hooded to hide his disfigured features. No doubt the servant had instructions not to make too intimate an examination. Hamed would be reserving that delight for himself. Marietta felt her stomach clench with revulsion.

Hamed must be hideous indeed if he would not reveal his face.

And she and Leyla now belonged to this monster. Leyla had told her that Hamed was Kasim's sworn enemy. How better to wound one's enemy than by hurting the things he loves best?

When the handsome, bare-headed servant turned and led the way to the stronghold the robed figure waited and fell in behind her and Leyla. Marietta walked forward haltingly towards the gate that led to their prison. Everywhere there were armed guards. Sita glanced at her once with mock pity.

The soft footfall of the robed figure behind them might have been as loud as a skin drum, the way it

21

echoed inside her head. Her knees were shaking so much that she could hardly walk.

Kasim knew that something was wrong the moment he set foot inside his house. He was not unduly alarmed, at first, by the fact that Mehmet was waiting to speak to him.

Whatever the matter was he would see to it at once, then he would be free to visit Marietta. All the days of the journey he had thought of her, imagining the delightful things they would do together. There was Leyla, his Turkish favourite, and Claudine also, but none of the women delighted his spirit the way the pale Frenchwoman did.

'What is it?' Kasim asked the servant equably, impatient to have the conversation over and done with. 'Has there been a dispute amongst the slaves?'

Mehmet bowed his head and Kasim noticed for the first time that the man was white to the gills. His hands clasped together at chest level were trembling slightly.

'Tell me,' Kasim said, his strong featured, angular face alert now and focused wholly on the servant.

'Oh, Master. I fear I am the bearer of ill news. A crime . . . in your absence . . .'

'What crime? Come now Hamed. I'm not a man who'd slay the bearer of bad tidings. Tell me plainly.'

'It is Marietta and Leyla. They have been stolen, abducted while in the souk. The guards were overpowered.'

Kasim was too stunned to speak. For a moment he could not move. The coldness that gripped his heart felt perilously close to fear.

'When was this?' he heard himself say.

'One day hence, Master. A search was mounted at once, but they have not been found. Our guards are searching still.'

Kasim nodded shortly. 'I will bathe quickly and

22

change my clothes, then join the search. Are you certain there is no news? Sita is always thorough. I would expect her to find some trace, some clue to whoever abducted the women.'

Mehmet blanched. 'Forgive me Master. I omitted to tell you that Sita has gone also.'

'What? She was captured too?' Kasim said softly in disbelief.

'Ah, no. A witness at the souk saw someone of Sita's description riding off. She was not under restraint. And a figure wrapped in a blanket was slung across the front of her horse.'

Kasim raked his fingers through his shoulder-length black hair. An icy calm settled over him as he realised the true enormity of what had happened. For a moment more he was rooted to the spot. His mind worked quickly.

Sita gone. That meant bribery. There were not many men in Algiers who could offer Sita the incentive she would demand to change camps. His enemies were many, but few would have the audacity to attack him so openly.

This crime was designed to humiliate him. That narrowed the field further. In fact it narrowed it to one.

Hamed. His old maritime adversary. Cultured, intelligent. And the one man in all the World who carried his personal grudge against Kasim marked for ever on his flesh.

Kasim strode into the courtyard of his house. He was stripping off his travel-stained clothes as he walked. Mehmet running behind him, gathered them up. Kasim barked out orders for food to be brought to him, arms to be gathered, and the slaves and guards ran to obey. One look at his set face, at the muscle working in his left cheek, and their eyes fell.

Kasim's black eyes blazed in unfocused rage. Someone is going to pay dearly for this, he thought, his blood pounding in his ears. He was aware of the irony, even as he formulated the thought.

For behind his stony façade, there was an emptiness, a raw grief. He refused to think of what might be happening to the two women. They might be dead already. No. Surely Hamed would not harm them. Not even to wound his old enemy.

But he could not be certain of anything. Hamed was not like other men. His desires were reputed to be even more refined, more esoteric, than his own. And Kasim well knew the basis for the rumours.

May the One keep you safe, Marietta, Leyla too, he prayed.

It seemed that he was paying already, just as Hamed wanted him to.

Chapter Two

The courtyard of Hamed's stronghold was thronged by people and animals. Lean-to shacks and animal pens butted up against the outer walls. The area resembled a souk more than a palace. There were smells of goats and boiling greens. Chickens scratched in the dust, setting up a fluttering and squawking as they avoided the path of the guards.

The building was a once splendid Moorish castle. Much of it had fallen into disuse, but a large tower and a jumble of smaller buildings showed signs of habitation. A ragged flag sporting the skull and crossbones fluttered from the tower.

The two women were hurried through the noisy bustle and taken through an archway in the tower, which was gated with huge doors of studded ebony. Inside the main building the noise of bustling humanity died away to a low buzz.

There was no time for Marietta and Leyla to look around or absorb their surroundings. All at once the stone passageway opened into a stairwell which curved around the inner wall of the tower. As they climbed, Marietta caught glimpses through the arrow-slit windows of the courtyard and canal area.

Many small side rooms and entrances to other passageways led off the stairwell. The place seemed to be a warren.

After climbing upwards for some time, Marietta and Leyla were ushered into a large furnished room. They were taken to a low divan, made to sit down, then their wrists and ankles were secured with silk ropes.

'Wait here,' a slave ordered.

It was quiet and cool inside the room. There was the smell of citrus wood from a smoking brazier. The guards, the handsome servant, and the tall hooded figure melted away. They were alone. For a while neither of them spoke.

Marietta looked around fearfully, inspecting their prison for the first time. Painted plaster hung in flakes from the walls, and here and there tiles were missing from a colourful, waist-high frieze. Embroidered tapestries covered two of the walls, many of them dusty and tattered. Paintings hung on the far wall above a platform covered with silken cushions. The paintings were rich and dark, glowing with jewel-like colours. They looked Spanish and Dutch in origin, the frames being of richly carved and gilded wood.

Everywhere she looked Marietta gained an impression of richness and luxury, touched with decay and disrepair. Did Hamed not notice that his stronghold was falling to bits around him? She decided that he must be either uncaring or supremely confident enough not to notice.

She caught a glimpse of a French cabinet and felt an unexpected pang. There had been one just like it in her father's house on Martinique.

Leyla too had been lost in contemplation. 'Who is Hamed that he lives like this?' she said.

'From the flag flying outside, I would say he obtained his riches from the piracy you mentioned.'

Leyla nodded. 'He must be powerful. Did you see the great number of guards and all those people who live inside the courtyard? This place is a town within a castle.'

Marietta tried not to think that they might never escape from their new master; that enigmatic, brown-robed figure, so ominously silent and brooding.

'Kasim will have discovered our abduction by now. However powerful Hamed is, Kasim will rescue us.'

She spoke with confidence. If she allowed herself to think otherwise, her fear would rise up and choke her.

Leyla's indrawn breath alerted Marietta to the fact that someone had walked into the room. She looked around and found herself staring at one of the most beautiful women she had ever seen. The woman had bright-red hair, dressed high into coils and ringlets laced with strings of pearls. Her face was heart-shaped and piquant as a cat. Her large eyes, rimmed with kohl, were a clear green.

She was dressed in startling costume, consisting of a corset so tightly laced that her waist was but a handspan in width. The top of the corset supported and pushed up her bare breasts, causing them to jut out in a most provocative manner. Her nipples were rouged a deep red. Under a frilled, transparent skirt, reaching to mid-thigh, she was naked. Her feet were encased in ornate, high-heeled slippers which were fastened to her ankles and part-way up her calves with criss-crossed, silken ribbons.

Marietta stared at this vision as she walked over to her and Leyla and stopped in front of them. Marietta attempted a tremulous smile, which the woman did not return.

'So, you are the prized favourites of Kasim Dey,' she said coldly, in perfect French. 'I am Roxelana, chief of Hamed's women. You will do obeisance to me.'

She stood looking down at them both, a haughty expression on her face. Marietta felt the instant dislike flare between her and Roxelana. She straightened her back and stared boldly at the exquisite, flame-haired beauty.

'I am Marietta de Nerval. An aristocrat by birth,' she said proudly. 'And I bow to no one, save Kasim who is my acknowledged master.'

She flashed a glance sideways at Leyla who was also bridling at the audacity of this Roxelana. Leyla's dark eyes were angry but wary.

'I am Leyla,' she said. 'Marietta speaks for me too.'

Roxelana laughed, a tinkling, infectious sound. 'How spirited!' she grinned. 'But you have no choice, you little fools!'

In one swift motion she seized both Marietta and Leyla by their long hair and flung them to the floor. Taken by surprise and hampered by her bonds and robes, Marietta sprawled headlong. Roxelana moved over to where Marietta was struggling to get to her knees.

'Better,' she said softly. 'But you must learn what it is to obey me. I have much influence over Hamed. If you wish to have an easy time here, you would do well to remember that. Watch and learn, Leyla.'

Ignoring Leyla, who had managed to get into a sitting position, Roxelana pushed Marietta back down with the pointed toe of her shoe. She straddled the recumbent Marietta by placing one foot either side of her head. Marietta struggled but she was pinned by the weight on her outspread hair.

'You wretch!' Marietta cried, trying to twist free. 'Let me up! Just set me free and you'll see who is mistress here!'

Her lips whitened with fury but she could do nothing but gaze up between Roxelana's parted thighs, where she could see the slightly parted pubis, covered with a light frosting of curling red hair.

Roxelana spread her thighs wider, affording Marietta an intimate view of her moist, red-brown folds. She seemed to take a perverse pleasure in displaying herself.

'Like looking, do you?' she jeered. 'Look well. This flesh-jewel is the seat of power. The means by which a woman can gain control over a man. But of course you know that. You have been well trained for pleasure, have you not?'

She thrust her hips back and forth in a grossly lewd manner, using her fingers to splay apart her flesh-lips. Marietta saw that Roxelana's secret flesh looked swollen. The inner lips hung down a little, like the petals of an exotic flower. Roxelana's fingers grew wet. She was quite plainly becoming aroused by assuming a position of power over Marietta.

One fingertip stroked the little flesh-hood in a circular motion, until the erect bud slipped from its protection and appeared like a shiny pink bead. Roxelana moaned and threw back her head to expose her white throat. Her bare breasts trembled, the rouged nipples hardening to pointed cones. She pushed her stomach forward and Marietta could not help but notice the rich swell of her hips, exaggerated by her tight-lacing.

'Look at me, am I not beautiful,' Roxelana said silently with every gesture, every sigh, as she continued to stroke and manipulate her sex. Marietta wanted to close her eyes, but she found that she could not look away from Roxelana's openly displayed vulva.

The sight was powerfully erotic to a woman who had been trained to be acutely aware of her own and other's sensuality. And Roxelana knew it.

'Do you not relish this position Marietta?' she murmured. 'Are you truly submissive I wonder? And will you be my slave as well as Hamed's, should I request that you pleasure me?'

'You'll have to beg first!' Marietta retorted.

Confused thoughts raced through her mind. She fought her natural reaction to such wantonness. Roxelana's sexual heat acted on her like an aphrodisiac. But Roxelana must not see how affected she was, how her own mound burned and throbbed in response.

Oh, she hated being made subject to this woman. There must be some way to stop this. Roxelana shifted position and Marietta winced at the pain in her head where the roots of her hair pulled tight against her scalp. She strained against the bonds at her wrists, itching to get her hands free to slap the woman's triumphant face. But there was nothing she could do. The silken ropes were deceptively strong.

Very soon Roxelana gave a shuddering sigh. Her head dropped forward and Marietta was enfolded by the perfume of her hair; sandalwood and roses. Roxelana paused for a moment to run her tongue over her small sensual mouth, then removed her hands from her pubis. She made an odd little sound of satisfaction.

Marietta felt it in her belly, as if a fiery dart had lodged there. It is over, she thought with relief. Her humiliation was at an end. Roxelana would never know how enticing she had found the experience.

Leyla made a sound of shocked disgust at Roxelana's wanton display. 'Now are you satisfied? Let Marietta up. You have proved your power over her.'

Marietta gathered herself for the moment when Roxelana would stand free of her hair. Bound or not, she would fly at her and reach for her face with her long nails. Then she gave a sound of outrage as she felt the first warm drops on her face. Shock made her speechless, but Leyla spoke out on her behalf.

'Oh no! How dare you. This is insufferable,' Leyla cried. She looked on with horror as Roxelana squatted down, opening her knees wide and letting the full rush of her urine spatter Marietta's face.

Marietta closed her eyes, but she was intensely aware of the full musky scent of Roxelana's sex, only inches from her face. The urine smelt strongly female and the drops on her lips were salty and slightly bitter. After what seemed an age, the flow lessened, then stopped.

Roxelana bent down and wiped Marietta's face clean on a fold of Marietta's dark robes. Then she stood up and stared down at her.

'Open your eyes,' she ordered.

Reluctantly Marietta did so. She was burning with renewed anger and humiliation. Her hair was soaked. Urine had splashed onto her robes. She saw that trickles of pale yellow liquid snaked down Roxelana's inner thighs. Amber droplets sparkled on the curling red hair of her sex.

'So, have you learnt your lesson?' Roxelana said sweetly. 'Or must I force you to cleanse me thoroughly with your tongue?'

Knowing that Roxelana was fully capable of carrying out this new threat, Marietta nodded reluctantly.

'I would hear you say it.'

Marietta swallowed hard. 'I honour you and give you the respect you deserve,' she said through her tight throat. Inwardly she was fuming, but now was not the time to give way to her fury.

'Ah, good. Now we understand each other fully, do we not? Remember this lesson. It will be the first of many. I must go now, Hamed may have need of me. I will send someone to attend to you before you are allowed to eat. You look like paupers in those ragged clothes. And you both need a bath, especially you Marietta!'

Again came the infectious tinkling laugh. And on that note she swept from the room.

31

'Oh the vixen!' Leyla cried. 'I swear we'll have our revenge. Are you hurt?'

Marietta struggled to a sitting position. 'Just my pride,' she said with a wry smile. 'It seems that I have made an enemy.'

Leyla made a sound of disgust. 'It's clear that that one has had things her own way for too long. That's about to change. I swear it!'

Marietta looked at Leyla in surprise. For as long as she had known her, Leyla had been gentle and sweet natured. Now her face was flushed with anger.

'Take care, dearest friend,' she said. 'Roxelana seems capable of anything.'

There was no time for any more talk as, just then, the same brown-robed figure who had met them from the barge entered the room. He was followed by a number of female slaves. Marietta tensed as the figure gave an order and Leyla was taken from the room.

'Where are you taking her?' Marietta said. 'Wait! Oh, please! Can we not stay together?'

Leyla flashed Marietta a frightened look over her shoulder, before she disappeared through a decorated archway.

Marietta struggled as two slaves led her towards a side door, but it was no use. She was conscious that the robed figure was following her. After giving the order to separate the women, he remained silent. His malevolent presence caused her to come out in a cold sweat.

A short way along a corridor they entered a small chamber. Thick Persian carpets covered the floors, some of them threadbare in places. The interior of the room was dim. A chandelier of Italian glass hung at the centre of the room. The light from many candles cast rainbow patterns from the cut glass droplets.

Marietta's bonds were loosened and her robe taken

from her shoulders. The scraps of ruined silk were removed next, until she stood naked, clothed only in her hair which hung in rich curling waves to her hips. She hunched over, clasping her hands to shield her body, waiting to see what was required of her. One of the slaves lifted a strand of wet hair with distaste.

'Roxelana's work, no doubt,' the robed figure said without surprise. The voice was cold, but she detected a slight tremor as if the man was in the grip of some strong emotion.

She knew that the man was studying her intently from within the shadows of his hooded robe. His anonymity was calculated to put her at a disadvantage. She was angry that her response was so obvious. Hamed must be fully aware that he terrified her. Gathering her courage she stood up straight and forced her hands down to her sides. Her body was beautiful, she had no need to be ashamed of being naked. Let him look.

'Bathe her, dress her as I have instructed, and bring her to my private apartments,' he said shortly. Marietta heard the grudging admiration in his voice.

The robed figure left the room. Marietta was led to a side room, where the walls were covered with green tiles. A wooden cabinet held bottles of oil and perfume. Set into a wooden platform was a sunken marble pool with steam rising from it. She climbed into the pool. The hot perfumed water felt wonderful against her skin. For a few moments she forgot everything in the luxury of feeling clean again. She ducked her head under the water, cleansing away all traces of Roxelana and the last remnants of the guards' treatment of her.

The female slaves washed her thoroughly, scrubbing her skin with pads of vegetable fibre to soften it. She was aware of their curiosity in the way they handled her. It was the same as it had been when she first entered Kasim's harem. The slaves there had admired her fairness, her pale skin, the slenderness of her waist and the unusually pale, silky hair of her mound.

She tried to speak to the slave women, asking them about Hamed, but they shook their heads, only giggling behind their hands and rolling their eyes at each other. Either they were stupid or they had orders not to give her any information. Soon she gave up trying to speak to them. Her hair was lathered and rinsed, then combed out and perfumed. She remained silent while they massaged and perfumed her skin.

Clothes had been placed ready for her use. The outfit was similar to the one Roxelana had worn. Hamed seemed to favour a sort of uniform dress for his women. A corset made of velvet and trimmed with silk ribbons, was fitted around her waist. One of the slaves fastened the front busk, then the other tightened the back lacings, pulling the laces at the waist more tightly than over the hips.

The lined fabric against her skin and the tight-lacing gave her the strangest feeling. It was as if her two worlds suddenly collided. In Martinique she had been corset-trained since the age of twelve. It had been part of her everyday life to wear a garment that reduced her waist. In Kasim's harem she had been allowed a certain freedom of dress. The clothes were loose and flowing, except for the high slave-collar and the fine chains he had loved her to wear. An extraordinary sense of *déjà vu* awoke within her at the familiar feeling of constrainment around her waist.

How oddly satisfying it was to feel the top of the corset pushing against the underswell of her breasts. Her back seemed straighter, her posture altogether better. She breathed in deeply, loving the feel of the air filling her lungs and swelling her breasts, so that they bulged upwards in a most becoming manner.

It was as if something almost forgotten awoke within her. Her personality, which had been changed and modified by the months spent inside the confines of the harem, seemed to stretch and reassert itself.

'Lace her more tightly at the waist,' one of the slaves said, smiling at Marietta's obvious pleasure in her appearance. 'She can stand it. I could almost span her waist with my hands when she was naked.'

Marietta let them dress her in the rest of the costume, knowing that it would do no good to protest. But secretly, she revelled in the sight of her body, which was clothed almost in the under-garments of her homeland. The strangeness of the fact amused her. She wondered how Leyla would take to this costume.

When they had finished tying the frilled, transparent skirt around her waist and were bending down to push her feet into a pair of high-heeled, backless slippers, Marietta glanced at her reflection in a green tinged looking-glass.

She was amazed and pleased by what she saw. Her waist seemed smaller even than Roxelana's; a fact which gave her a perverse pleasure. The swell of her hips flowed richly outwards, emphasised by the constriction above them. The bottom of the corset dipped down to a rounded point, flattening her stomach and drawing attention to the 'V' shape between her thighs. At the back the corset hem curved up, leaving her rounded bottom and thighs exposed.

The top of the corset was moulded to support her breasts and to force them up high. A frill of black lace covered the bottom of her breasts, leaving most of their fullness and the nipples on view. Marietta assumed that her costume was complete, but she was mistaken. After rubbing a rose-pink rouge into her nipples, a slave twisted and teased them until they were erect. Then she secured a gold clamp to each. Single pearl droplets dangled from the clamps.

Marietta suppressed a gasp. She had never worn jewellery of this kind. The pinching of the clamps was not uncomfortable enough to hurt, but the steady pressure caused her nipples to throb and burn in a most disquieting manner. She lifted her hands to cup her breasts, so openly displayed and wanton-looking. The pearl droplets glowed dully, a perfect contrast against the pinkish-brown colour of her nipples. Her lips parted in a secret smile. If only Kasim could see her. She knew that he would be unable to resist her.

'You like what you see?' the slaves smiled. 'Hamed will be pleased. Indeed you are beautiful. Roxelana had best look to her merits!'

At the mention of Hamed, Marietta felt a chill. What was she thinking of, admiring her reflection when he waited for her in his private apartments – hooded and silent, an unknown quantity. She averted her eyes, her pleasure in her appearance quite lost.

The silk ribbons that secured the backless slippers were wound upwards around her calves. Then the slaves stood back to admire their work. One of them ran her hands up the curved bones of the corset, looking longingly at her own broad waist and thick hips.

'One thing more. Spread your legs.'

Wonderingly, Marietta did as she was told. The slave took hold of her lightly furred sex-lips and attached a small gold clamp to each one. Tiny gold chains, ending in a pearl droplet dangled partway down her thighs. Again they were designed not to pinch too much, but Marietta was acutely aware of their unfamilar weight and the way they drew atten-tion to the triangle between her thighs. She felt the tickle of the warm chains as she placed her legs back together. A final glance in the mirror showed her that the chains with the gently swaying pearl droplets were clearly visible through the short frilled skirt.

Hamed placed his eyes close to the gaps in the wall, which corresponded with the eyes in a painting in the chamber next door. He reclined on his stomach on a divan, placed so that the watcher could relax while spying on the occupants of the other room.

Ah, the Frenchwoman was indeed a treasure. How Kasim must hate losing her. The thought gave him immense satisfaction.

Hamed had watched every detail of the bathing, oiling, and dressing of Marietta. It was all the more enjoyable as the Frenchwoman had no idea that she was being observed. Her questions to the slave women had made him smile. So, she was curious about him, was she? He would soon set her mind at rest.

Marietta had a quality that drew him strongly. Her sensuality was touched with innocence. Something rare in a woman who had lived for many months in a harem. Her pleasure in the beautiful garments he had provided for her use was, he felt sure, natural and unforced. She might be withdrawn and afraid when he next met her face to face, but from the secret room he had glimpsed her true personality.

It was truly touching. Marietta was as fresh as the first flower of spring, especially compared with the somewhat jaded delights of Roxelana. Hamed smiled. And the habitual hard lines around his mouth softened a fraction.

Lying his cheek on his bent forearms, he relaxed while Roxelana sponged away the sweat he had accumulated during a bout of sword practice. He sighed with pleasure as Roxelana dried him, then dug her fingers into his neck and shoulders, massaging away the pressure marks left by his armour.

In a while he'd have her cream him well, then pleasure him with one of the exquisite toys in the way he loved. Truly the sight of the Frenchwoman had heated his blood.

He ached to take full advantage of Marietta's many charms. The old bitterness rose within him, but he pushed it down resolutely. He managed well enough. He had long since resigned himself to his physical limitations. There were many compensations, many spiked pleasures, for a man with imagination. Where was the sense in crying for the moon when he had the velvet night and all the stars? Madness lay that way.

Besides, at this precise moment, the taste of triumph was sweet indeed. He knew that Kasim must be suffering. How could any man not mourn the loss of such a jewel? And he had not only Marietta under his dominion, but Leyla too – the sultry Turkish beauty. Leyla's capture had not been part of Hamed's plan, but he was delighted that Sita had abducted her too. Sita would expect extra payment, of course, but he was as rich as the Croesus of legend. Inanimate objects meant little to him. Marietta and Leyla were worth any price.

Kasim would learn that soon enough. No doubt he was even now engaged in a search for his women. It would not be long before he approached the stronghold with a proposition. Let him. Kasim did not know it yet, but his torment had only just begun.

Hamed's mouth curled in a smile as Roxelana made a sound of impatience. He waited. She was silent for a while, then she thrust back a lock of wild red hair that fell onto her forehead and gave a grunt of irritation. Her curiosity was obviously getting the better of her.

'You may look,' Hamed said, raising his head and

positioning himself to once again spy on the Frenchwoman.

Roxelana stopped her ministrations and approached the wall. Bending forward she peered through another set of spy-holes. Her small sensual mouth tightened as she watched the Frenchwoman being laced tightly into the corset. Roxelana said nothing. She was absorbed totally by the scene in the other room.

Marietta was now being fitted with nipple and labial clamps. Hamed licked his lips and made a hoarse sound in the back of his throat. For just a moment, Roxelana drew back from the spy-holes. Her face looked sharp and cruel.

Hamed could not resist teasing her. 'A tiny waist she has, eh?' he said. 'And those pale limbs, that hair. What a feast for any man. Or woman.'

Roxelana turned a furious face to him. She tossed her upswept red curls, so that the ropes of pearls were in danger of being shaken loose. 'She is not as beautiful as I am,' she said, challenging him to agree with her.

Hamed was deliberately silent. Roxelana's green eyes narrowed.

'You are enamoured of this woman,' she said, careful to keep her voice light. 'I can see it in your face, Master. Only command me and I will arrange an entertainment for you. The Frenchwoman will do my bidding, be assured of it.'

'Resume your attentions to my person,' Hamed said evenly. 'Do not presume to anticipate my wishes.'

Roxelana seemed about to speak, but obviously thought better of it. She took up her place and began massaging, her fingers digging cruelly into Hamed's broad scarred shoulders.

'Gently now, my sweet,' Hamed said with an edge

to his voice. 'Do not forget your place. It is not as secure as you seem to think it.'

Roxelana leant forward to kiss the nape of his neck. 'Your pardon, Master. The Frenchwoman brings out the basest feelings in me.'

'Then direct your ire into the task at hand,' Hamed said directing Roxelana's fingers downwards.

'Your pleasure is my pleasure, Master,' Roxelana said smoothly.

Hamed felt the first cold touch of the perfumed cream as she smeared it onto the crease of his buttocks. Her fingers kneaded his flesh, working the cream well into the inner surfaces of his crevice. As the cream warmed and liquefied she slipped two fingers into Hamed's anus. Sliding them in and out, she exerted a subtle pressure on the sensitive place inside his body which caused Hamed to shiver with pleasure. Bending forward she placed a line of kisses up his backbone, her pointed tongue snaking out to tease his tautly muscled back.

'Now the toy,' Hamed groaned.

Roxelana warmed the ivory head of the phallus between her palms. Applying a generous amount of cream to the bulbous end, she placed it against the puckered mouth of his anus, and pushed slowly. Hamed let out a deep sigh.

In the other room, Marietta twisted and turned in front of the looking-glass, admiring her costume. Hamed's eyes flickered to the short, transparent skirt that revealed more than it concealed. The lightly shadowed mound of her pubis was a pale gold triangle. He could see the gold chains, with their pearl droplets, brushing gently against her white thighs as she moved.

One day, he thought with measured anticipation, he would spread those thighs and taste that neat little sex. And the Frenchwoman would moan and sigh against his mouth just as she had for Kasim.

Hamed was learned in the ways to bring pleasure to a woman. It was his delight to watch as they melted and begged for him to do more to them, to do anything he wanted. And he would. Oh, soon, he would.

Then all his thoughts became concentrated on the sensations that flooded his body. And there was nothing in the World but Roxelana's clever fingers. Hamed's whole body tensed as he strained towards the fragmented pleasure, which was all that Kasim had left to him.

Marietta was led into the main room and told to wait. The slaves left her reclining on a low divan. After reminding her of all the guards that were present within the stronghold, lest she should be considering escape, they went their way.

When no one came into the room immediately Marietta relaxed. She was hungry. She and Leyla had not eaten since before they went shopping in the souk. It was almost a full day since their capture. She wondered what Leyla was doing. Was she being bathed and dressed? Or was the dreadful Roxelana now tormenting her friend?

The tall hooded figure appeared silently in the room.

Marietta jumped with shock. She had heard no sign of the man's entrance. She gazed up fearfully as he approached. The man's gait was smooth and studied, almost insolent and graceful in its way. Drawing close, the figure raised its hands and drew back the hood. He unclasped his outer robe and let it fall to the carpet.

Marietta held her breath, not daring to look away. A leather mask, such as she and Leyla had worn outside the harem, covered the whole of the man's face. Sun-streaked blond hair tumbled around the mask. He wore a black silk tunic, open at the neck,

41

over baggy leather trousers which were tucked into high leather boots.

She saw his strong neck and wide shoulders. His chest was broad, well muscled and tapering to a slim hard waist. The hips, encased by black leather, were also slim. His thighs looked solid and powerful. Whatever Hamed's face looked like, there was nothing wrong with his physique. He was superb. Against her will she found herself responding to the predatory maleness of him.

Marietta realised that she was staring openly, searching for signs of deformity or injury. Such a commanding man had no need for subterfuge. Unless his face was hideously ugly.

The man drew near, stood looking down at her. No word had passed between them. She did not know what her reaction ought to be. Her mouth was so dry that she doubted she could speak. Fear of the unknown kept her rooted as he slowly looked her up and down. The glitter of his eyes was apparent behind the mask. She could not see what colour they were.

Reaching out a hand he caressed one of her breasts, taking hold of her nipple-clamp and pulling it gently. A sliver of sensation jolted right through her. At her indrawn breath, she thought he smiled. He let go of the pearl. She felt it brush against the swell of her breast. The droplet was warm from the touch of his fingers.

The masked man spoke then, and the contempt in his voice was palpable. 'Is this the way you greet your Master? Have you not been taught to assume a position of submission?'

Marietta slid off the divan hurriedly. Sinking to her knees, she clasped her hands in the small of her back and straightened her shoulders. Lifting her chin high, she stared straight ahead. This was the classic pose which Kasim had insisted all the harem women adopt at any time he ordered it. She had been trained to obey him on the instant.

'Part your thighs,' the masked man ordered.

Trembling, Marietta did so.

'Wider. Display yourself for me.'

Marietta opened her thighs as wide as possible. She felt the lips of her sex part and the unfamiliar weight as the little clamps, with their chains and pearl drops, swayed from side to side at the movement.

The masked man bent towards her; touching her lightly on her shoulders he traced a fingertip over the creamy skin. He cupped her breasts, plucking again at the nipple-clamps, until she had a strong urge to draw back from his touch. Her nipples felt hot and sensitive, almost to the point of discomfort. He reached inside the top of the corset and lifted her breasts free from the rim of black lace. They jutted out almost obscenely, the nipples taut and glowing. Gently he slapped her breasts as if testing for firmness. He weighed the flesh in his hands and bent to draw in the perfume that rose in a sweet cloud from her cleavage.

Then his hands roved down over the corset, following the curved lines of the bones. He ran an admiring fingertip up the front busk, plucking at the hooks that fastened the garment. Moving around her he stood gazing at her back view.

He took time to admire the way her buttocks flared out richly into a perfect heart shape. Her thighs, compressed by the weight of her upper body, were full and round. A light touch played over the laces. She felt the warmth of his fingers on the flesh of her back where the laces bisected it into diamond shapes.

Then came his touch on the open valley between her buttocks as he tickled the tight little anus. One fingertip rubbed at the creased little mouth, tickling it and nudging a little way inside it. Marietta waited for him to insert his finger fully. She tensed against the expected invasion, but it did not come. Instead he reached between her legs and cupped the whole of her warm mound in his open palm.

His wrist rubbed against the whole of the area between her legs as he reached further upwards. The moistly parted folds of her sex and the shadowed valley between her buttocks was pressed closely to his wrist and lower arm.

Marietta steeled herself to relax as he began to massage the pouting plum of her sex. He pinched the folds closed, exerting a referred pressure on her pleasure-bud. Now and then he tugged on the little chains, rolling the pearls between his fingers. The clamps pulled on her swelling flesh, giving her a subtle pleasure. Despite her fear of him, Marietta felt herself becoming moist.

The masked man stopped touching her sex and began feeling the texture of her pubic hair, twisting it into curls and tugging gently at it. Walking around to her front, he lifted the frilled skirt and gazed at her parted thighs and the rosy bud that nestled within its fleece of silver-blonde hair.

All these things he did slowly, as if with wonder, and in complete silence. His concentration and tension transmitted itself to Marietta. He seemed to be familiarising himself with her body. There was a strange dense intimacy to his touch. It was not the measured examination of the victor over the vanquished. It was something far more complex.

Despite his control, his calm deliberation, she was very conscious that, after a time, his breath began to come faster. No longer did she feel such a sense of his coldness. Whatever he thought about her, he was becoming strongly aroused.

The strain of remaining rigidly in the submissive posture caused her thighs to tremble slightly. She wanted desperately for him to say something.

Finally, she could stand it no longer. The silence was utterly unnerving. She knew that she risked punishment, but she had to speak.

'Master. I beg you – '

'Silence!' he ordered. 'You were not given permission to speak. Get onto the divan and lie on your back. Quickly now! Or you'll be sorry.'

She hurried to do as he said. The silk cushions were soft against her skin as she lay back amongst them.

'Raise your thighs up to your chest. Place your hands on your calves and open your body completely to me.'

Heat rushed into Marietta's face as she did as he asked. He was once again remote and menacing. It was dreadful to have to obey him. Her thigh muscles ached as she drew her legs in tightly. Her hips were raised up to him and the tight half-closed plum of her sex, presented for his view. The two gold chains trailed across her outer sex-lips, tickling the already sensitive skin. She hoped he could not see that she was wet. But he noticed at once that the line dividing her intimate folds was moist. He gave a growl of satisfaction.

She looked fixedly over his shoulder, not meeting his eye, as he removed the labial clamps and laid them aside. For a moment he massaged the pressure points where they had pinched, using just the tips of his fingers. Then he reached out and exerted pressure so that her outer sex-lips peeled apart like a ripe fig and the moist, deep-pink flesh within was revealed.

Marietta moaned with distress as he plucked at the sensitive folds, and rubbed her flesh-hood back and forth. Soon her bud began to throb sweetly. As she opened her thighs wider on his command, the reddened morsel stood proud of the surrounding flesh.

He laughed with open delight. She was struck

again by the familiarity of the sound, but she was too aroused and anguished to think straight. His next words sent a deep shiver through her body.

'How shameful and wanton your sex is. It's hungry for pleasure. So beautifully swollen and eager for any caress. I can smell the heat rising from you. But it's not your pleasure I crave. It's my own.'

He moved away from her for a moment and loosened his belt. Stripping off the tunic, he discarded it. The full, leather trousers fell in folds around his boots. His upper body was magnificent. The skin was a uniform light gold in colour, the tight male nipples like copper coins. She looked down at his strongly erect cock, rearing up from a nest of crisp, dark-blond hair. The cock-head was moist and glistening, protruding fully from the cock-skin. The balls in their hairy sac were round and firm.

Marietta's eyes widened as the masked man fell to his knees between her drawn-up thighs. She felt the warmth of his body as he leaned in to her. He smelt of lemon-grass cologne mixed with the musk of male arousal.

He placed his palms on her inner thighs, stretching them wide apart, digging his fingers into the petal-soft skin. She moaned as the head of his swollen shaft nudged against her hungry womanhood. He pressed in a little way, so that her inner lips opened around the bulbous end. He worked himself in her juices until he was thoroughly wet, then with a sigh of pleasure he pushed fully into her.

His eyes glittered through the slits in the leather mask as he thrust strongly. His warm cinnamon-scented breath was hot on her face. She was filled up completely by the hardness of him. The cock-head rammed into her, so far up inside that she felt it against the neck of her womb. He looked into her face the whole time he was working himself in and out, his hips jerking back and forth.

Marietta moved under him, lifting her hips to meet his thrusts. She could not hold back her sighs of pleasure. It had been weeks since a man had taken her like this. The sensation of his member slipping wetly into her was wonderful. Her own slick flesh clung to the cock-stem as it moved, as if reluctant to release it.

The warm pleasure spread into her belly. She could fell herself building to a peak. Oh, she was near, so near . . .

The masked man convulsed and thrust a final time, then he collapsed onto her. Frustration made her reckless. She did not care that she might be punished for wilfulness. Reaching between their bodies she rubbed her bud until she brought herself rapidly to the pinnacle. The sweet waves consumed her. Her vagina pulsed around his still-hard cock. She screwed her eyes shut as the pleasure gradually began to fade. A sexual flush stained her cheeks.

The masked man seemed locked in a world of his own. Shudders still wracked his powerful body. For one insane moment she thought he was weeping. Instinctively, she put her arms around him and drew him close. The moment was poignantly tender. What was it about this man that stirred her so strangely? One moment she was terrified of him, the next she was moved to comfort him.

She heard him whisper something in a low voice and realised with a shock that he had called her name.

'Marietta, My sweet. Oh, God . . .'

The way he said it, with sadness and longing, seemed to reach into a secret compartment of her heart. And that voice. It was achingly familiar. She had thought there was something about him from the beginning. Now she knew why. This was no ex-pirate named Hamed.

But surely it could not be . . . In an instant her

suspicions became a certainty. She forgot how menacing this man had seemed. Pushing herself up on one elbow she reached out and tore the mask from the man's face.

'By all the Saints! Gabriel!' she croaked and reached up her arms to draw his head close for a kiss.

Gabriel jerked his head back like a whiplash. His beautiful face was convulsed by rage. Tears streaked his cheeks. He threw himself from the divan and began struggling into his clothes. She watched with amazement as he turned his back on her.

It was impossible, but he was here. She had never thought to see him again. But he was changed. So bitter. She did not know him.

'Gabriel. What has happened to you . . .?' she began, tentatively.

'Be silent!' he spat. 'Don't pretend you are innocent. I know what a schemer you are. Now you're going to pay for your betrayal. I persuaded Hamed to bring you here. And now, I'll have my revenge.'

'I don't understand. How came you to be here?'

He gave a harsh laugh. 'All in good time. I intend you to know everything. I have suffered, Marietta, but now I am to be rewarded. Hamed has given you to me – we are both his slaves of course. But I may do with you what I will.'

Though she was shaking inside, she made herself smile.

'Then I am safe. I know that you will never hurt me. Even when you try to be cold – as just now – you draw pleasure from me like honey from the comb. Did you not feel my tenderness for you?'

Gabriel looked up. For a moment his stormy grey eyes met hers. She felt him soften. His face assumed an expression of confusion.

'Can it be so?' he said gently, almost to himself.

She reached out her arms to him.

'Embrace me, Gabriel. It warms my heart to see you again.'

With a low sound like an animal in pain, he whirled and strode from the room.

Chapter Three

Gabriel stopped in the passageway and leant back against the tiled wall.

The picture of Marietta's stricken face filled his thoughts. If she only knew what it cost him to appear cold to her. Part of him longed to go back to her, gather her into his arms, and clasp her to his chest.

She was even more beautiful than he remembered. Impossible to remain unmoved by her. He had meant to take her without tenderness, use her for his pleasure alone. But somehow he had responded to the spell of her flesh.

The way she had hidden her fear had been touching. He had seen how she shrank from him at first, yet there was only the slightest tremor to her mouth; a certain wildness of those incredible blue eyes to betray her inner turmoil.

Gabriel had long anticipated the sweetness of revenge. He had wanted to see Marietta trembling with fear, her bright beauty dulled by ill-treatment, as his had been. But when he saw her there at the canalside, helpless, wearing only torn rags under her dark robes, his hatred wavered like a candle-flame in a breeze.

He recalled the first time he ever laid eyes on her. It seemed a lifetime ago. Covered in black robes, from head to toe, she had stood watching, with Kasim, while he, Gabriel, was being whipped on the public punishment block. The shame and the erotic intensity of that meeting flooded him with emotion even now.

How he had twisted and turned in his bonds as the public punisher ran rough, hard hands over his body. He had tried to stop the flooding pleasure of submission, but it had overcome him; the way it always did when Selim, his master, chastised him. The public punisher too knew just how hard to beat him, measuring the strokes of the lash to allow a riot of warm pain to penetrate every nerve, every sinew.

And Gabriel's arousal was horribly visible to all. His cock was so strongly erect, his balls shrunk to hard stones. When a lash-stroke snaked across his thigh and sent smarting heat to his engorged sex, he had broken.

Marietta had watched in silent fascination, her pale face stark inside the black hood of her concealing robes. He had felt her like a presence in his mind. Even the roar of the crowd as his semen spattered the boards could not detract from that first sight of her. His painfully beating heart had almost stopped when their gazes locked. He had never seen eyes like hers. Bluer than the summer sky; bluer than flax flowers.

In Kasim's harem he had begun to get to know her a little, even to believe that she returned his affections. Only once had they come together in love. In Kasim's carriage Gabriel had taken her with gentleness and skill, opening her body for the first time to the invasion of his erect male flesh. He had hardly believed that she was virgin still. So many pleasures she had been taught, but that final one, Kasim had reserved for himself.

Gabriel stole the last of her innocence, but the victory of conquest was hers. As they moved together in timeless rhythm he knew that part of him had become hers for ever.

Then Kasim discovered them together.

Gabriel's action that day was the catalyst that decided his fate. Kasim would not countenance a rival for Marietta's heart. Marietta had been forced to choose between them. She chose Kasim.

Pain knifed through him. Even now he could not bear to think of those final moments – the way they had looked, Kasim and Marietta rapt in each other, all excluding. The two of them had betrayed him. For in his darkest moments he owned up to the fact that it had indeed been a double loss. For Kasim, with his dangerous, male beauty, his restrained desires, had woken Gabriel to new and powerful pleasures. Once he would have been content to serve the two of them, selflessly, as long as he was secure in their love.

But that security had been torn from him. It was unforgivable. Now, Marietta was a prisoner inside Hamed's stronghold. The costume Hamed insisted she wore added a new dimension to her beauty. Gabriel had been prompted to torment her a little, while he still remained unknown to her. Later he intended to reveal his identity.

How smoothly she had assumed the position of submission on his order. How docile she was as he handled her body. Ah, she was obedient and well trained now, the fire within her concentrated into willing servitude. By her own choice, she was Kasim's creation. That's what hurt him most. He could have put the past behind him, rejoiced in being reunited with her, if he truly believed that Kasim had forced her into any action against her will.

Kasim was too clever for that. He never forced anyone who did not wish to be dominated. He was dangerous in the way that he compelled his slaves to discover their most secret wants and desires. Kasim desired that his victims collude with him in their own debasement; and this they did willingly. Gabriel had seen how Marietta responded to the spiked pleasures of chastisement. He knew that something within himself resonated to those same dark desires.

Ah, Marietta. She had looked so sensual, lying on the divan after he withdrew from her body. Her cheeks were flushed and her neck and shoulders were imprinted with the after-glow of her climax. So much for taking his own pleasure and leaving her wanting. He grinned suddenly. She had taken her pleasure for herself, reaching between their bodies to stimulate her well-trained sex. What a rampant and shameless little baggage she had become.

He was captivated anew by the changes in her.

The Marietta he had known would not have dared to be so self serving. She had grown in confidence and poise over the past months. It made her even more delectable. Would he never get her out of his blood? It seemed not. And it was that realisation that had broken him.

He should have got up and left her immediately he had sated himself. Left her with no word, no backward glance. But his resolve had crumbled when his emotions rose up to choke him. Her arms crept around him, holding him tenderly, soothing away the hurt she must have sensed within him. He had mumbled something incoherent . . .

And it had been in that instant that she recognised him and tore the mask from his face. Terror had almost overcome him. The love and anger rushed together so that he could hardly breathe. He had not known whether to strike her or kiss her. Flinging himself away from her, he had begun pulling on his clothes, not trusting himself to speak.

With her thighs parted and smeared with his semen, her lovely mouth curved in a smile of gladness, she had called for him to embrace her again. Oh, God. How could her eyes hold such innocence? Was it possible that she was not at all the schemer he knew her to be?

The cold of the wall tiles seeped into his back through the black silk tunic. He despised his weakness. Through all the things he had suffered since Kasim betrayed him he had remained steadfast, his hate of his gaolers sustaining him until Hamed gave him new hope. And now he was unmanned, made pathetic by his love for a woman without honour. He was furious with himself. How was it possible that she moved him still? He pushed back the damp blond hair from his forehead, fighting for composure.

After a few moments he moved on, his thoughts still full of Marietta. He made his way to his private apartments. Every detail of Marietta was imprinted anew on his senses. The taste of her, her smell, the feel of her hair. And the heat and wildness of her passion. Her perfume clung to his fingers; sweet feminine musk.

Where was the sense in denying it – in struggling against the truth? He had never been free of her. He realised it fully only now. He was so absorbed that he did not notice the woman until she spoke.

'Well. Well. How elevated you have become.'

Gabriel looked up to see Sita leaning idly against one side of an arched doorway that led to a small courtyard where a fountain played amongst fruit trees.

'And no thanks to you,' he said curtly.

She laughed. 'Come now. Why hold a grudge? I was only following Kasim's orders when I gave you over to the gaoler. And all's well now, that's plain. I knew you'd prosper. Beauty creates its own fortune. And you are beautiful indeed. Whatever was done to you has not diminished your looks.'

She paused, her narrow dark eyes sliding side-ways, then coming back to rest on his face.

'Enough of the past,' she said softly. 'It's done with. Let's make our peace. We share the same master again, only this time it's Hamed.'

With a sound of disgust he pushed past her and then stopped and glanced back. Her audacity amazed him. Did she really think they could ever be friends?

Sita's thin lips parted and she moistened them with her tongue in a nervous gesture. Her normally sharp features softened as she absorbed his scrutiny. She took a step towards him, encouraged to move closer by his stillness. Her slim soldier's body moved gracefully in the closely-fitting leather garments; the livery of Hamed's guards.

'Do you remember the time you were sent to the stables for punishment?' she whispered urgently. 'You were not cold to me then.'

'I remember,' he said levelly, recalling how she had mistreated him and forced him to pleasure her.

Incredibly, he had desired her briefly. It had been in a moment of madness when he was confused and afraid for Marietta's safety. Self disgust had flooded him as soon as his need had been assuaged. He knew that he had responded to Sita's advances precisely *because* she was cold and scheming – the very antith-esis of Marietta.

Or so he had once thought. Marietta had turned out to be more like Sita than he cared to imagine.

'If you know what's good for you, you'll keep away from me,' he said coldly to Sita and began to put distance between them.

Her eyes glittered. Her thin face grew pale with anger. 'I thought we were even,' she shouted after him. 'You have your Frenchwoman back don't you? I got her for you. That must count for something!'

He did not look back. She gave a hiss of rage.

'How was she? As good as you remembered!'

'Better,' he called back, closing his ears to Sita's taunts, but her mocking laughter followed him to the stables.

Marietta lay curled up on the divan for many minutes after Gabriel left. The pleasure of their joining faded quickly, leaving her feeling sad and confused.

Gabriel loved her still. She knew he did. But for some reason he was fighting it. He seemed determined to hurt her, to punish her for some imagined crime. Part of her was afraid of the coldness in his troubled grey eyes, but a larger part rejoiced. Gabriel was here. She had never expected to see him again. A tiny core of heat inside her burned just for him. Gabriel, the beautiful golden slave. The first to thrust his hard male flesh inside her.

A woman always remembered her first time.

She loved Kasim completely, having accepted long since that the dark tides within him were reflected in her. She delighted in serving him. But Gabriel, so strong, so perfect of form, was often in her thoughts. Now he was here. And new possibilities presented themselves. If only she could break through the barrier he had erected . . .

After a while she got up and began to explore the room. She found a brass ewer and jug behind a carved screen and cleansed herself, drying her skin with embroidered towels that hung on a rack.

She could not forget the look on Gabriel's face as he drew away from her. What could have happened to him? He had promised to tell her everything, but the way he said it chilled her to the marrow. She shivered, wishing Leyla was here to confide in.

As if in answer to her call the door opened and Leyla stepped inside, followed by a servant-girl holding a tray of food.

'Oh, I've been worried about you,' Leyla said.

'When they separated us I imagined all kinds of awful things. But I see that you are well.'

She stopped and her long dark eyes became shadowed with concern. 'What is it?' she said softly, hurrying towards Marietta.

Leyla was wearing a long flowing cloak of scarlet silk which billowed out behind her as she moved. The door clanged shut behind her and a key turned in the lock. Marietta was on her feet in an instant. She flung herself into Leyla's arms.

Leyla enfolded her in a scented embrace. 'I'm here now. Tell me about it,' she murmured, stroking Marietta's hair.

Marietta told her everything that had happened, explaining that Gabriel had been one of the hooded figures who welcomed them at the canalside.

'Gabriel? Here? I cannot believe it,' Leyla said at length. 'Kasim set him free. I thought he would have travelled far from here. Made a new life.'

'I thought so too. But he is Hamed's slave, just as we are,' Marietta said. 'He told me that he persuaded Hamed to bring us here. Oh, Leyla, he means to punish me for some imagined crime! And I believe that he will. I tried to see the man I knew in his face, but his eyes . . . They were so . . . so bleak.'

Leyla disgested this information in silence. She led Marietta to a small couch set next to a low table of carved and inlaid bone.

'You must eat,' she said practically, sinking down in a cloud of scarlet silk. 'You cannot think clearly on an empty stomach. You are weak and still shocked by all that's happened. No wonder you are distressed. Come, eat now, talk later. There is sure to be an answer to all this.'

Marietta smiled shakily. 'And I thought I was the strong one.'

Leyla took her hand. 'I can be brave when someone

I care for is in distress,' she said softly, caressing Marietta's palm with the pad of her thumb.

The servant, whose name was Bishi, arranged silver dishes of rice, spiced meat stew, and baked aubergines, on the table. Then she poured cool mint tea into tall glasses. Smiling and inclining her head gracefully, she backed away and went to stand beside the door.

Marietta's mouth watered at the savoury aroma of the food. She piled a plate with the bright yellow rice, which was flavoured with saffron and studded with apricots. Then she helped herself to lamb stew and vegetables and began to eat with relish. Leyla was right. Everything would look better on a full stomach. She began to feel better after just a few mouthfuls.

For a while there was silence while they ate. Leyla rolled the rice into little balls with her fingers and deftly tossed the food into her mouth. Soon they finished eating and sat sipping the sweet mint tea. Marietta asked her where she had been and Leyla explained that she had been fitted with a similar costume to Marietta.

'Nothing exciting happened to me,' Leyla said, trying to make light of the present situation. 'No masked lover bent me to his will, then pleasured me so soundly!'

Put like that, the edge of danger seemed diminished. Marietta laughed, her eyes sparkling.

'I could not help responding. Gabriel is magnificent as you know. And I was hungry for male flesh. It had been so long since I experienced the thrust of a hard male member.'

Leyla rolled her eyes in agreement. A look of understanding passed between them. She too had been eagerly anticipating Kasim's return.

'How could Gabriel resist you? You look enchanting in that costume. Ah, if only I had been here. I burn too. Perhaps he would have taken pity on me.'

Marietta gave a scandalised laugh. 'Leyla you are quite shameless!'

Leyla leant over and kissed Marietta's cheek. 'I know,' she smiled. 'I've always been that way. Tell me. How do you think I look?'

She stood up and Bishi ran forward to take her red cloak.

'Thank you, Bishi. Bishi is to be our attendant,' Leyla explained. 'I am told that Hamed wants us to be comfortable. He wishes us to consider ourselves his guests rather than his prisoners. Bishi will see to all our needs.'

Bishi blushed prettily as she heard her name mentioned, then flashed Marietta a dazzling smile before lowering her eyelids and looking down demurely. She was about eighteen years old and fresh-faced, with an open expression.

Marietta hardly noticed the servant-girl. She could not take her eyes off Leyla. She knew that Leyla was trying to divert her from thoughts of Gabriel and she was succeeding. Leyla looked magnificent. Her corset was made of scarlet velvet, embroidered with gold thread and trimmed with magenta leather strips. Her large breasts spilled voluptuously over the top of the corset. The clamps that clung to her wine-red nipples were shaped like circles with open centres. Each tiny, hard nipple-tip had been teased through an opening so that it was collared by a ruby-studded circle.

Her short, transparent skirt was also red and her backless slippers glittered with red jewels. Red velvet ribbons secured the slippers to Leyla's ankles. Leyla's creamy skin and abundant black hair made a startling contrast to her costume.

'And look at this!' Leyla parted her legs and rocked her hips from side to side.

Marietta looked at the fine gold chains hanging

from the labial clamps adorning Leyla's plump hairless sex. More rubies, winking red light from their facets, trembled at the ends of the chains.

'Are they not beautiful? And they feel so strangè. The slight weight makes me want to touch myself and bring pleasure to my body. Is that not dreadful?' She put both hands to her cheeks in a gesture of modesty that was so out of character that Marietta laughed.

'You have never needed prompting to give yourself pleasure! You are a flower of passion, my dearest Leyla. How well I know that!'

All at once they were both laughing. Marietta pirouetted so that Leyla could see the details of her own costume. She leant forward so that the pearl clamps on her nipples shook enticingly.

'Have you no clamps for your pretty golden sex?' Leyla asked, looking down to Marietta's unadorned thighs.

Marietta remembered that Gabriel had removed them before stroking her intimate flesh with his knowing fingers. The memory of his touch sent a tug of heat to her stomach.

'They're here,' she said, walking over to fetch the labial clamps which Gabriel had dropped onto the carpet next to the divan where they'd lain. 'I'll attach them.'

'No, my treasure. Let me,' Leyla said, her voice slightly breathless and her eyes shining. 'It will be my pleasure.'

Marietta lay back and settled herself comfortably amongst the silken pillows. The heat in her belly coiled and increased. This act of opening her body to another's gaze always drew a unique sensation from her body.

Slowly, teasing Leyla by prolonging the moment when her vulva would be laid bare, she parted her knees and let them fall open. She drew up her legs so that the transparent skirt fell back and her pouting mound, closed and plum-like, came into view.

'Push out a little for me, my treasure,' Leyla said huskily. 'And part your thighs more.'

Marietta loved to hear Leyla speak when her voice was roughened by passion. She anticipated the moment when Leyla would touch her.

Leyla's fingers trembled as she took hold of each of Marietta's plump, outer flesh-lips in turn and attached the clamps. Marietta felt the pinching bite of each hinged fastening as it closed on her flesh.

The coolness of the clamps and the slight weight felt pleasant against her warm sex. Smiling at the Turkish woman, Marietta stretched like a cat. The fine chains tickled her thighs as she moved. She felt relaxed and at ease, as she always did after making love. Leyla had succeeded in making her forget the unpleasant aspects of the exchange between Gabriel and herself.

She saw how Leyla's long dark eyes glowed, how her full red mouth looked soft and inviting. She smiled inwardly, feeling her body begin to respond more strongly to Leyla's exotic beauty.

'I would like to make pleasure with you now,' Leyla whispered in Marietta's ear, biting the lobe playfully. 'The thought of you and Gabriel sharing pleasure has heated my blood. I must have you first. Then will you grant me release?'

She kissed Marietta deeply, probing her mouth with her tongue, then sucking in her under-lip and nibbling at it gently. Marietta moaned softly as her arms came out to embrace Leyla. The feel of her soft scented skin pressing against her, the coils of dark perfumed hair brushing against her arms was intoxicating.

After a moment Marietta pulled away.

'Bishi?' she said breathlessly.

'Will be discreet. I'm sure she would not dream of

61

telling tales. Would you, Bishi?' Leyla chuckled deep in her throat.

'No lady,' Bishi said, her face red and her eyes like saucers. 'I'll . . . I'll clear away the food dishes while you take your ease.'

Bishi began gathering up dishes and empty glasses, averting her eyes from Leyla and Marietta. Leyla smiled as Bishi hurried from the room. 'Such modesty. I did not think to find it in this place. Bishi is so fresh and innocent. She reminds me of you when I first met you.'

Marietta stroked Leyla's pale cheek and ran her finger along the delicate jaw-line. 'You taught me to coax pleasure from my own body. I had never done that.'

'Never touched this place?' Leyla said throatily as she slid her hand up Marietta's thigh and began stroking her pubic fleece softly. 'I love your paleness and the way this pretty fleece crowns your sex.' Her fingertips threaded through the silky curls, tickling them.

'No . . . I . . . never had.' Marietta breathed, as Leyla's fingers opened her and slid inside the moist flesh-lips.

She lay back on the low couch as Leyla slid to the carpet and positioned herself between Marietta's spread knees. Leyla kissed her inner thighs and licked the creamy flesh. She worked upwards and nuzzled Marietta's sex-lips apart with her mouth, before teasing the tender inner flesh with long loving licks.

Under the expert ministrations Marietta began to moan aloud. Leyla smoothed back the little flesh-hood and sucked softly on the erect bud she exposed. Marietta's flesh turned to liquid and she tossed her head from side to side.

* * *

Hamed moved the curtain covering the spy-hole aside.

Ah, what exquisite timing. The Frenchwoman was spread across the couch, her legs opened wide, and the Turkish woman was at work on her.

He watched avidly as Leyla moved her head up and down. Sometimes she moved from side to side, her mouth brushing across Marietta's sex in a subtle intense rhythm. The tumble of Leyla's black hair fell in waves to her hips, brushing the floor on either side.

Marietta's white thighs trembled and jerked, now pressing against the sides of Leyla's head, then straining to open more widely. Her beribboned calves and the delicate high-heeled slippers looked beautiful to him. She looked somehow more naked than if her legs and feet had been bare. This was a fact that forever fascinated him.

He watched enthralled as Marietta's legs waved and her slippers dug into the velvet of the couch, her knees flexing in helpless arousal. The ankles were so slender, imprisoned by the ribbons that wrapped them round and round. He imagined the little pink toes, curling with pleasure, pushing against the imprisonment of the bejewelled brocade slippers.

Marietta's fingers meshed in Leyla's hair, clutching and releasing the silky midnight strands as her pleasure flowed over her. Then she put her arms back behind her head, in the attitude of an innocent child when it sleeps, and thrust the whole of her lower body towards the other woman's mouth. The contrast between innocence and fully sexual woman-hood was devastating.

Hamed's eyes roved over both women. His tongue snaked out to moisten his full lips. His handsome, strong-featured face grew slack with desire. God, what beauties. Light and dark; a perfect foil for each other.

Marietta's pale hair was draped over the silken pillows. Her slim shoulders and shapely arms were arranged now in a relaxed posture, which was at once erotic and possessed of supreme tenderness. Again he was struck by the contrast in her nature. The corset that constricted her waist and caused her breasts to bulge upwards added to the impression of bodily delicacy. He saw how the clamps pulled on the tender nipples, each one now taut and strongly erect. The pearls shimmered and swayed as Marietta writhed, straining for her moment of release.

Her pale face was intense, the rose-petal mouth pursed and her cheeks flushed. There was a blankness to her expression. Marietta seemed to have given up her whole self to the woman who knelt between her thighs, as if in supplication.

Hamed absorbed the tension between them and gloried in it. He tore his eyes away from Marietta's pale perfection for a moment to concentrate on the other woman. Leyla too was possessed of great beauty. In contrast to Marietta's pale slenderness, Leyla's was the lush, full-blown beauty of the classic Venus.

Leyla's strong shoulders and long slender back flowed into a perfect heart-shaped bottom, made more enticing by the transparent red skirt. Her waist was not as slender as Marietta's, but then she, being Turkish, would not have been corset-trained from birth. As she moved, he caught a glimpse of the swell of her breasts and saw that there were compensations for her larger waist.

Leyla's breasts spilled over the top of the corset like large ripe gourds. Her nipples were prominent, especially so at this moment. They were very long and a lovely, deep wine-red. Just looking at them made him long to take them in his mouth.

He congratulated himself on the choice of her costume. Her black hair and white skin were startling against the deep-red and magenta of the embroidered velvet, and the gauze of her short skirt. The circular, ruby-studded nipple-clamps were perfect for her. He longed to see the labial clamps that gripped her sex-lips – Marietta's too.

The soles of Leyla's feet were upturned to him. She, like Marietta, had small, neat feet. He saw the slender backless slippers she wore, the ribbons that were stranded tightly around her shapely calves.

He fretted that he could not see every detail of their bodies, though he longed to gaze at every feature, every swell, every enticing crease. What a torture to imagine the shape, colour, and odour, of each rosy sex – that part which he considered to be a woman's most intimate beauty, beside her feet, of course.

Leyla's body partly hid Marietta, affording him a clear look at her from the waist up. And Leyla herself presented only her exquisite back view, but like a connoisseur he was content to wait. There were so many delights to discover and he would savour them, individually – one by one.

As they were now, the two women made a uniquely charming tableau. Hamed watched, lost in admiration and erotic longings.

Soon Marietta reached her peak of pleasure. Hamed feasted his eyes on her face, the half-open lips, the closed eyes with their fluttering lashes. And the breathy moans she uttered. She fell back onto the couch, with Leyla in her arms. They kissed passionately.

Marietta's skirt was still bunched up and he saw that she had a light frosting of pale blonde hair on her pubis. He was delighted by the novelty of it. Surely Kasim ordered that all his women be denuded of body hair. Why was Marietta alone spared? If only she would move a little, then he would be able to see her more clearly.

What a jewel. What perfection of form.

Hamed waited. His breath came fast. His mouth felt dry. It had been many long months since he had felt like this. Oh, he would have such pleasure from these two. How fortunate that Leyla had been taken along with Marietta. The reason why he had ordered them to be abducted paled. It did not matter why they were here. It was enough that they were.

For a while the women embraced. He could hear them whispering endearments, but did not catch what they said. Then Marietta pushed herself half upright and reached out to caress Leyla's breasts.

Yes. Oh, yes. Hamed felt a dart go straight to his belly as Marietta took one of Leyla's nipples between her lips and drew the tightly-fitting clamp into her mouth. Then she slid it in and out between wet parted lips. Leyla threw her head back, exposing a long pale throat. Her hands clutched at Marietta's shoulders as little tremors passed over her face.

Marietta gave a low, husky laugh at the evidence of the other woman's enjoyment. She kissed Leyla lightly on the mouth, then moved down the couch until she was kneeling on the carpet. Leyla moved to accommodate her. Marietta's hands swept down over the red corset, lingering on the velvet covered bones that held Leyla's waist in so sweetly. Then she pushed up the short, red skirt, so that Leyla's naked sex came into view.

Hamed had only a brief tantalising glimpse of Leyla's lower body, before Marietta's form obscured it from view. He saw that the Turkish woman's vulva was naked, as he expected. It was plump, the pubis well-developed. The inner lips showed slightly, their frilled red edges seeming to invite the caress of an admirer.

How sweetly the plump sex nestled between Leyla's thighs, shadowed by the bottom edge of the corset and framed by the soft folds of the red skirt.

He leant forward, pressing his face against the dusty panel, but his view was limited.

He could only imagine how Marietta used her mouth to draw pleasure from Leyla's womanhood. Marietta's hands crept upwards to cup the rich over-flowing swell of Leyla's breasts, to tug and toy with the nipple-clamps, as she moved her head slowly up and down between Leyla's thighs. Leyla gasped and moaned and moved her hips in an almost obscene manner.

Hamed ached to see what Marietta was doing. To watch as she teased the deep-red folds of Leyla's pubis with tongue tip and lips – to hear and see, more closely at hand, how Leyla groaned and shud-dered in the grip of sexual ecstasy. Did Marietta relish the salt-musk of Leyla's sex-taste? Leyla too must have the taste of Marietta in her mouth. How would Marietta taste? Like musk-honey and silk, he thought. He longed to taste them both, to smell them, to rub their rich juices all over his face, to bury his tongue in their silky inner warmth.

His imaginings ran free. His whole body seemed to be in a state of rampant desire. A desire that could normally only be slaked in a certain way. For the first time in many years he felt potent. He moved his hand downwards feeling for the unfamiliar tumes-cence. Dared he hope . . . ?

Finally he could stand it no longer. The women were so absorbed in themselves that they would not notice if he slipped into the room.

It was time he made his presence known.

Bishi folded clean towels and put them in the marble-lined bathroom.

She resisted the urge to go back into the room where Marietta and Leyla were pleasuring each other. She was not unduly concerned by their display of desire for each other. Indeed, she might have liked to watch from one of the spy-holes in the adjoining rooms, but she felt afraid of them and of the changes they would bring to the stronghold.

Her hands shook as she went about her tasks. Never had she seen such beautiful women. They were exquisite. Perfect. No wonder they were the pampered favourites of Kasim Dey.

How could Hamed help himself? He would be bewitched by them both. Her spirits sank as she thought of it. Once she had hoped that his eye might alight on her, but she was not beautiful – not like Roxelana, or the two new women. In her village she had been considered comely enough. But she knew that she was merely pretty, with the transient freshness that youth brought.

Bishi filled bottles of coloured Venetian glass with scented oils of carnation, lily and rose. If only Hamed could see beyond her face and into her simple, honest heart. He would discover something unique there – something that belonged to him alone.

She felt sorry for her master and was shocked at herself. It was not seemly to pity Hamed. Her master had so much and was rich beyond imagining. Still, she knew that he was not happy and it saddened her.

Roxelana brought him no joy. Neither did the erotic tableau that Gabriel arranged to fill Hamed's lonely nights.

She sighed. Sometimes, all the pleasures of the flesh and the delights of the senses were not enough.

Sometimes, men did not see what was in front of them.

Chapter Four

Marietta felt Leyla's flesh convulse against her mouth.

She exerted pressure against the well-developed bud of pleasure with her tongue, holding back Leyla's moment of release.

'Oh, please . . . please,' Leyla begged, her head lolling back as her eyelids fluttered open.

Smiling against the slick, rain-scented flesh Marietta gave two more gentle licks upwards and felt the little flesh-hood slip back completely, leaving the jutting bud exposed. She took the little nub between her lips. As she sucked it gently in and out, Leyla shuddered and reached her peak of pleasure.

'Oh, my sweet. My treasure,' Leyla breathed as her hips rocked in diminishing paroxysms and she subsided against Marietta.

Marietta sank onto the sofa and cradled Leyla in her arms. Both of them were flushed and hot. The hair clung damply to their foreheads. Leyla's breath came unevenly. After a moment she let out a long sigh of contentment. Marietta allowed her head to rest on Leyla's shoulder. Her eyelids drooped. She felt drowsy and ready to sleep.

It was a while before either of them noticed that a man had appeared in the room. Then, both at once, they became aware of a subtle difference in the atmosphere. Turning their heads they saw the tall figure standing in the shadows of a velvet tapestry. He was staring at them with undisguised absorption.

Leyla gave a little cry of alarm. Marietta was suddenly fully awake. Adjusting their clothes quickly they sat up, both regarding the silent figure with suspicion. Marietta recalled how Gabriel had seemed to appear out of the air in the same way.

She looked closely at the man as he approached them and recognised him as the well-dressed servant who had met them at the canalside.

'I assume there is a secret way into this chamber,' she said boldly. 'Are we to be spied on at every moment? Even those of private intimacy?'

The man's hard, handsome face creased in a smile. 'You assume correctly, on all counts,' he said evenly in the deep rich voice that she remembered. 'You have been brought here on my instructions. And whilst you are here, your every action is for my pleasure. Mine alone. As you have guessed, my stronghold is a warren of secret passages and rooms. They allow me to observe what is happening wherever and whenever I wish. Sometimes to my immense satisfaction.'

The dark-brown eyes which studied them with a mixture of appreciation and hauteur were shadowed and intense.

Realisation dawned on Marietta. 'You are Hamed,' she stated.

Hamed inclined his head. 'At your service,' he said, his large sensual mouth curving with wry humour.

His thick brown hair was brushed straight back from his wide brow. The wings of grey at his temple gleamed softly in the light from the Italian chandelier.

His broad, powerful body was clothed in a tunic and closely-fitting trousers of dark-green figured leather. High black boots fitted snugly around his powerful calves.

Marietta could see no sign of the mutilation Hamed was supposed to have suffered at the hand of Kasim. He was handsome in a strong-featured, implacable sort of way. She knew that Hamed had been a pirate, but he seemed cultured and intelligent, not at all the boor she had expected. He extended a hand to her and she saw again the ring set with a single cabochon ruby.

She hesitated for a moment, but realised that she had no choice but to respond to the gesture. She put her slim hand in his and felt his strong, warrior's fingers close over hers. He drew her to her feet, then did the same for Leyla.

Marietta could sense his tightly leashed desire. She was nervous. Hamed had an air of unpredictability about him. This was the man who hated Kasim. Where they in danger? As Hamed continued to look them both over, a half-smile on his face, she relaxed a little. Of course Hamed would wish them to pleasure him. It was a way of establishing his ownership, and letting them know that they must bend to his will – if they wished to remain safe until Kasim came for them.

Hamed sat down on the couch and stretched himself out, linking his hands behind the back of his neck. Marietta and Leyla remained standing, looking down at him. They waited for Hamed to speak, but he remained silent. His dark, brown gaze flicked over them in a leisurely fashion. He seemed to relish their discomfort. Marietta stared back at him boldly.

Then Hamed smiled slowly, acknowledging her spirit. 'What delight Kasim must find with you beauties. It pleases me to have deprived him of such singular pleasures. That erotic tableau I witnessed just now has inflamed my own passion. You will attend to that, at once. Both of you. I would experience the expertise I witnessed, first hand.'

Marietta's cheeks grew warm as she realised that Hamed had indeed watched everything she and Leyla had done together. They had pleasured each other thoroughly, using all the skill acquired during the long hot nights in the harem. When Kasim was engaged with matters of state they often solaced each other. Sometimes Kasim enjoyed them both at the same time, but the pleasures that Marietta and Leyla shared were usually private and unobserved. She could tell that Leyla too was mortified by the thought of Hamed having witnessed their private pleasure.

Hamed parted his legs and rested his high black boots on the rolled arm of the couch. The tumescence at his groin was plainly visible through the soft leather trousers. Hamed half-closed his eyes and relaxed. He said nothing more. This was a man who expected to be obeyed, at once.

Marietta hesitated. She did not think she could do as this man ordered. Kasim was her soul and her life. For him she would do anything, but something within her rebelled at the thought of pleasuring Kasim's sworn enemy.

Leyla, ever practical, flashed a glance of encouragement at Marietta, then stepped forward and laid her hands on Hamed's leather-clad thighs. She kneaded the firm muscles gently and began stroking upwards towards his groin. Hamed sighed. He turned his head towards Marietta and gave her a questing look. His dark eyebrows drew together in a frown.

'Well?' he said coldly. 'Surely this is not disobedience? I gave an order to you both. If one does not comply, both will be punished.'

Marietta moved forward quickly. 'How may I serve you?' she asked in a small voice.

Hamed smiled. 'Ah, better. Unfasten my tunic, then caress my torso with the tips of your breasts.'

Marietta fumbled with the fastening. Her fingers trembled and she was clumsy, but this seemed to amuse Hamed. Leyla was caressing the bulge at his groin. He gave a grunt of pleasure as she unfastened his belt and opened the leather trousers. Underneath he was naked. Leyla drew out the half-erect cock-stem and heavy sac, then peeled back the trousers so that Hamed's lower body was exposed from hips to thighs.

She gave a gasp and paused. Marietta, opening the tunic at the same moment, glanced down and barely controlled a similar response. A great puckered scar ran down one side of Hamed's taut stomach and disappeared into his groin, narrowly missing his penis and disappearing between his thighs. It showed pale against his otherwise golden-brown skin. The dark-brown curls at the base of his belly were bisected by the great ugly scar.

'Handsome, is it not?' Hamed said unperturbed by the double scrutiny. 'My manhood was not stolen, but it was affected. Is it not ironic that fate has declared that Kasim's exquisite pleasure-slaves shall coax me to a singular release?' His deep beautiful voice held such venom that Marietta almost recoiled. It seemed that his hate sustained him.

She would have pitied another man, but Hamed was so strong and vital that such emotion seemed misplaced. The wound was terrible and must have been a long time healing. Indeed his potency had clearly been affected. His cock, though thick and of a good length, was still only partly erect, despite Leyla's best efforts. She suspected that Hamed made light of this affliction for his own sake. His partial impotence must be a source of great shame to him. She knew how all men prided themselves on their ability as lovers.

It was a challenge to pleasure Hamed. She felt he was giving them some kind of test, a test they dared not fail. Her hands were steady now. She knew that she must work hard to assist Leyla in bringing this man to fulfilment. Bending forward she did as he asked and dragged the tips of her breasts across his broad chest. Slowly she described circles on his warm skin. The scent of him filled her nostrils. Vanilla and cinnamon, and clean maleness.

The pearl nipple-clamps played across his bronzed skin, tickling the slabs of muscle and teasing his tight male nipples which nestled in thick curls of brown hair. Hamed arched his back, pushing up to meet the pearl clamps as they swayed back and forth. His lips parted on a soft groan as Marietta lashed the pearls across his nipples which crested to form hard brown pips. They seemed extraordinarily sensitive for a man, perhaps in compensation for the loss of feeling in his groin. Lowering her head she closed her mouth on one of the pips and circled it with her tongue, then bit down on it gently. She did the same with the other one, then using just her tongue tip, she flicked the reddened nipples, blowing gently on the spittle-damp cones.

Hamed subsided onto the couch, his mouth slack, a look of mixed pleasure and anguish on his face. After a moment he thrust his hips towards Leyla as she worked on his penis, sliding the partially engorged glans in and out of her mouth. She gripped the base of his shaft and squeezed tightly, then flicked the underside of his glans with the tip of her tongue. Searching between his bottom cheeks she found the puckered mouth of his anus and pressed on it with a fingertip. She put just the tip of her long nail inside him, working it in and out, exerting a subtle scratchy pleasure. Hamed bucked against her hand.

'Yes. Oh, yes,' he grunted. 'Deeper.'

Leyla smiled and pressed gently so that her finger

entered him slowly at first, then she buried it to the knuckle. Curling her finger inside Hamed's anus she pressed on the sensitive spot which was separated from his sac by only a thin membrane. Drawing away for a moment she circled the tiny mouth of his cock-head with a fingertip, which she wetted by sucking on it first. A drop of clear salty fluid formed and rolled slowly down the engorged shaft-head. Leyla licked it clean, then closed her warm, soft mouth over the cock-tip. Keeping her lips relaxed she sucked its rim with rapid shallow movements.

As Marietta claimed Hamed's mouth and plunged her tongue into his throat, he hollowed his back and sank down onto Leyla's finger. His hips worked back and forth as Leyla now pleasured him with strong downward strokes of her mouth and throat. One hand worked his cock-stem, while the other penetrated his body and at the same time cupped his hairy sac.

The phallus was almost fully erect now. As the cock-stem was drawn clear of Leyla's mouth, the engorged glans emerged full and purplish, shiny with Leyla's spittle. His sac had shrunk to a hard tight ball. Hamed's release was approaching. Leyla gave a sound of satisfaction deep in her throat and moved her finger gently in and out of his anus.

Hamed made a sound like a sob as the two women pleasured him thoroughly. Marietta pinched his nipples hard as she kissed him, running the tip of her tongue around the inside of his mouth, then curling her tongue around his and sucking it strongly. Tremors ran down Hamed's thighs as his crisis overcame him. He clutched at Leyla's hair, meshing his fingers in the rich, dark waves and clutching her closely to him.

Suddenly his whole body convulsed. He threw his head back and screwed his eyes shut as the semen jetted into Leyla's throat. Marietta drew away a little and kissed him tenderly. She loved the moment when a man's pleasure was upon him. For just an instant, even the strongest man was as vulnerable and as weak as a baby.

Hamed recovered quickly. Without a word he stood up and adjusted his clothing. Then he stretched and ran his fingers through his thick brown hair. Marietta and Leyla waited warily for him to speak. Leyla remained on her knees beside the couch. Marietta stood at the head of it.

Hamed did not spare them a glance. 'Poor Kasim,' he said at length. 'To be deprived of his favourites. Now I know what he will be missing and why he prizes you so highly. Shall I send him a message, describing how I have enjoyed you? No. I think I'll wait a while. There is much more I shall do to you first. Then I will send him a scroll, beautifully written and graphically illustrated, detailing all the ways you have given me pleasure!' He gave a harsh laugh. 'Will that not madden him?'

'It is not enough that you have captured us? Must you taunt Kasim as well?' Marietta burst out.

She regretted her brief moment of tenderness. Hamed had accepted the pleasure they gave him as due tribute, brushing them off the moment he had spilled his seed. It was the expected action of a master over his captives, but perversely she was disappointed, having thought him capable of more nobility. It seemed that he had simply used them in an attempt to avenge himself on Kasim.

Hamed looked surprised at her outburst. For a moment his eyes softened with something like respect. Then his sensual mouth formed a hard line. 'Nothing I do to Kasim will ever be enough,' he said. 'You will be a witness to that soon enough.'

'What do you mean?' Marietta said, alarmed by his tone. 'What other treachery have you planned?'

But Hamed did not answer. He strode towards the

door. Before leaving the chamber he paused and said over his shoulder, 'I advise you both to rest now. Your real work begins on the morrow.'

'Work?' Leyla said.

'The work of entertaining me. And from now on I do not want you dissipating your energies by pleasuring yourselves idly with each other. Heed me well. Unless I expressly order it, all your talents are to be directed towards me. I am your new master. Serve me well and you will live here in luxury. Disobey me and you will be punished severely. Remember that I see and hear everything.'

He looked directly at Marietta and said on a final note, 'If I did not trust Gabriel so well I would not believe what he says of you. Well – he too will have his revenge.'

Hamed walked across a small courtyard on his way to Otsami's apartments.

He felt replete, sated, aware of every part of his anatomy. His body gave him back the tingle of perfect health. Even the slight ache from the old scar could not detract from his elation. Physically, he had not felt so good in a long, long, time, but his mind was more troubled than he cared to admit.

He was dangerously close to becoming obsessed with Marietta and Leyla. There had been no warning, just the sudden and certain reality of his emotions, but it was something he could not afford to feel. He could not possibly become ensnared by his enemy's creatures.

He needed to slow down, cool off, put matters back in perspective. In this mood he needed the gentle ministrations of his Japanese slave. Whenever he was troubled, needing to get his thoughts into order, he came to Otsami.

A nightingale in a gilded cage, hanging in a lemon tree, gave out a sweet song as he passed. The heavy perfume of roses and lilies rose on the sweet summer air. Leaves rustled in the breeze, dappling the marble floor-tiles with coins of gold and blotches of purple shadow.

Hamed was acutely aware of all these things. His senses seemed stirred to new levels. And he knew why. Kasim's pleasure-slaves had brought him to the sort of release he had once only dreamed of. Despite his injury, for a few moments he had been potent. A rare thing for him. Even Roxelana was only able to stir his body to a certain level. His pleasures were fragmented usually, dull-edged at best. Yet Marietta and Leyla together had wrought a miracle. At his moment of release he had almost wept.

Somehow, he had hidden the fact from them. It had taken a supreme effort to remain detached, when he had been tempted to fall at their feet and humbly thank them. That would never do of course. They must never know how he felt. But one thing he knew already. Whatever Kasim offered, however much he threatened and begged, Hamed would not return his slaves. There was nothing that would persuade him to relinquish them. Well – almost nothing . . . Hamed considered a few possibilities and smiled as he walked under an archway, festooned with a purple flowering creeper.

Reaching Otsami's apartments he nodded at the servant who opened the door to him. On the threshold he slipped off his boots and pulled on the indoor shoes that were there waiting, always ready for him, on the tatami that covered the floor tiles.

The peace and sparse beauty of Otsami's chamber reached into his soul, exerting a calming effect on him. A paper partition, painted with a landscape of waterfalls and mountains screened by plum blossom, separated the chamber. On one side was her sleeping space with its rolled futon and red lacquer cabinets for her clothes. On the other was her living space. In front of the screen was a long table with a number of shallow dishes containing miniature trees.

Otsami was at work on her painting in the far corner of the room. Seeing him she looked up and smiled. Gracefully she rose to her feet and came towards him with her smooth shuffling steps which he had found so entrancing when he first met her all those years ago. Her jet-black hair was held back by a scarlet ribbon. It hung in a straight fall down her back, sweeping the bottom edge of her scarlet and black kimono. She bowed from the waist, her slender white hands crossed on her chest.

'Welcome Hamed-*san*,' she said in her soft sing-song voice. 'Will you take some tea?'

Hamed followed her over to a wooden platform where a low black lacquer table stood. A beige-coloured paper lantern stood on the table, matching the cushions that surrounded the table. Light streamed in through white paper blinds. Seating himself, he made himself relax.

He watched Otsami's graceful movements as she made tea and chatted about inconsequential things. He answered absently, studying the half-finished painting, a tranquil scene of birds alighting on a vase of yellow chrysanthemums.

Already he felt calmer, soothed by the timeless atmosphere, the monochrome colours of Otsami's room, and her gracious unobtrusive presence. After tea he would ask her to sing and play the shamisen. Perhaps they would share a hot bath and he would have her massage his scalp with lotus-scented oil.

Nothing, save Otsami's cool oriental beauty, her studied and gentle artistry, could provide a foil for the dangerous and oh so compelling delights of Kasim's exquisite pleasure-slaves.

Marietta slept badly.

Her dreams were full of Kasim. How lonely and

sad he would be without her and Leyla. Kasim had not given his heart easily, but in the end he had fallen hard. She imagined how he must be searching for them, how he would be amassing a great sum to pay the expected ransom. Every one of his creditors would surely be trembling in their beds. Kasim could be ruthless when necessary. He had proved that to her time and again. She and Leyla were essential to his happiness. Not for a moment did she stop to consider the possibility that he would abandon them.

In her sleep she found herself cradled in Kasim's strong arms. Her cheek was pressed to his bare chest. His lips moved in her hair, then he tipped her face up for his kiss. She tasted his mouth and felt the liquid warmth of his tongue as he probed the inside of her mouth. She awoke with a jolt in the early hours with tears on her face. Brushing them away with her hand, she fitted herself to the curve of Leyla's back, finding comfort in the warmth of the other woman's naked body. Soon she slept again.

When she woke completely the chamber was still in shadow. For a moment she did not know where she was, then she saw the dusty tapestries, the Italian chandelier, and the dark tracery of the wrought-iron at the windows, against the lightening sky.

Her stomach lurched sickeningly as she remembered all that had happened. Gabriel had been instrumental in bringing her here, so that Hamed could wreak some kind of twisted revenge on Kasim. Gabriel seemed to have become her enemy. Her world had been turned upside down. She and Leyla had a new master, Hamed, who appeared only to want to use her and Leyla for his callous momentary pleasures.

How soundly they had drawn sweetness from Hamed's body, but he had spoken no words of praise or thanks. Instead he had left them abruptly, uttering veiled threats.

She felt afraid and insecure and wished that Leyla would wake up and offer comforting words. But Leyla was asleep beside her, her dark hair spread out in rich waves across the pillows. Marietta bent over her, but Leyla did not stir, her breathing was deep and even. She murmured in her sleep and buried her head more deeply into the pillows.

Marietta knew that she would sleep no longer and Leyla looked so peaceful that she could not bear to wake her. Pushing herself upright she padded across the room and poured herself a drink from the covered pitcher on a silver tray. A cool breeze blew in through the open window, smelling of dust and brackish water.

She could not judge the time, but thought it must be near dawn as the first birds were beginning to herald daybreak. From the window she could see the canal a long way below. The water gleamed darkly. A boat slid past the window, the lantern at its stern bobbing gently with the motion of the water.

She turned back to the room, feeling oppressed by the thickness of the walls standing between her and freedom. In a sudden panic she had a vision of the future. Perhaps they would never escape. Kasim might never find them. It would be unbearable if they were to stay here. More so, if Gabriel was to remain her enemy.

Suddenly, she wanted to talk to him. To ask him what crime she was supposed to have committed. She could not believe that he would turn away. Surely he would listen, give her a chance to redeem herself. And if not, there were other ways to appeal to his senses. She knew how he had always desired her and his actions earlier had proven that he still found her irresistible.

On impulse she reached for Leyla's red silk cloak and wrapped it around her nakedness. Putting her ear to the door she listened. Silence. Twisting the ornate brass handle, she pulled, holding her breath as the door swung silently inwards.

There was no guard in sight. She could not believe her luck. Pulling the door closed behind her she hurried down the corridor. The floor tiles were cool against her bare feet.

There were doors set at intervals down the corridor, each of them identical to the one that led to the chamber she shared with Leyla. She hesitated, suddenly unsure of the wisdom of her actions. Her hand reached out to grasp the handle of the first door, but she did not turn it. It would be sheer chance if she found Gabriel's room at the first try. She had no idea if he even slept in this part of the stronghold, or if he slept alone.

What if she was to stumble upon Roxelana? Or even Hamed? She would be punished for sure if she woke the occupants of the wrong room. There were so many doors, she could not possibly try them all. There seemed nothing for it, but to turn back. She had been foolish to venture into the corridor in the first place. Whatever had possessed her to take such a risk? She cursed her impulsiveness. Now she worried that Leyla would wake and find her gone.

She whirled and began to retrace her steps. With luck she would be back in the chamber before anyone realised that she was gone. Too late, she heard heavy steps coming towards her from the direction of her chamber.

There was the chink of metal, the sound of studded boot soles, the rumble of male voices. The guards. No time now to flee. She thought fast. Pulling the hood of the cloak to cover her head she walked resolutely towards the bend in the corridor, intending to meet the guards head on.

'Well, well. And who's this abroad so early?' said a cheerful voice. 'And what's she doing prowling around like a cat who's been out all night?'

Marietta made her steps languid. She slowed to a halt and sidled up to the guard who had spoken.

'Now that's a silly question,' she purred, keeping her chin lowered so that he caught only a glimpse of her face. 'You look like a man of the World. Can you not solve such a simple puzzle?'

The second guard gave a chuckle. 'Your lover's waiting and you've lost your way, eh?'

Marietta nodded, darting him a look from lowered lashes. 'And I'm likely to be beaten if my mistress discovers me gone.'

'Can't have that now. It'd be a shame to mark your pretty back with stripes.'

'Aye. We'll take you where you're going – for a small price,' the first guard said, drawing close and laying a hand on her shoulder. 'Show us how grateful you can be, eh?'

He pulled at the red silk and it slipped to reveal a bare creamy shoulder and the swell of the top of her bosom. The second guard gave a growl of appreciation and took a step closer. Marietta steeled herself not to cringe back from them.

She smiled. 'Thank you kindly. And will I tell Master Gabriel what price I had to pay you?'

The guards jumped back as if she'd burnt them.

'I jest only. Master Gabriel, you say?' the first guard said, sheepishly. 'A fine man. He has the ear of the illustrious Hamed. We're going past his quarters. Come. We'll accompany you.'

Smiling to herself, Marietta followed the guards through a door and ascended a stairway that led into the upper reaches of the tower.

They left her outside a pair of double doors.

'You'll need no more help from us,' they chuckled. 'Tell Master Gabriel how we aided you.'

'I will,' she smiled boldly, opening the door on one side and slipping inside the room.

With her back pressed to the solidness of the wood, she waited, allowing her eyes to become accustomed to the gloom inside the chamber. She heard the guards move off. Her heart beat rapidly, she felt its pulse heavy in her throat. Fear made her feel sick, but she forced herself on. It was too late to give in to faint-heartedness.

There was silence in the chamber. By the light of a single red lamp she could make out the shapes of furniture and see the curtained alcove that must house Gabriel's bed. She could smell burnt sandalwood and see the thin blue smoke that curled upwards from a small brazier set next to the lighter shape of a large window.

Slowly, she moved across the room, her silk cloak sweeping across the cool tiles. Her feet felt the softness of a carpet as she approached the alcove. Now she could see a little more clearly. Fine embroidered drapes partly concealed a low spacious bed. Against the pale sheets she saw a dark form, swathed in thin silk covers. Gabriel seemed to be deeply asleep. Intent on the shape curled up in the centre of the bed, she put out her hand to draw back the drapes.

Acting without thought, not daring to waver, lest she should lose courage, she bent down and leant over the still form.

'Gabriel?' she whispered.

So quickly that she had not time to register the movement or to recoil, the figure sprang up and threw off the bedcovers. There was a muffled expression of female rage. Marietta gained a confused impression of pale slimness and long tangled hair, then two strong hands gripped her from behind.

Marietta could not move. The grip was like iron. She felt her back resting against a solidly muscled chest, hard thighs held her legs in a vice-like grip.

The scream died in her throat as a palm was pressed over her mouth.

'Don't move or you die,' Gabriel grated in her ear.

The woman on the bed cursed and reached for a lamp which stood on a chest nearby. In a moment a golden glow illuminated the room. The woman on the bed was naked. Her red-tipped breasts shook as she scrambled to the floor. A heart-shaped face, topped by bright red ringlets, was thrust forward.

'You!' Roxelana spat and threw herself at Marietta, fingers extended to claw at her face.

Gabriel moved so that Roxelana crashed harmlessly into his side. Removing the hand from Marietta's mouth, he grasped both her wrists and twisted her round so that she was crushed against his chest. His loose blond hair brushed against her cheek. The scent of lemon-grass and musk enveloped her. At his proximity she felt a sudden and unexpected rush of longing.

'Leave this to me,' he said to Roxelana. 'Go back to your quarters. I'll join you later.'

Roxelana tried to reach for Marietta. Gabriel fended her off with one hand.

'But the little bitch is probably armed! She meant to murder you while you slept. Let me call the guard.' Roxelana's green eyes flashed dangerously.

'No!' Gabriel said firmly. 'Do as I say. I'm in no danger.'

As if to prove the fact he used his free hand to examine Marietta for weapons. Roughly he ran his hand over the curves of her body. Under his careless touch she trembled. She heard his quick intake of breath as he discovered her nakedness.

'She's harmless,' he said tersely to Roxelana. 'Now go.'

With a final venomous glance at Marietta, Roxelana shrugged on a velvet wrap and stalked from the room. 'Hamed shall hear of this!' she said as a parting shot.

Gabriel let go of Marietta and walked across the room to a carved wooden cabinet. He poured two glasses of wine and handed one to Marietta. She glared at him, rubbing her bruised wrists.

'That woman is a hell-cat! Can you find no one better to fill your bed?' At once she wished she had remained silent. Even to her own ears she sounded jealous, even petulant.

Gabriel's eyebrow lifted with amusement. His beautiful face was still flushed with sleep. 'What else did you expect? You come creeping into my room without so much as a by-your-leave. If I'd known you were going to visit me I'd have arranged to sleep alone.'

Marietta bit her lip. This was not going the way she had planned at all. How dared he make fun of her!

'Here. Take this wine,' Gabriel said evenly. 'It will calm you.'

She looked at him in amazement. 'Wine?'

'Hamed is no Muslim. He keeps a good cellar.'

Marietta took a sip. She had not tasted wine since she left the convent. And that had been a thin, sour liquid mixed with water. In Kasim's house she drank only fruit sherbets. She took another mouthful of wine. It was delicious, fragrant and sweet, rich with fruit flavours.

Gabriel watched her over the rim of the Venetian wine-glass. 'Are you going to tell me why you are here?'

She took a deep breath and closed her fingers tightly on the glass as if to steady herself. 'I had to come. I could not bear to think that you hated me. What you said back there . . . it made no sense. I need to know what you think I did.'

Gabriel narrowed his eyes. They glinted like slate

in the lamplight. 'If you have come here to regale me with more of your lies—'

'But I haven't told you any lies. Ever. You must believe me. Would I have risked punishment to come to you if I cared nothing for you, as you seem to think?'

In an instant he was beside her. He reached out a hand and drew back the silken hood. Her pale hair tumbled around her shoulders. Tipping up her chin he looked down into her wide blue eyes. He stared at her intently as if searching for something, then cursing softly he turned away.

'I cannot believe that you knew nothing of Kasim's plans.'

'What plans? You talk in riddles. Will you tell me what happened to you? Something has made you change towards me. I cannot believe you are so bitter, so cold.'

'Can you not? Then listen to what I have to say, and then tell me that I have no reason to hate Kasim and anyone who is close to him.'

Chapter Five

Gabriel began to tell Marietta what had happened to him in Kasim's house. It was as clear as yesterday. Every detail imprinted indelibly on his memory. As he began to speak the months fell away, the raw wound within him awoke. And he was back there at the precise moment when he slammed the door on Marietta and Kasim.

Tears had blinded him as he ran from the scene he had just witnessed.

He had lost her. The one woman he desired above all others. Marietta had lain full-length on the carpet behind the ornately carved door, her lips pressed to Kasim's booted foot in an eloquent gesture of submission.

What use was the freedom Kasim had promised, without Marietta to share it?

Reeling down the corridor away from Kasim's private apartments Gabriel had had no idea where he was going or what he was to do. At that moment he did not care. He was naked, his hair still damp and sweat-darkened. Straw from the stables had clung to his skin in patches. He had worked loose the bonds that Kasim had put on him, rubbing at his sore wrists where the ropes chafed them.

Gradually he had become aware that he must formulate a plan. However painful, he must put all thoughts of Marietta and Kasim from his mind. But it was impossible. His body had still ached for sexual fulfilment. Kasim had stirred him to hot lust as he pressed Gabriel face downwards onto the velvet bedcover and thrust into his oiled anus, taking a final exquisite pleasure and leaving Gabriel wanting. Gabriel's tumescence had not abated. His superb, well-trained body had continued to burn, even while his mind and soul sorrowed.

He passed groups of guards who put out their feet to trip him or taunted him as he stumbled past, finding it amusing to slap his naked buttocks or pull at his jutting cock. He let them jostle him, not caring how they ran their calloused soldier's hands over his golden skin. When one of them fell to his knees and took Gabriel's straining shaft into his mouth he had closed his eyes and given himself up entirely to the sensation of lips and tongue.

The sweetly tearing pleasure came upon him swiftly. He gasped and moaned, bucking against the soldier's mouth, delving deeply into the silken throat, his tight sac bumping against the man's bristled chin. The others watched, making sounds of encouragement. Gabriel was sunk in his own world of anguish. Everything was locked out except the clamouring of his body. For a while he cared for nothing, not even himself, glad of the diversion, the hiatus of emotion. There was only heat and wetness and the intoxicating smell of the soldiers, a mixture of sweat, leather, and male arousal.

When another of the soldiers had put his arms around him from behind and drawn him against his hairy groin he did not protest. The blunt edge of a cock nudged between his buttocks and he shifted his legs to accommodate it. The oil Kasim had anointed him with still streaked the inner flesh of his buttocks. The soldier slid smoothly into him. Gabriel sagged back against him, welcoming the penetration, the feeling of being opened. He was jerked back and forth by the power of the soldier's thrusts. Warmth gathered within him, crowding out the freezing shock, the sensation of being adrift and unwanted.

With a grunt the soldier had spilled into him. After that there was another. And another. Gabriel closed off his mind and slid past caring. He hardly noticed that they had finished using him. He came back to himself when he heard a familiar female voice and felt a leather boot-toe nudging at him.

Looking up from where he had slumped against the tiled wall he had seen Sita's narrow spiteful face. Hands on hips, she stared down at him. Behind her were a number of the female harem guards. All of them regarded him with pity and contempt.

'Well. Well. What a mess you're in,' Sita had said coolly. 'The golden beauty brought low, eh? No longer a favourite, but an outcast. How fortunate for me. You'd better come with me to see a friend of mine.'

'But I'm to be set free,' he had murmured, stirring himself. 'Kasim promised me.'

'For certain he did,' she said. 'You can tell that to Dimusen the gaoler. You and you take him. You others secure him with chains. We're about to restore you to the life you were made for, Gabriel. The life of a pleasure-slave.'

'Keep him here until he's learned what it is to be truly docile,' Sita said to Dimusen. 'He's cowed now, but he's spirited and troublesome when in his right mind. I want him ready to display himself willingly. Then I'll spread the word that a choice slave is to be offered in the market. When there's enough interest, we'll make a killing.'

Dimusen's small eyes glittered in his fleshy face. His bald head was topped by a dirty pigtail. The heavy gold rings in his ears and through the septum of his nose gleamed in the flickering light of the rush candles on the walls.

He extended a massive arm and closed thick fingers around Gabriel's biceps. 'A choice morsel,' he said wetting his thick lips. 'Should fetch a pretty price. And in the meantime I'll take great pleasure in taming him.'

Gabriel twisted round and spat in his face. 'Get your filthy hands off me! I'm a free man you tub of lard!'

Sita's narrow mouth curved in a grim smile. 'Not any more. I'd advise you to get used to the idea. Dimusen is not known for his patience.'

As Dimusen laughed richly, the fat around his enormous waist jiggled and his breasts wobbled. He took a ponderous step forward and picked Gabriel up bodily. Gabriel struggled against his chains, but it was no use. Dimusen was incredibly strong. Slinging Gabriel over his meaty shoulder he carried him to an open cell and slung him down on a pile of straw. Winded, Gabriel lay curled into a ball.

Before he could recover, the chains securing his wrists were attached to a ring set into the wall of the cell. Dimusen threw him a dirty wolfskin, then put a bucket and a jug of water next to him. The cell door clanged shut and darkness descended.

The sounds of Sita's and Dimusen's voices grew fainter as they moved away. Gabriel was alone. He wept tears of frustration and anger. There was a hard ball of pain in his stomach. He could smell his own body. It was sour with stale sweat. The soldiers' semen had dried on him, leaving a crust that streaked his buttocks and thighs. In self disgust he burrowed into the scratchy straw and pulled the wolfskin to cover his nakedness.

He no longer cared what happened to him. Nothing mattered if Marietta was lost to him. But during that first long night he had ample time to think and, gradually, he felt a new anger sink and take hold deep within him. He realised that it was unlikely that Marietta was innocent. She must have known what Kasim planned. No wonder she had thrown herself at his feet.

They had betrayed him. No doubt they had planned it together. Well they hadn't heard the last of him. He wanted revenge. The promise of it would sustain him throughout whatever was to come. His stomach roiled and acid rose to burn his throat. Revenge would be the saving of him. It would have to be enough – for now.

The days of early summer lengthened and grew hotter. In Kasim's gardens, lilies scented the air and lemons and oranges ripened on the trees. Peacocks sent their echoing calls to mix with the sound of fountains that tinkled and sparkled in the sun.

Dimusen rubbed his hands together as he arranged a bunch of wild flowers in a cracked stone jar. He set them to decorate the wooden table in his room.

He felt good. Another day had dawned fair, sending a pale light to penetrate the musty lower reaches of the palace. This place was his domain. He took pride in his work and wielded the whip with the same degree of pleasure he got from abusing his prisoners sexually. His name sent a shiver down the back of anyone who heard it.

It was time to visit the prisoner again. Inside his dirty leather breech-clout Dimusen's stubby cock stirred. Anticipation made his mouth water. He passed his tongue over his thick lips.

Gabriel was a beauty and no mistake. He hadn't

had a toy like him for many a long day. Over the weeks he had taken full advantage of that fact. It was a pleasure to have him all to himself. Too bad that he would be sold one day. Well, at least the money would be a compensation for his loss. But the day of the sale was far away and for now he could do as he wished with the most perfect specimen of maleness he had ever laid eyes upon.

Gabriel sprang up the moment the cell door creaked open. He backed away from the smiling Dimusen, eyeing him warily. His once golden hair hung in dull, greasy ropes, straggling over his shoulders and down his back. Though his powerful shoulders and heavily muscled torso were still superb, he had lost weight. His cheeks were hollowed and his eyes over-bright, giving his beauty a touch of other-worldly fragility.

'Well, my pretty,' Dimusen smiled, showing broken teeth. 'What are you going to do to earn your breakfast this day?' His hand trailed down to his bulging breech-clout and moved a corner of the garment aside to display his rampant cock. It was thick and short, topped by a reddish and angry looking glans.

Gabriel glowered at him, eyes burning with contempt. 'You can keep that swill you call food. And if you try to touch me I'll fight you tooth and nail!'

'Oh ho, fine words. Please yourself. But hunger makes for an eager bedmate. You'll not last long. I'll call back later, when I've done my rounds. See whether you've changed your tune.'

He pulled the cell door closed and went on his way. Gabriel sagged with relief as he heard the gaoler's wheezing laughter and the sound of the bucket of steamed wheat clanging along the wall. Dimusen was in the mood to wait today. He wasn't always. Gabriel's gorge rose as he recalled the many times he had been forced to pleasure the gaoler –

held captive by his chains, pressed face down in the stinking straw, while the fat man heaved and sweated over him.

His stomach gnawed with hunger and he knew that, despite his brave words, he'd do anything Dimusen asked him to on his return. He sat on the filthy straw and put his head in his hands. Despair threatened to overcome him. How long had he been here? He would have lost count of the days except for the marks he had scratched on the crumbling bricks with a link of his chains.

He squinted at the marks, counting them in the dim light. Five weeks and six days. It felt like years. He tensed as he heard footsteps approach his cell. Surely Dimusen had not finished his rounds yet. The spy-hole in the door was uncovered and a face blocked the square of light. The light from a lantern flooded the cell, causing him to hold his arm up to cover his eyes. Soon after that he heard voices raised in anger. He listened closely and thought he recognised Sita's voice.

He waited with bated breath until his cell door was unlocked and Dimusen shuffled inside. The gaoler was sweating and seemed agitated. He carried the usual bowl of steamed wheat, but there were pieces of stringy meat on top. In his other hand he had a jug of watered milk and a hunk of rough bread. Gabriel's mouth watered at the feast.

Dimusen put the food on the floor. 'Seems that you're to be fattened up and allowed to have a bath every day,' he said. 'You're to be sold a week from now. Pity. I was getting used to having you here. It's a lonely occupation . . .'

Gabriel was surprised to hear real regret in the gaoler's voice. Dimusen's eyes were moist. His thick lips trembled. He paused as if waiting for Gabriel to speak words of comfort. Gabriel was incredulous. He could find no pity in him. The marks of his mistreatment were too fresh. The gaoler enjoyed his work too much. His eyes flickered towards the food. Dimusen caught the movement and recovered himself. He grinned.

'What do I get then? For this food and enough hot water and soap to wash the lice away? Be good to be clean again, eh? And have a nice full belly.'

Gabriel closed his eyes and gritted his teeth as Dimusen came close. The gaoler's breath quickened as he caressed Gabriel's torso, squeezing his nipples with his thick fingers. He grunted as he buried his face in Gabriel's neck and began to lick his skin.

'Eager for Dimusen's lusty cock are you? Better enjoy it this day. You'll be the plaything of some old man soon enough.' His wheezing laughter tickled Gabriel's ear.

Gabriel emptied his mind and tried to think only of the food and the bath, but somehow Marietta's face imprinted itself on his mind. He fastened onto the image with eagerness. It was her hands that caressed him, her mouth that travelled over his skin, tasting and suckling.

Dimusen would be finished quickly and now he had hope. Soon he would see the sky and smell the clean fresh air.

Every day after that the opportunity for revenge would come closer and closer.

Marietta sat in stunned silence when Gabriel finished speaking. Her wine stood on a side table, the glass still half full.

Gabriel gazed out of the window as dawn spread a stain of salmon and peach across the sky. His face was set in a mask of pain.

What could she say? Nothing seemed adequate to compensate for his suffering. No wonder he hated Kasim. There was no denying that he had been treated shamefully, but she could not believe it was

Kasim's doing. And yet . . . She knew Kasim to be ruthless. Where she was concerned he would dare anything. Was she not counting on that very same attribute at present?

Her throat was dry. She took a gulp of wine before she spoke. 'Gabriel,' she began, her voice low and filled with emotion.

'Don't!' he rapped. 'Spare me your pity. And don't tell me again that you knew nothing about what was to happen to me. I had ample time to think things over and I cannot be persuaded of your innocence.'

'Then what am I to say?' she said softly. 'You have tried me and found me guilty.'

His grey eyes were calm as they fastened on to her. 'Say nothing,' he said. 'Just listen to me as I finish my story. In some strange way it helps to tell it all to you. God knows why.'

'Tell me then,' she said. 'So that I may understand fully why you despise me.'

He blanched. And she knew that she had touched a nerve. Ah, Gabriel, you deceive yourself, she thought. I know what is in your heart, but you must rediscover it for yourself.

He poured more wine and refilled her glass, then settled himself in the padded window seat. The pink light, streaming through the carved lattice work, made a lacy pattern on his face. He was naked to the waist. The smooth, gold skin of his magnificent torso was flawless. The deep-blue folds of his velvet robe covered his lower body. He rested the hand holding his wine-glass on one bent knee.

He looked beautiful and mysterious and, in some indefinable way, more brittle than when she last saw him. Her heart went out to him. Deep in her belly the flame that burned for him burst into new life. It was that quality of human frailty, clothed in strong male flesh that drew her to him. Kasim too, had that same streak in his nature; it was the flaw in the gem that pronounced its perfection; the overblown quality of a rose, foreshadowing the moment when its beauty must fade. The hint of fragility made those things more poignant than mere beauty.

A rush of emotion brought tears to her eyes. She wanted to feel Gabriel inside her again, to be filled with his hard male flesh and to ride him to a blistering climax. Almost she got up and went over to him, but he began to speak again and she steeled herself to bide her time.

'Sita came for me a week later. I was taken to the market-place and displayed along with all the other slaves. It was deeply humiliating to be put on show like an animal. All day long I had to stand there, while all who pleased examined me. They stuffed their fingers into my mouth and forced me to display my teeth. Looked inside my ears, checked my hair for lice and made me bend my knees and jump up and down. But, you know, I did not care what they did to me – for the sun shone down on my naked skin and a clean breeze caressed me.'

He looked at her and smiled without warmth. 'After Dimusen's foul touch the hands that cupped my balls, worked my shaft, and pulled back my cockskin seemed innocent. The fingers that poked deeply into my body and tugged at my pubic hair were nothing to me. I was broken somehow. And I did not heal until Hamed bought me and brought me to his stronghold. Then we found solace in each other. I discovered that we had both felt the poisoned touch of Kasim's influence and suffered in different ways. Both of us have been scarred by him, but I wear my wounds on the inside.'

'And are you to be scarred for ever by your experiences or will you allow yourself to live again?' The words were out before she could stop them. She had not meant to sound so callous.

Gabriel's head whipped round. 'Easy to say,' he

97

said. 'Tell me. How am I to do that when I am haunted by your betrayal? In all this, it is the one thing I cannot come to terms with. Not a night has passed when I am free from you. Every woman I pleasure wears your face.'

Slowly, he uncurled from the window seat and came towards her. The look on his face made her tremble, but she held his eye. He reached out and grasped her chin, holding it so tightly that her eyes watered. The pad of his thumb stroked teasingly across her soft mouth.

'You came here of your own accord, seeking, no doubt, to beguile me with sweet words and your sweeter flesh. What am I to do with you?' he said softly. 'How can I make you tell me the truth?'

She felt his restrained violence. The way he fought with himself. His desire for her was written plainly on his face. So was his wish to hurt her. The truth – he did not want that, she realised. His suffering had blinded him to everything but the pursuit of revenge. More denials were of no use. Gabriel wanted to hear her confession. Only then would he be able to forgive her. And seeing him so damaged, she knew she had to give him what he wanted. Later there would be time to set things straight. Haltingly at first, she began to speak.

'I . . . I did not stay with Kasim of my own free will. He threatened to have you killed if I chose you over him. I knew that he would never set you free, but any chance at life was better than nothing.'

Gabriel bowed his head. 'So you *did* know that I was to be given to the gaoler.'

'No. I . . . I knew only that you were to be sold.'

He put his hands on her shoulders, holding her so tightly that she could not move. She felt him trembling. 'And if you had been given an unconditional choice – who would you have chosen?'

Marietta looked directly into his troubled grey

eyes. Forgive me Kasim my love, she said inwardly, but I must tell him what he wants to hear.

'I would have chosen you,' she said without faltering.

Gabriel groaned and pulled her close, grinding his mouth against hers in a kiss of agonised longing. 'I knew it,' he murmured against her lips. 'I knew it was all the doing of that Devil!'

Marietta pressed a fingertip against his mouth. 'Hush. Let us speak no more of Kasim. We have found each other. Gabriel, I want you so. I never stopped loving you.' Tears glittered in her wide blue eyes. It was true. Part of her did love him and always would.

'You were so cruel and harsh when you took me back there in my chamber,' she said huskily. 'Won't you love me now with gentleness? Forget your hate. It will destroy you if you do not. Come, find healing within my flesh.'

He looked dazed as if he could not believe his good fortune. Gently she disengaged herself and stood up. She undid the single hook that held the red silk cloak around her shoulders. The thin fabric slipped to the floor with a soft rustle and she faced him, clothed only in her unbound hair.

He gazed at her, drinking in all her pale beauty. Then he scooped her up in his arms and carried her to the couch. She wrapped her arms around his neck and clung to him, breathing in the warm scent of his nakedness. His sun-bleached blond hair brushed against her cheek as he laid her on the couch then sank down beside her, cradling her in his embrace.

She felt his heartbeat as he pressed her against his hard chest and his touch was gentle as he stroked her tumbled curls back from her forehead.

'My own Marietta,' he whispered as he placed light kisses on her eyelids, her cheeks, the tip of her nose, and finally her mouth.

Her lips opened under his and she tasted him, teasing the inside of his mouth with the tip of her tongue. A hot stab of wanting speared her belly as his hands stroked her arms and shoulders. He seemed to be exploring her afresh, as if they had never lain together. She strained against him and he laughed thickly.

'So eager for me, sweeting? Be patient. The waiting will be worth it.'

He pressed his lips to the hollow of her throat, circling the indentation with his tongue. His hands stroked her breasts, cupping the underswell and bringing them together. He pressed his face to her cleavage, inhaling her perfume, then nuzzled the tips of her breasts. With tender lips he mouthed her nipples, sucking them in and collaring them with a curled tongue. The light touch of his lips, the warmth of his mouth, was maddening. Her nipples swelled to hard little cones. As he nibbled the taut flesh, the sensations rippled down her belly and found an echo in the pulsing between her thighs.

Turning in to him, she closed her hands over his, lifting and offering up her breasts to his eager mouth, suckling him like a child. The sweet pulling sensation opened a well deep within her. Her sex felt heavy and the wetness gathered at her entrance, ready for the moment when he would thrust into her.

She meshed her hands in his hair and drew his face close, kissing him deeply, murmuring his name. There were tears on her cheeks. She had not expected to feel so much. This was no mere pleasuring of the body. It was truly a healing, a new beginning.

Smiling tenderly he stroked her face, then moved down her body to kiss the soft mound of her belly. His long hair was spread across her hips and thighs, like a skein of yellow silk. The strands tickled her skin. Tremors passed over her belly. Gabriel positioned himself between her thighs, exerting a gentle pressure with his palms, so that she spread her legs.

'Bend your knees up, my sweet. I want to gaze on that adorable mound with its unique fleece. Let me breathe in your fragrance and taste the sweetness of your secret flesh.'

For a moment he just looked at her, stroking the pale blonde pubic curls back from the sex-lips to reveal the pink inner flesh. He cupped the perfect globes of her bottom, drawing his fingers along the inner edges of her cheeks, where the skin was a darker shade. Then he bent forward and took a long loving taste of her sex.

Marietta almost cried out at the exquisite sensations as he licked slowly up the inside of each of her flesh-lips. He paused at the spot where they joined and nuzzled at the little hood of flesh that covered her bud of pleasure.

Slipping two fingers inside her, he moved them in and out as he flicked the covered bud with the tip of his tongue. Marietta moved against his hand, feeling his knuckles grow wet with her juices as her womanhood gave up its honey. Removing his fingers, Gabriel pressed his mouth to her soaking vulva and covered it completely, burrowing into her, sucking the slippery folds in an erotic kiss.

Marietta emitted a series of high-pitched little cries. Her pleasure threatened to peak. Surely she could not stand much more. Her reactions tipped Gabriel over. Kneeling up between her spread thighs, he tipped her hips up and grasped the back of her waist. As he slid into her, he moaned deep in his throat and pulled her fully onto his swollen shaft. In one smooth movement he was all the way inside her, his cockhead pressed against the entrance to her womb.

For a moment he paused, savouring the silken heat inside her. Marietta worked her hips, urging him to move.

'Now, Gabriel. Oh, now.'

Leaning into her he thrust strongly, drawing almost all the way out before plunging back inside her. Marietta's whole body tightened as her flesh-tube pulsed around him. Gabriel felt the tiny inner jerks around the head of his cock and knew that she was near to a climax. Leaning forward he laid her flat, loving the way her sex gripped and milked him even more tightly in that position.

Slowly now, he drove into her, supporting himself on straight arms and arching his body so that he could watch her face as he drew her on towards her peak.

Marietta's hands clutched at the rumpled sheets. Her pale hair was spread out all around her. Her swollen, half-opened lips, her intense blue eyes, and the languidness of her limbs acted on him like heated wine. She had never looked more beautiful to him.

At the moment when she climaxed, her face screwed up into an expression of sublime anguish. A pain seemed to pierce Gabriel right through his heart as he watched the play of emotion across her features. Oh, God he loved this woman more than life. Marietta contracted around his shaft so tightly that he lost control completely and spurted his seed into her. The sweet agony of it seemed to go on and on.

At last, he collapsed, gasping, onto her.

Marietta held him tightly as he sobbed openly. She cradled his face against the hollow of her throat, stroking his hair and murmuring endearments. It was a long time before he was able to speak.

'Marietta. Marietta . . .' he whispered brokenly.

'Hush. We have no need of words. Sleep now. And let there be peace between us.'

He sighed with contentment and closed his eyes. It would be wonderful to slip away, knowing that he would wake later and still be in her arms, but he could not sleep until he had told her what was in store for their former master.

'Never fear, Kasim will get his just deserts, my love.'

He felt her tense and thought she was afraid. He leant on his elbow and looked down at her. 'I'll keep you safe. He won't hurt you. Hamed is going to lure him here. You and Leyla, my sweet, are the bait that will bring him.'

Marietta drew in her breath sharply. 'Hamed means to capture Kasim?' she said incredulously.

'Nothing so simple. To do such a thing to the Public Administrator of Algiers would cause an all-out war. Hamed does not seek that. He will put a proposition to Kasim. If our former master will agree to spend a specified time as Hamed's willing pleasure-slave, then you and Leyla shall go free. Hamed is known to be a man of his word. Kasim knows this.'

Marietta hid the horror she felt. Everything in her cried out against this outrage, but she dared not let Gabriel see how profoundly his words had affected her.

'Kasim won't agree to that,' she said with forced confidence.

'You think not? You underestimate your worth. I could not forget you. Do you think he can?'

Gabriel pulled Marietta down to lie against him as he snuggled contentedly under the bedcovers.

'I'll sleep well now,' he said, kissing her temple. 'And my dreams will be full of the sight of Kasim brought low. Is that not a pleasant thought?'

'Yes. To be sure,' Marietta whispered, biting her lip.

Long after Gabriel had fallen asleep she lay awake thinking about Kasim. Surely he would not agree to Hamed's terms. She conjured a mental image of Kasim, his sharply angled face and mysterious dark

103

eyes. Eyes that glistened with constrained desire when he chastised her so sweetly that her whole body dissolved with willing submission. The love she felt for her master was very different to the tender emotion that Gabriel stirred within her.

It had always been difficult for Gabriel to accept how much Kasim meant to her. He did not understand that Kasim had showed her what she truly was. Something in her cried out for the spiked pleasures, the humiliation, that only her acknowledged master could supply.

It was easier for Gabriel to believe that Kasim had forced her to stay with him, than to face the truth. Yes, she loved Gabriel. But she could not live without Kasim. Gabriel's pronouncement had thrown her into confusion.

Oh Kasim, I am eager for you to come for me, but not at the price that Hamed demands, she thought. She could not imagine Kasim as a slave. He was so proud, so rigidly self-contained. She thought she was familiar with every turn and facet of his dark, jewel-sharp intellect, but she did not know how he would react when he learnt that Gabriel was now Hamed's slave.

Kasim had once desired Gabriel strongly. She was not certain whether or not he had betrayed him. Once she would have sworn on the strength of Kasim's integrity, but Gabriel had been promised freedom and he had been misused. What was she to make of it?

She no longer knew what to believe. The truth was becoming ever more blurred. And where did that leave her? She was guilty of deceiving Gabriel too. There had been no other choice, but she did not like what she had done.

She lay staring up at the embroidered bed-curtains, while morning sunlight spilled into the room. Beside her Gabriel slept, a half-smile on his well-shaped mouth.

Roxelana clenched her fists together so hard that her long scarlet nails cut into her palms.

She had waited in the corridor for Marietta to emerge from Gabriel's chamber, planning to seize her and drag her before Hamed. Moments had passed and stretched into minutes, until she had to face the fact that Marietta was not coming out. That meant one thing only. Somehow the French bitch had managed to curl Gabriel round her little finger. It seemed impossible. She knew how Gabriel felt about his former master and his favourite female slave.

Surely she would hear Marietta's pleas for mercy, her cries of distress as Gabriel took his revenge. But there was only silence. She imagined the scenario. Marietta on her knees, her hands raised in supplication. Gabriel falling for her lies and gathering her into his arms.

Roxelana stormed back to her chamber, almost numb with fury. How dare Gabriel dismiss her so that Marietta could take her place in his bed! She had never been so insulted. Before Marietta came to the stronghold, she had been everyone's favourite. Gabriel had not been averse to her charms. Oh, no. He liked it well enough when she crept into his bed unexpectedly. Hamed too, looked to her alone for his physical pleasures. Now she was not so certain of her supremacy with him.

For Hamed had come straight from an erotic interlude with Leyla and Marietta and gone to visit Otsami, something he always did when his mind was troubled. Luckily Roxelana's spies kept her well informed. She would act swiftly and take steps to see that Marietta fell from favour.

But first, the Turkish woman. Leyla must be alone in the bed-chamber. She would start with her.

She finished dressing in a dark-green corset and matching short skirt.

'Lace me more tightly,' she ordered, holding herself in until her waist was compressed to its limit.

It did not matter that she could hardly draw breath, or that her breasts were thrust up higher than ever. It was imperative that her waist become as small as Marietta's. She turned this way and that, admiring her shape in a looking-glass. Emeralds glinted in her upswept red hair and at her throat.

Almost ready, she waited impatiently while a servant slipped her feet into high-heeled slippers and twined green velvet ribbons around her calves. Putting the pointed toe of her shoe to the servant's chest, she pushed hard. The servant overbalanced and sprawled on the floor.

Roxelana laughed, a light infectious sound. Then with one of her quicksilver changes of mood, she frowned.

'Get up! You look ridiculous,' she rapped. 'Now get out. Bring me some hot food and leave it covered. I have to go out, but I won't be long.'

Reaching for a flexible riding crop she left the room. Quickly she made her way to the chamber, where she hoped Leyla still slept. Her breath quickened with excitement as she paused outside the door. All was silent within. Excellent. It was still early, only the servants and guards were abroad at this hour. She suppressed a laugh: and women bent on revenge!

The door opened silently. She saw Leyla immediately, lying half-uncovered and flushed with sleep. Her dark wavy hair formed a pillow for her head. Against the blackness of her tresses her profile showed as pure and clear as a cameo.

Roxelana felt an unwilling admiration. The Turkish woman was possessed of a lush curvaceous beauty.

106

She imagined how the crop would sound as it struck the creamy flesh. Leyla's half-exposed buttocks would look beautiful when criss-crossed with pink marks.

Roxelana's body grew tense with anticipation. Between her thighs a pulse began to tick strongly. She looked down on the sleeping woman, relishing the feeling of power over her. How pleasant would be the sight of Leyla's terrified face as she woke her abruptly to pleasure-pain.

And how satisfying when Marietta learnt what had happened to her friend during her absence.

Slowly, with studied deliberation, she raised the crop.

Chapter Six

Kasim rose early and prepared himself mentally for what was to come. His usual meal of fruit, bread, and mint tea stood ready, but he drank only cold water and ate nothing. Until his task was complete he had forsworn all food.

Two coffers, filled with a fortune in gold coins, stood in the centre of his chamber. It had taken days to collect and half the merchants and burghers of Algiers simmered and chafed at the loss of the better part of their profits.

Kasim cared nothing for them, nor for the fact that he had made new enemies with his demands. His mind was centred on Marietta and Leyla. The messenger he had sent to Hamed had returned the day before last. Hamed had refused to speak to him or even acknowledge him. Red faced, the messenger had been obliged to wait for hours outside the locked gates of the stronghold, until he finally gave up and left, to the accompaniment of jeers and a hail of abuse.

Hamed's unspoken message was clear; he would discuss his terms with no one except Kasim himself. So now, Kasim would enter Hamed's stronghold and challenge him face to face. If threats and a show of force did not work, then there was the money to fall back on.

Hamed must respond to the latter surely. He well remembered how Hamed had been motivated by riches in his days of piracy. Kasim had not seen his old adversary for many years. Had Hamed changed? He would soon see for himself. Kasim concentrated on what he knew of Hamed, going over and over their exchanges, remembering that Hamed was no fool. He was cultured and intelligent. It would be a mistake to underestimate him. Consumed by hatred Hamed might be, but he was unlikely to be provoked to rash actions. The situation needed careful handling and would call for all the diplomacy Kasim was capable of.

He was alone, having elected to dress without the aid of a bodyservant. The intricacies of putting on full dress-armour concentrated one's mind wonderfully. After washing his spare, tightly muscled body with cold water, he dried himself with a rough towel. As he dressed in a high-collared black tunic and loose red leather trousers, he schooled himself to do everything slowly and deliberately. No one must guess that beneath his icy exterior, he was besieged by self doubts.

He pulled on the padded undershirt, then buckled on a fitted breastplate of Moorish armour. Flaps of hinged metal protected his groin and thighs. Sturdy armoured boots, the toes curving upwards into stiff spikes, clothed his legs from mid-thigh downwards. He walked stiffly towards the window, where there was a looking-glass on an angled stand.

The carved and enamelled gold of the armour reflected morning light onto his starkly handsome face. His cheeks looked pale, almost bloodless, above the dark smudge of his morning stubble. Only his wide, sensual mouth had a little colour. He smiled grimly into the glass as he brushed his long black hair straight back from his forehead and secured it at his nape, prior to fitting on his dress-helmet.

His fingers were clumsy as he attached his black silk cloak to the shoulder-fittings of the armour. He felt the urge to rip the cloak off and throw it to the floor. Cursing under his breath, he clenched his teeth and forced himself to complete the task. There, it was done. Now the helmet. He pulled it on so that it rested low on his forehead. The weight of it was oppressive, but he hardly noticed. Shaped armour plate, moulded and curved, cupped his cheeks. The peak of the helmet rose into a point, adding inches to his already impressive height.

At last, he was ready. He swept from the room, the black cloak swirling out behind him.

In the courtyard, his horse and retainers awaited. Mehmet waited with Kasim's mailed gauntlets, another servant handed Kasim his weapons. He thanked them and managed a grim smile. The coffers were loaded onto a cart. As the servants stood back, Kasim urged his mount forward. His mouth was set in a thin, hard line. His sharp cheekbones were shadowed and there were dark smudges under his eyes.

No one spoke. Those nearest to him lowered their eyes. All who stood in the courtyard were aware that wars had started over lesser things than the insult offered to Kasim Dey by his old enemy.

The horses' hooves clattered on the metalled road as Kasim's entourage headed out of the city. They must take a circuitous route to Hamed's stronghold, as the horses and carts could not go by barge.

Kasim leant back in the saddle and breathed in the cool, mist-scented morning air. Inside the heavy gauntlets his fingers tightened on the reins. An image of Marietta formed in his mind. He held it still, like a

110

lamp in his inner darkness. Her pale, lovely face was his talisman.

'Never fear, my loved ones. I'm coming for you both,' he breathed. 'And one way or another I swear I'll get you back.'

That vow must be enough to sustain him. Let Hamed ask for anything; anything at all. Whatever it took, he would succeed in rescuing Marietta and Leyla. He would not allow himself to think of the consequences of failure.

Gabriel escorted Marietta back to her quarters.

The guards who now stood steadfastly on either side of the door stared straight ahead, too well trained to pay any attention to the comings and goings of the masters and pleasure-slaves. Some time ago the flame-haired Venetian had crept inside the room. The muffled cries and sobs that reached them had been intriguing, but they knew better than to comment or interfere. Roxelana emerged minutes later with her cheeks flushed becomingly and a look of satisfaction on her exquisite face. Without a sideways glance she swept down the corridor, the high heels of her backless slippers clicking on the floor tiles. A look passed between the guards, but they did not pass comment. The Venetian woman was a law unto herself and woe betide anyone who incurred her displeasure.

At the door Gabriel raised Marietta's hand to his lips.

'I must leave you here for a while, my sweet. Hamed will expect me to attend him as usual, so that he can give me his orders for the day.' He bent close and whispered. 'I will say that I ordered you to come to my chamber. Then you will not be punished for roaming the corridors without permission.'

Marietta watched Gabriel walk away before slipping into her chamber. For the first time in days she felt at ease. Her step was light as she crossed the room.

'Not still abed, surely,' she said teasingly, seeing that Leyla was spread face-down in the tumbled bedcovers.

It was a moment before she realised that Leyla was sobbing quietly. At once Marietta was beside her. The red silk cloak settled into a pool around her as she knelt by the bed.

'What is it? What's wrong?'

The question died on Marietta's lips as she pushed aside the heavy black hair that was spilled across Leyla's prone body. She saw the angry red marks that streaked Leyla's naked bottom. Leyla pushed herself to a sitting position, wiping away her tears with the back of her hand. She turned towards Marietta and Marietta drew in her breath. The same marks coloured the backs and sides of Leyla's thighs. One long red weal slanted across the fullest part of her breasts and another had caught her across her side.

'Who did this thing?' Marietta said tightly.

'Roxelana,' Leyla said tremulously. 'She crept into the room while I was asleep and began beating me. I had no chance to put up a fight. She . . . she tangled me in the sheets and held me down while she used a crop on me. I tried to twist away, but she kept hitting me. It was best to lie still and let her have done.'

Marietta made a sound of outrage. Many times she and Leyla had been chastised by Kasim, but never had either of them been so cruelly used. Roxelana must have put all her strength behind the crop. The skin around some of the raised marks was discoloured and already turning purple. Though the skin was not broken, Leyla would be badly bruised.

'She – Roxelana – said that this was to be a warning to you. You are to keep away from Gabriel, unless

112

Hamed orders it. Is that where you were? I called to you for help—'

'Oh, Leyla, forgive me! I have been selfish. I ought to have told you where I was going, but you were so deeply asleep. Yes, I went to find Gabriel's chamber. I could not bear for there to be such hatred between us. I wanted to speak to him. Roxelana was with him when I entered the room, but he dismissed her. It never occurred to me that she would come here and take out her anger on you. This is my fault. You've been hurt because of me.'

Leyla smiled painfully. 'Do not blame yourself. I don't think Roxelana needs much provocation. It seems that we must ever be wary of her. She's been the favourite here for a long time and she resents our presence. She . . . she said that she knew that Hamed had taken pleasure with us both. That seemed to enrage her more than anything.'

Marietta put her arm around Leyla and drew her close. 'Roxelana should be taught a lesson. I'll wager that Hamed knows nothing of her actions. We'll see what he has to say about this.'

Leyla clutched at Marietta's hand. 'Take care. Do not do anything rash. You'll only provoke Roxelana further.'

Marietta did not answer. She was filled with anger on her friend's behalf. She did not know how she was going to do it, but she would make Roxelana pay for this morning's work.

'I'll ask Bishi for some salve to put on those weals,' she said practically. 'They're nasty, but I don't think they'll scar. Now you lie down and rest until Bishi arrives.'

Leyla lay on her stomach and Marietta gently pulled the bedcovers around her, leaving her sorely abused buttocks and thighs uncovered. A short time later, Bishi arrived with a tray of food and set it down

113

on a low table. Her eyes widened as she took in the scene on the bed.

Marietta told the servant-girl what had happened and Bishi went at once to fetch a soothing oil. She hurried back, bursting into the room, her eyes as round as saucers. Another servant followed her.

'We're to help you bathe and dress as soon as you have eaten. You're to look your best. Hamed orders you to come to his private apartments.'

Marietta tensed. Some sixth sense told her that this was no ordinary summons.

Hamed's private apartment, a round room at the top of the tower, was filled with the light that streamed in through the many glazed, arched windows. Coloured spots speckled the tiled floor and turned the faded colours of the carpets jewel-bright. Playful dust motes danced in the sunbeams.

Carved wooden panels covered the walls, the gilding and paint patchy in places. A curtained alcove held a platform that was bordered on three sides by a huge padded couch, upholstered in gold brocade. Fringed silk cushions were piled around it. Enormous cabinets and a chest of rare inlaid wood stood around the walls.

Marietta and Leyla, clad in their 'uniforms' were led into the chamber. Marietta was all in black and Leyla wore white. They made a striking pair, the contrast in their individual colouring enhanced by their chosen costumes.

Hamed, magnificent in robes of emerald, figured velvet lounged on the gold couch, drawing scented tobacco into his lungs from a copper narghile – the water pipe of the East. Roxelana sat at Hamed's feet, curled up on one of the silk cushions. All around the room stood uniformed guards.

Hamed narrowed his eyes appreciatively as Marietta and Leyla approached him. The red mark across

Leyla's exposed breasts and the stripes on her buttocks were clearly visible under her short, transparent skirt. Though she moved as smoothly as always, it was evident from her face that she was in some discomfort. Hamed turned to Roxelana and raised a quizzical eyebrow.

Roxelana smiled confidently up at him. 'The woman displeased me, my lord,' she purred, reaching up to rest her red-taloned hand on his thigh.

'They are not yours to command,' Hamed said tersely, removing her hand.

Roxelana pouted prettily. 'Must I suffer their insults in silence, then? Am I not allowed to chastise these wayward creatures?'

Hamed bent close. 'You know you are not. Come to me with any problems you have. Unless I order it, you are to stay away from them. Do not take too much upon yourself, my dear. This is the second time in two days I've had to reprimand you. We shall have to discuss this later. You need a lesson it seems.'

Roxelana's face fell, but she smiled tremulously and tossed her unbound red hair over her shoulder. Hamed clapped his hands and Marietta and Leyla were led to a curtained alcove and told to remain there until summoned forth.

'You make a sound at your peril,' Hamed said to them.

'It's Kasim, I just know it,' Leyla whispered to Marietta, reaching for her hand and holding it tight. 'He's come for us. We'll soon be leaving this place.'

Marietta recalled Gabriel's words and felt a shiver of foreboding. Hamed had lured Kasim here deliberately. He would not give them up easily. And where was Gabriel? He was nowhere in sight. Then she forgot everything as the main doors opened and Kasim stepped into the room. Her legs turned to water as she gazed at him. She had not seen him for weeks. And never had she seen him dressed for combat.

In the gold dress-armour, he looked magnificent. A black silk cloak flowed down from his broad shoulders and brushed the ground behind him. His starkly handsome face was laid bare by the clean lines of the helmet. She felt the heat flood her belly as she looked at him. Everything else was forgotten, Hamed, Roxelana, even Gabriel paled into insignificance beside the commanding presence of Kasim, her master and lover.

'Welcome to my stronghold,' Hamed said. 'It has been many years since you graced us with your presence.'

'I come not for pretty speeches, nor to visit,' Kasim said coldly, 'but to discuss the return of those whom you stole from me.'

Hamed affected a look of innocence. 'Ah, so this is why you come surrounded with armed men and dressed for war?'

Kasim ignored him. 'State your terms.'

'First things first. I would not have you think that I am a barbarian. Sit. Take some refreshment. See, I have ordered iced, melon sherbet, since you do not touch wine. Roxelana serve our guest.'

Kasim climbed the steps to the platform and sat down stiffly, facing Hamed. Kasim's eyes flickered appreciatively over Roxelana as she poured a glass of the cool drink. She looked up at him from under her lashes, pleasantly surprised by the good looks of her master's old adversary. Her small sensual mouth curved in a smile. She allowed her fingers to brush against Kasim's as she handed him the tall glass and bent low so that his face was only inches from her bare breasts.

Kasim thanked her for the sherbet, appearing not to notice the other gestures. He took off his helmet and gave it to his bodyservant to hold. As he sipped his drink he looked around the room.

116

Behind the curtain, Marietta shivered as if Kasim's night-dark eyes had touched her as they slid past. She ached to press her palms to his cheeks and kiss his hard mouth. In the brightness of the sunlight Kasim's features seemed to be all sharp angles, like a marble sculpture of his own image.

Hamed sipped his glass of wine, slowly, taking the time to study Kasim. He looked cool, but Hamed knew what a sharp mind, what depth of emotion, there was behind those seemingly relaxed features. For a while longer he savoured the feeling of being in control, then suddenly he grew impatient. He wanted the details of the terms over with and Kasim brought low, not sitting looking haughtily around with that self-contained look on his proud face. Somehow his very stillness made Hamed ill at ease.

'Well then, to business,' Hamed said.

There was no change of expression on Kasim's face, but Hamed knew that he was instantly alert. He decided to be candid.

'I will not insult you by denying that I have the two women, Marietta and Leyla, staying here as . . . my guests.' He gave a small smile. 'You wish me to return the women to your safekeeping – and I am willing to do that on one condition.'

'Name it,' Kasim said at once. 'What payment do you require?'

'Payment?' Hamed said, as if the notion had not occurred to him. 'No. You misunderstand. That would be far too easy. Any sum I named you could procure at once.'

'Then you seek to fight!'

'No. Not at all. I require only that you come willingly to this place – after due time to set your affairs in order, of course – and stay for a specified period.'

117

Kasim allowed a flicker of puzzlement to cross his features. 'For what purpose?'

Hamed smiled broadly and paused before he answered. 'You will consent to become my pleasure-slave. The fact need not be made public. Indeed, you will tell your ministers that you are quite safe and will take up your duties again in due course.'

Marietta saw Kasim blanch. He will refuse, she thought, his pride will not allow him to consider such a profanity. She felt an odd mixture of emotions. Perversely, she almost wanted him to accept. There was something so intoxicating in the image of Kasim's splendid body, naked and adorned for pleasure, as hers was. Oh, to see him on his knees, servicing a master or groaning under the lash . . . But it was not right, nor possible, that he abase himself for the sake of Leyla and herself.

A little moan of distress lodged in her throat. Hamed's terms were too much. It seemed that they must remain Hamed's prisoners, while Kasim laid siege outside the stronghold walls. Then Kasim spoke and Marietta's chin jerked up in shock. Leyla gripped her hand so tightly, that she winced at the pain.

'I accept your terms,' Kasim said coolly. 'How long am I to stay here? I will have an official document drawn up, you understand. A treaty, which we both shall sign.'

Hamed stared at Kasim in stunned amazement. He had not expected him to agree so readily. He felt a grudging admiration for his enemy. It took great strength of character to accept the terms he set down.

'I . . . I had thought one month would suffice.'

'Agreed.'

'Good. Good. How long will it take you to make the necessary arrangements?'

'I can be back here within a week.'

'Then it's settled. Marietta and Leyla will be

released on the last day of your month's stay. Let me be clear about this. You do know what is expected of you?'

Kasim nodded. 'I know.'

Hamed's full mouth curved richly. 'Then I trust that you will be a most obedient slave? How interesting it will be for you, a master, to learn what it is to serve others. I almost envy you.'

A muscle jerked in Kasim's cheek, but he gave no other sign of his feelings.

'That seems to be all then—' Hamed began.

'Not quite,' Kasim interrupted. 'One thing more. I wish to see Marietta and Leyla – alone. To establish that no harm has come to them.'

'Ah. To see them alone will not be possible. But you may judge for yourself whether they are safe.' Hamed clapped his hands and the women were brought out of the curtained alcove.

Kasim's eyes flashed with pleasure at the sight of them. He did not speak, but Marietta needed no words to read what was in his heart. She saw the love and the naked desire in his eyes and was proud of her beauty; the beauty that had stirred this deeply passionate but restrained man to offer himself up as a willing slave.

Many times she had appeared before Kasim naked, or clothed only in thin gold chains and silk veils, but never had she worn such a provocative costume. The paleness of her hair and skin was more startling than usual when set against the deep black of the leather and velvet costume. Kasim's dark eyes took in all the details of her dress. The cinched waist; her lifted and exposed breasts – with the nipple-clamps of sparkling black obsidian; the black transparent skirt which revealed her lower belly and the shadowed triangle between her thighs. Conscious of his gaze on her she moved her thighs apart slightly, so that the delicate

119

labial clamps – with silver chains that ended in black pearls – moved slightly against her white skin.

Kasim permitted himself a small secret smile before his eyes strayed to Leyla. Immediately he narrowed them as he saw the weals on her skin.

'What is this?' he demanded.

'Ah, yes,' said Hamed. 'An unfortunate incident. Not of my doing. The matter is in hand. Never fear, I wish no harm to come to such beauties as these. They will be safe until you return, then you will see for yourself how they are treated.'

'That had better be, or our agreement is void. You do realise that if you break your word, this stronghold will be razed to the ground?'

'I am fully aware of that. But I shall keep my word. You know me to be a man of honour. And besides, all I desire will come to pass. Why would I wish to harm anyone?'

Kasim nodded curtly. 'Then so be it.'

'Excellent. Now please be seated. I have arranged some entertainment for you before you leave. Take your ease.'

He clapped his hands and Gabriel walked slowly into the room. He wore a breech-clout of white leather. His superb body glowed with health. A strip of studded white leather encircled his forehead, holding back his long blond hair. Freshly washed and gleaming, it streamed over his shoulders. Deep wristbands, also studded and glittering with jewels reached almost to his elbows. He carried what looked like a whip. The stranded ends of the lash swayed as he walked.

Kasim leant forward, obviously surprised to see Gabriel. He seemed intrigued, Marietta thought, and not at all dismayed. If anything Kasim was looking Gabriel over with a mixture of pleasure and desire. Gabriel was, as ever, magnificent. No one, not even

Kasim, could be unmoved by his powerful male beauty.

Marietta recalled Gabriel's bitterness. How he must be looking forward to having Kasim in his power. She made herself a promise. She would do everything possible to make Kasim's time as a slave an easier one. Perhaps if she took pains to please Hamed in some special way he might listen if she asked for lenience on Kasim's behalf. There might be a way. Something Hamed had done when he first examined her at the canalside came to her mind. Ah, yes. That was the way . . .

She felt sure of herself. If only Bishi could be persuaded to help her. Hamed would not be able to resist her charms. And it would serve Roxelana right if Hamed turned away from her.

'I have had little chance to test the obedience of these pleasure-slaves,' Hamed said, breaking into Marietta's thoughts. 'I thought it would amuse you to watch as I put them through a few paces. Gabriel here is my slavemaster. He is most thorough, as you will see for yourself, soon enough.'

Kasim nodded as if unconcerned, though his dark eyes took in every detail of Gabriel's appearance. He desires him still, Marietta thought, as she saw the absorption in Kasim's face; the way his glance lingered on the perfect musculature and the pronounced fullness in the white breech-clout at Gabriel's groin.

Marietta felt a little thrill of fear as she absorbed Hamed's words. She and Leyla were to be chastised while Kasim watched, as indeed he had watched many times before, but this day it was to be Gabriel, Kasim's ex-slave, who was going to draw down the pleasure of submission from their bodies. She could only guess what Kasim must be feeling. Did he long to be the one who handled them? Perhaps he longed

121

for the attentions of Gabriel. Or was he burning with anger at the cavalier treatment of *his* pleasure-slaves?

Marietta dared not meet Gabriel's eyes. The memory of their loving that morning was still fresh in her mind. She could not reconcile that with what he was about to do to her and Leyla. Even though she knew he had no choice, as Hamed's slavemaster, she cringed at the implacable set to his mouth. There was no sign of the tenderness she had seen earlier.

Gabriel held out a hand for each of them, his beautiful face expressionless. Marietta was led to a narrow, waist-high bench which had been placed in front of the platform. Leyla followed her.

'You will see how well I work my – or should I say your – pleasure-slaves,' Hamed smiled. 'Marietta was served by Gabriel personally, in his chamber last night. Is that not so Roxelana?'

Roxelana smiled cruelly. 'That is so, my Lord.'

Marietta flushed deeply as a spasm passed over Kasim's face. It was the first real sign of any emotion. Damn Roxelana, she thought. Her interfering had prompted Hamed to say the one thing designed to twist the knife for Kasim.

'Gabriel will demonstrate his artistry for you. Much of his skills were learnt while he was your slave, I believe.'

He gestured to Gabriel. 'Ready them. Display them for our guest. You know what to do. And you Roxelana. Stand by. Gabriel may need assistance.'

'Yes, Master,' Roxelana said, positioning herself on the far side of the bench.

Marietta and Leyla stood with their backs to the bench, facing the platform. Though her eyes were downcast, Marietta could feel Kasim's gaze on her. She determined to give a good account of herself for him alone. What did it matter that Hamed and Roxelana were determined to humiliate Kasim by displaying Leyla and herself in front of him? If she enjoyed what they did, and showed the fact to Kasim for his pleasure, then they failed to wound him.

On Gabriel's order she and Leyla turned around and bent forward over the bench. The wooden bar was padded and shaped for comfort, fitting neatly into the curve of her belly. It was broad enough to support the whole of her torso, but her shoulders and bare breasts were thrust forward. The pale globes hung free and the dangling nipple-clamps swayed gently.

Marietta's upswept curls flopped forward to partially cover her eyes. She was glad of this, as Roxelana's narrow green eyes never left her face. Roxelana watched avidly for any sign of distress, any evidence of suffering. Marietta was determined that Roxelana would be disappointed. Lifting her head she flashed her a dazzling smile. Roxelana's mouth twisted with rage, but she could do nothing but watch as Gabriel walked around the two women, arranging them in the most provocative position.

'Lean over further,' Gabriel ordered Marietta, tapping her gently with the coiled whip and pushing the short skirt up to lie in folds around her waist.

He did the same to Leyla, exclaiming at the colourful stripes on her pale flesh. As he ran a fingerip ever so gently over one of the raised weals, tremors passed over Leyla's skin.

'Have no fear. I can see the weals are still sore. I'll not hurt you,' he whispered to her, then raised his voice. 'Flex those pretty buttocks both of you. Display the darker tint inside those globes. You provide a wonderful contrast in colouring. Leyla so dark and Marietta so fair.'

Marietta felt the heat flood her face as Gabriel described her own and Leyla's bodies in colourful details. It seemed an insult to describe to Kasim, those intimate parts which he so loved and desired.

Hamed does not own me, she thought, this is for you Kasim.

'Stretch your legs apart so that your bottom-mouths are visible. And part your legs to display the labial clamps. Hurry up!' Gabriel slapped Marietta on her bottom with the flat of his hand when she hesitated. Not hard, but hard enough for her to realise that he meant her to obey instantly.

Marietta arched her back and pushed out her bottom, as Gabriel ordered, at the same time spreading her thighs. Leyla did the same. The little chains on the clamps swayed back and forth, tickling the soft skin of Marietta's inner thighs. She knew that they were to be beaten and felt a sort of horrid expectation of the pleasure-pain to come.

Gabriel reached between her legs and gave the clamps a little tug, rolling the black pearls between his fingertips. Then he grasped each of her flesh-lips and smoothed and pulled them down, so that the neat little purse of her sex was parted slightly and displayed to best advantage. Tweaking the golden curls, he fluffed them into shape, then stroked the few damp tendrils away from the pursed little opening between her bottom-cheeks.

He moved to Leyla and did the same to her hairless sex-lips. Hamed commented on the delectable naked-ness of Leyla's sex, and remarked on the silky smoothness, the taste of her intimate flesh against his mouth. He was plainly trying to provoke Kasim, having never pleasured himself with Leyla in that way. Leyla turned her face towards Marietta. Her full underlip was nipped in by her teeth. She was flushed deep red with shame.

There was a pause, then Marietta felt Gabriel's fingers slipping into the groove of her buttocks, stroking gently and anointing her flesh-valley with oil. His touch was warm and gentle as he caressed the inner skin of her buttocks. She pushed against

Gabriel's hand, drawing in her breath when he pressed the pad of his finger softly against the puckered mouth of her anus. Using one finger, then two, he slid the oil deeply inside her bottom, lubricating and loosening the tight little orifice.

A tiny sigh escaped her as the strong fingers penetrated deeply into her body. She heard Roxelana's grunt of disapproval. Marietta was not supposed to be enjoying being displayed in this way. The humiliation was meant to shame her before her old master. Marietta smiled. This was not so bad. Kasim would be enjoying the sight of Leyla and herself spread so enticingly for him. She felt a pool of warmth gathering in her belly as she anticipated the moment when Gabriel would use the lash on her taut bottom.

She had been beaten many times by Kasim. Though the shame of it was hateful, it was also addictive. After the initial soreness, a burning warmth followed; a warmth that always reached inside her and tapped the well of her feminine moisture. Soon, oh, soon, the wetness would begin to seep out of her, heating and softening her sex, ready for the thrust of Gabriel's hard cock.

A sort of dreamy anticipation settled over her. She was lulled into a realm of sensual delight. Beside her Leyla's breath came fast and shallow as Gabriel gave her his full attention. Marietta relaxed, pushing her belly against the padded bar of the bench, and arching her back even more deeply.

Her rounded bottom was thrust high as if begging for the cruel kiss of the lash. She knew that the deep-pink inner flesh of her vulva was glistening and the darker coloured flesh-valley between her parted cheeks had never looked so inviting. The feeling of helplessness, of exposure, washed over her in a wave of truly awful delight. What sweet punishment this was.

But Hamed's next order cut into her thoughts like

a knife. It was so unexpected, and so inexplicable, that she tensed. Her eyes must have showed her dismay, for a flicker of satisfaction crossed Roxelana's face.

'Fit them with the tails,' Hamed said. 'Show them what they are about to receive.'

And Gabriel walked slowly around to the back of the bench, so that Marietta and Leyla could see him unwind the coiled whip. Only it was not a whip he held. The thongs separated into two objects; Gabriel held one in each hand. Marietta saw something like a phallus formed all of leather. The short stubby handle was rounded on the end, looking impossibly large and cruel. The shaft of it ended in a number of long hanging thongs. One of the 'tails' was white and tipped with pearls, the other was black and tipped with drops of shining black obsidian. She appreciated the jewelled beauty of the objects, even while she cringed as the realisation of what they were to be used for came over her.

For Hamed had never planned to have them beaten. Their punishment was to be refined and altogether more subtle. A deep flush of shame stained her cheeks and spread down to cover her breasts.

How foolish she had been to think that Hamed would allow her and Leyla to keep any dignity at all. As Gabriel moved around the bench and positioned himself directly behind her, Roxelana reached out and grasped her chin. She jerked Marietta's head up, so that Marietta had no choice but to look directly into her face. Marietta immediately squeezed her eyes tight shut. She would not allow Roxelana to see her distress, she just would not!

But Roxelana was determined to relish the moment. She bent and brushed her lips across Marietta's mouth, then bit down viciously. Marietta winced with the pain and opened her eyes on a reflex. She glared her dislike and anger at Roxelana. The pain in her swollen lip brought tears to her eyes.

'That's better, Frenchwoman. Keep your eyes open, or I'll hurt you more next time. Let me see your shame. All of it. Give it to me.' Roxelana's little mouth was slack, her green eyes luminous in her beautiful cat-face.

Marietta felt the rounded tip of the leather-bound handle nudge between her buttocks. Not there. Oh no. She was so tight and the phallus was so very bulbous at the end. She could not suppress a tremor as the head of the object pressed against her anus. Surely it was too big. It would hurt.

But it hurt only a little and only at first. Gabriel worked it into her slowly, dripping more oil onto the handle to make its passage easier. He moved it back and forth until the tight orifice accepted the intrusion. With a subtle scratchy sensation the phallus slid fully into her, stretching the little mouth obscenely.

Oh, how terrible that Kasim could see her orifice, so well-filled, so horribly eager for the leather phallus. The fleshy pad between her anus and vagina was firm, pushed out by the pressure of the object that filled her. She wanted to close her legs tight, to shield the protruding object between the lush curves of her bottom.

'Hold it inside with your muscles,' Gabriel said severely. 'Don't struggle against it. If it slides out, it will be the worst for you.'

Marietta tightened the muscles of her buttocks, thighs, and belly, trying to keep the object inside her. It filled her completely, invading her body, exerting an inner pressure on her sex, which throbbed and burned maddeningly. The long trailing thongs, tipped with beads of cold obsidian, hung down to cover her mound. As she writhed with anguish the thongs brushed lewdly against the parted lips of her vulva and stroked her burning flesh-hood.

127

Never had she felt so ill used. It was far worse than the time she had been spread in a similar way on the public punishment block. Then, the faces that gazed at her had been the faces of strangers.

Leyla whimpered when her 'tail' was inserted, though Gabriel was careful to go very gently on account of her abused buttocks. She threw a tearful glance towards Marietta, her full red mouth trembling with mortification. Roxelana laughed throatily when the objects were in place.

'Excellent,' Hamed breathed. 'Is Gabriel not an excellent slavemaster? You can begin to see what he has in store for you.'

Kasim did not answer. Marietta realised that the demonstration was for Kasim's personal benefit. Hamed wanted him to realise fully what was in store for him when he returned. Tears gathered in her eyes. She imagined Kasim bent into this same position, a leather 'tail' inserted into his body. How would he bear it? She and Leyla revelled in being subservient. Yes, if she was honest, even in being displayed in this humiliating way.

But Kasim was proud and reserved. It might break him. She was more determined than ever to put her plan into action. Hamed would not be able to resist her.

Then she felt Gabriel's warm hand move between her legs and she could think only of the pulsing of her demanding womanhood. He pinched her flesh-hood between two fingers and moved it slowly back and forth. She felt her pleasure mounting, her insides seemed to curl as his knowing touch coaxed her to a slow and melting release. Her hips worked against his hand and the thongs brushed softly against her skin as she reached for her climax. Gabriel's fingers plunged deep into her silken sheath and slid wetly in and out.

He gripped the leather 'tail', protruding a short

way out of her anus, and twisted it gently. The oiled leather turned inside her, sending ripples of sensation through and through her. That final touch tipped her over.

She did not care now that Roxelana watched her face. She sensed how Kasim gazed longingly on the moist little jewel between her thighs – decorated so beguilingly with the labial clamps that pinched the swollen flesh-lips and the trailing jewel-tipped thongs. This release was for him, only for him.

As the inner pulsations began she bit her lower lip and let out a series of breathy sighs, spreading her legs as wide as possible and working her bottom so that the leather thongs danced up and down. Let Roxelana see her pleasure. She hoped the Venetian woman envied her. And indeed it seemed that Roxelana did. For she let Marietta's chin drop with a sound of disgust and turned away, but not before Marietta saw the lascivious glint in her eye.

Roxelana gave her attention to Leyla, who was now being soundly pleasured by Gabriel. After tearing off the scrap of leather at his groin, Gabriel positioned himself between Leyla's spread thighs and pushed into her with a hoarse groan. Sighing and thrusting her shapely rump hard against him, Leyla rode Gabriel's strongly erect cock.

Marietta could only hang limply over the bench as Gabriel plunged into Leyla. In a short time he gave a grunt of release and collapsed over her. Marietta's breath returned gradually to normal. Now that her pleasure was over, she was flooded by renewed shame. The thonged handle still stuck obscenely out of her body. It required all her concentration to keep it buried inside her. She longed to grip the shaft and pull it free from her private passage, but she dared not. She must wait until Gabriel gave her leave. But no order came to remove the tail. It seemed that she was to be obliged to keep it in, even when the order came to stand.

'Get up and face the platform,' Gabriel ordered when he again wore the breech-clout.

Slowly, Marietta turned, her eyes downcast. The phallus itched and burned inside her. The jewelled thongs hung down, brushing the backs of her thighs. She could hardly bear to look at Kasim. But it seemed that she did not need to do so. He was even now descending the platform and striding from the room. His head was bowed and she could not see his expression. The manservant, holding his dress-helmet, scurried after him.

'I'll look forward to your return,' Hamed called after Kasim. 'Within a week, remember?'

Gabriel grinned at Hamed. 'Do you think he'll come back?'

'Certainly he will. What I offer is irresistible. How could any passionate man refuse such a challenge. Do not all masters envy their slaves? Even while Kasim is horrified by my terms, he is powerfully intrigued. Did you not see the fascination on his face? I'll wager that he was imagining how it would feel to be in the place of Marietta or Leyla!'

'Then our exhibition was a success,' Gabriel said, laughing richly. 'Your new pleasure-slave knows what to expect. So much the better. Let him think on this for the next few days. I cannot wait to train him.'

Hamed leant forward earnestly. 'Go ready yourself Gabriel. I want you at your most inventive. Devise some new distractions for me.'

Gabriel bowed his head. 'It will give me the greatest pleasure, my Lord.'

Roxelana wore a look of lewd excitement at the exchange and Hamed's handsome hard face was slack with desire. Hamed beckoned to Roxelana and she came and curled up at his feet. He meshed his fingers in her bright-red hair and ran the silky strands over his fingers.

'Did you enjoy that, my pet?'

'Immeasurably,' she murmured, rubbing against his velvet-covered thigh.

Hamed stretched and yawned. 'Take these two away,' he ordered Gabriel. 'And bathe them. Then bring them to me. I would sample that well-trained flesh.'

The satisfied expression left Roxelana's face. She thrust herself away from Hamed's leg and sat stiffly, watching with narrowed eyes as Gabriel led Marietta and Leyla from the room.

Marietta knew that Roxelana had a new grudge against her now. She would try to make her pay for her shameless enjoyment. For by finding pleasure in the display, Marietta had robbed the Venetian woman of the pleasure of seeing her sobbing with humiliation. The realisation of that fact gave her immense satisfaction.

As she reached the door of the apartment, she looked over her shoulder and smiled slowly and deliberately at Roxelana.

Chapter Seven

'You were wonderful, my darling,' Gabriel said later that evening, his lips warm against the skin of Marietta's throat. 'The way you gave yourself up completely to every sensation. When I pushed the tail into your body I found it almost unbearably arousing. It was all I could do to control myself. I wanted to take you at once, to bury my hard flesh inside you and ride you until you wept with pleasure.'

She smiled up at him and tapped him lightly on the cheek with one finger.

'But you did not. Instead it was Leyla you favoured. Ah, how cruel you were to deny me. Not at all like the tender lover of a few hours ago. And I saw what pleasure you took in provoking Kasim.'

Slipping his arm around her waist, Gabriel walked by her side. The garden was lit by perfumed candles that glowed through paper lanterns set in the trees. A sunken path, soft with a cushion of moss, wove through the overgrown flowerbeds and crumbling walls.

'Do you forgive me?' Gabriel asked softly.

Marietta lifted her chin for his kiss. 'You are

Hamed's slavemaster. What else should I expect of you? When he next orders you to prepare us for his entertainment, you will do so, won't you?'

Gabriel looked away. 'Of course. Like I watched whilst you and Leyla were ordered to pleasure Hamed in his chamber after Kasim left. Hamed is my only master. I owe him my life and my obedience.'

'And you will take every chance to humiliate Kasim, even if that means using Leyla and me to do it.'

He paused and turned so that he faced her. His voice was sad and tinged with the bitterness she now recognised. 'Hamed has a right to vengeance. I have too. You know what my true feelings are for you. But I have to settle with Kasim before I can allow myself to live again.'

'Can you not let it go, Gabriel? This hate will consume you.'

He turned on her in surprise. 'You ask me that? Surely you of all people can see that Kasim deserves to suffer. Did he not capture you and keep you against your will? And later, when you could have gone free, he kept you with him by using threats.'

Marietta nodded. It was partly true. Kasim had captured her and her friend, Claudine, when the ship carrying them home from the convent at Nantes had sunk in the Bay of Biscay. But she had long since ceased to think of herself as Kasim's captive. The role of master and slave had become blurred. Each was the captive of the other. And the harem was a prison no more, it had become her home. She regretted having to lie to Gabriel, but there had been no other way. One day she'd tell him her innermost secrets, but now was not the time.

In the soft violet light under the cypress trees Gabriel's beautiful face was a map of shadows. His eyes searched her face as he waited for her to answer. He did not entirely trust her, she realised. It was too soon for him to put away all his doubts, despite the fact that they were now lovers. She must keep up the pretence of hating Kasim for a while longer. She made herself smile.

'Yes. Let Kasim learn what it is to be a pleasure-slave,' she said as they emerged into a patch of moonlight. 'It will give me great satisfaction to see him brought low.'

Though she had no wish to see any such thing, she was aware that there was a sort of twisted justice in the situation. Kasim had brought forth and nurtured her most secret desires. He had taught her to relish the subtleties of servitude. Once she had asked him why he had chosen her and he had answered, 'I see myself in you. Your desires are an echo of my own.'

She acknowledged the truth of his words. She and Kasim were similar in so many ways. So might not Kasim desire to experience the pleasures of submission? How exquisite if he was to find fulfilment at Hamed's stronghold – even to tremble and beg for release from her. Oh, would Hamed allow it? she wondered. A tiny shudder rippled through her at the thought of it.

And Kasim would be here, nearby. He would sleep within the walls of the stronghold, separated from her by only the crumbling stone walls of his chamber. She knew that the place was peppered with secret passages and rooms. There must be a way for her to reach him, to be alone with him. Surely it was possible. But if she was to gain a measure of freedom it was imperative that she secure Hamed's trust. She had a few days only to bring him under her spell.

Time to put her plan into action. Bishi had been informed of it. While Bishi bathed her after her exertions at the 'entertainment' in Hamed's private apartments, Marietta had told her what she required.

134

Bishi's eyes widened, then she grinned showing strong white teeth.

'You like my master?' she said, looking pleased, as if Marietta had paid her a personal compliment. 'It will make him happy that such a beautiful woman desires him. He deserves to be happy. Such a kind man. He brought me here from my village where I was starving. For that I owe him my life.'

Bishi blushed and turned away. It was the longest speech Marietta had heard her make. It was plain that the little servant-girl was in love with her powerful master. She found the fact touching.

Marietta let Bishi believe what she liked about her motives. The servant-girl was only too willing to help. She had promised to have everything ready when Marietta returned from her walk in the garden. Bishi promised that Hamed would not be able to resist her.

But now she was with Gabriel. Why could she not forget everything but him? The scent of night flowers was heavy on the still air. Large orange moths fluttered around the lanterns. Others danced in and out of the waxy white blooms that festooned the creepers clambering over a broken trellised archway.

Gabriel looked into Marietta's shining eyes. 'Why so silent, flower of my passion,' he whispered huskily. 'What are you thinking?'

'I was remembering how you taste when you kiss me. And how you feel inside me,' she whispered, lowering her eyelids. Oh, she hated herself for deceiving him, but it was only a little lie.

'My thoughts were similar,' he said, pressing her against a stone wall. 'It is time to refresh my memory.'

The cool stone felt good on her bare skin as he pulled off her cloak of blue silk. Underneath she wore only an ankle-length tunic, slit up both sides to the knee. With eager fingers Gabriel pushed the tunic up to her waist. Cupping her buttocks he lifted her and linked her legs around the small of his back. In a swift movement he freed his erect cock and positioned it between her spread thighs.

His urgency communicated itself to Marietta. This was to be no slow and gentle loving. Despite her rioting thoughts she was affected as always by his proximity. It gave her a feeling of power to see Gabriel trembling with need for her. She moved slightly so that she was sitting astride his erect phallus. The warm, hard length of it was pressed closely against the groove of her parted sex-lips. Her pubic fleece ground against the curling hair at the base of Gabriel's belly.

She kissed his strong neck, mouthing the slightly damp skin which tasted of salt and lemon oil. Claiming her mouth, Gabriel kissed her deeply, filling her with his exciting taste. The tip of his tongue played with hers. She captured it and sucked it deeply into her mouth. His little moan of pleasure vibrated into her throat. Moving her gently back and forth along his cock-shaft, Gabriel exerted pressure on her inner flesh-lips. The moist tip of his cock-head rubbed against her pleasure-bud, drawing it a little way out of its hood and smoothing it back as he made each withdrawing motion.

She knew that he wanted to plunge into her. His whole body was tense with his need, but he was prolonging the moment before he penetrated her. His sexual urgency was tamed by the depth of his feelings for her. Knowing this, she felt a surge of tenderness for him. Oh, Gabriel, if Kasim did not exist, I would want only you. Only you . . .

'Holding you, wanting you, is such sweet torture,' Gabriel murmured in her ear. 'I almost went mad with longing for you all those months.'

The heady perfume of the flowering vines filled Marietta's nostrils. She lifted her face to the moon as

Gabriel moved his hard maleness against her. She was very wet now. Gabriel's shaft was slick with her moisture. The rhythm of their two bodies seemed as old as time. Suddenly she wanted Gabriel to penetrate her, to soothe her troubled thoughts. Her fingers moved in his long sun-streaked hair. She strained towards him, savaging his mouth. Yet he held back, still. The moment hung on the air, precious, eternal. The cold silver moonlight poured down. Marietta imagined she could feel it, caressing her skin, running down over her face and neck like silky-soft water.

Gabriel gave a groan and slipped into her at last. She gasped against his mouth as his hard flesh filled her. Tensing her thighs, she squeezed his waist, feeling the ridges of muscle against her skin. His hands slid under her buttocks, cupping them and drawing her forward. She linked her ankles and crossed them in the small of his back, surging against him as their bodies thrashed together. She was acutely aware of Gabriel's great strength as he supported her weight. Bending his knees slightly, he leant into her so that he could thrust more deeply.

His beautiful face was intense, transfixed by the grip of his passion. He was tender and violent at the same time. Such a strong man, but it was so easy to wound him. She felt possessed by the strange quality of the emotion he prompted within her. Theirs was surely more than a joining of two bodies.

A little sob rose in her throat. Oh, if only everything could be simply physical. Two healthy bodies taking pleasure in each other. That's all. This other feeling, so inexplicable – was it love? Obsession? Even pity for his sufferings? Whatever it was, she did not want it. But it was too late to fight it, she was ensnared by Gabriel. Why did they have to meet again? When Gabriel left Kasim's house she thought she would never see him again. It would have been better that way. Now everything was so complicated.

Gabriel buried his face in her neck. His breath seared her damp skin. She arched against him. The hardened tips of her breasts thrust against the bunched silk of the tunic. Even as her pleasure built and her body clamoured for release, she could not halt her thoughts. Her mouth twisted with anguish. Gabriel mistook the gesture for passion and murmured endearments. His grey eyes were dark and glazed with desire.

Marietta closed her eyes, unable to look at Gabriel's beatific face as his moment of release approached. Her own climax eluded her, but Gabriel had not realised the fact. He held her tight, breathing in the scent of her hair, while his seed jetted into her.

Tears pricked against her eyelids. She was flooded by tenderness and self-hatred.

Even at this moment, she was betraying him. For while it was Gabriel who claimed her body so sweetly, it was Kasim who had the firmest hold on her mind. Whatever happened, he always would have.

Marietta ate her evening meal alone in her chamber. She did not mind. Solitude suited her for the moment.

She knew that Leyla would be enjoying herself and she was glad for her friend. Marietta had never fallen prey to the petty jealousies within the harem. Other women formed brief attachments, then squabbled and fought over imagined desertions. Marietta's and Leyla's relationship was abiding, based as it was on a mutual generosity of spirit.

Leyla and Marietta had been introduced to Otsami earlier in the day. Marietta was fascinated by the exotic delicacy and the charming manners of the Japanese woman. She had never seen such hair. It fell straight and shining down Otsami's back, like a skein of black silk. And Otsami's longish, oval face, small red mouth, and narrow slanting eyes, were curious indeed. Marietta tried not to stare, but could not help it. Otsami looked so strange in her colourful silk robes, with their deep sleeves and the wide padded sash at her waist. She was not sure if she found Otsami beautiful or merely odd.

Her apartments also had a stylish austerity. The furniture of red and black lacquer, the woven mats which covered the tiles, and the wooden platform with its bed and floor cushions, struck Marietta as unnecessarily sparse. She felt ill at ease sitting at the low table, while Otsami knelt to serve them refreshments.

Leyla appeared to have no such reservations. She seemed to be perfectly at home, admiring the little row of miniature trees which were visible in the small courtyard outside. Otsami spoke perfect French and she and Leyla chatted animatedly over tea served in exquisite blue and white porcelain bowls. Leyla discovered that she shared Otsami's love of music, and eagerly accepted an invitation to spend the evening in the Japanese woman's company.

Alone now, Marietta nibbled spiced aubergines stuffed with almonds. She pushed the food around in her silver dish and slumped against the cushions on the divan. She sighed. It seemed that she and Leyla were to be allowed a measure of freedom as long as they did Hamed's bidding. They were like butterflies trapped in an exquisite silken net. The analogy depressed her. She sipped a long glass of lemon sherbet, then called for Bishi to attend her. From the servant-girl, she learnt that Hamed had sent away his retainers as he wished to spend the evening alone.

The timing was perfect.

'Have you brought the things I asked for?'

139

Bishi grinned and held out a carved wooden box. Marietta opened the lid and peered inside.

'Excellent. Now make me as beautiful as the morning star Bishi. Then go and ask, most humbly, if my Lord Hamed will admit me to his presence.'

Hamed was reading when she entered his chamber. She waited until he looked up before she closed the doors behind her.

Lamplight gleamed on his thick brown hair, picking out the wings of grey at his temples. His strong-featured face was a little harsh in repose, the sensual mobile mouth compressed into a straight line. He supported his chin with the heel of his hand as he leant over the book. He seemed completely absorbed. She had not thought him to be a scholar.

'You asked to be brought to me?' Hamed said, closing the book with reverence and laying it aside. 'I must confess, I am intrigued. Have you some complaint? Are you not being treated well?'

For the first time he noticed how she was dressed. He tried unsuccessfully to keep his eyes on her face. Marietta strode confidently into the chamber, aware of how minutely Hamed watched her. She hid a triumphant little smile. How could he help but be entranced. Bishi had done her work well.

'Your hospitality is faultless, my Lord. But there has been no chance for us to be alone together. I thought it might please you to get to know me a little better. I hope I am not intruding on your solitude.'

Hamed said nothing. He made a dismissive gesture with his hand. The cabochon ruby glinted on his finger. She could tell he was assessing her motives. Of course he realised that she wanted something, but he had no idea what it might be. Her clear blue eyes sparkled with mischief. He'd know soon enough.

Her high-heeled slippers made a staccato rhythm as she walked across the floor. She deliberately avoided walking on the carpets, knowing that the sharp sound of the metal-tipped, wooden heels would draw Hamed's gaze directly to the area she wanted it.

Hamed drew in a sharp breath, then hid it with a yawn. He was reclining on a low divan. As she approached, he raised himself up, supporting himself on his elbow. He still did not speak. She saw him swallow and permitted herself a tight little smile. Yes, your mouth is dry, she thought. I was right about you. I knew what would inflame your passions.

As she drew near to the divan, she stopped and bent down as if to adjust her slipper. She bent over from the waist in a smooth graceful gesture and drew her outspread fingers all the way along each foot in turn, then she encircled the ankle before sweeping her hands up her shapely calves.

Hamed's eyes followed her every move. He leant a little closer, studying her position which showed her long slim legs and richly curving hips to advantage. Turning her head sideways, Marietta treated Hamed to a look that was full of promise. Then she straightened up slowly and turned to face him. With her hands on her hips and her legs parted slightly, she let him look his fill.

Her long pale hair had been swept up and pinned tightly into little coils which resembled seashells. Crystal-topped pins glittered amongst the coils. The severe hairstyle made her skull look small and fragile and left her face bare. The pure lines of her bone structure, her neat nose, and the clear blue of her eyes were accentuated by the lack of decoration. The exposed nape of her neck added to the overall look of fragility.

The rest of her costume was frankly erotic. She knew that the contrast of her neat head, her naked face – almost childlike in its clarity, and the lush

141

adornment of her body was a powerfully stirring image.

Crystal studs decorated her ears. Her shoulders and arms were bare. A wide belt, shaped and boned and made of strong gold ribbon, constricted her waist and left her breasts exposed. Her nipple-clamps were of gold and crystal. A thin chain hung between the clamps, connecting the two.

'Come closer,' Hamed said hoarsely.

Obediently Marietta moved nearer. She placed each foot carefully, measuring her strides and swinging her hips as she walked. There was a padded stool next to the divan. Marietta halted. Keeping her eyes on Hamed's face, she lifted one leg high and placed her foot on the stool. The leather-covered heel of her slipper made a deep indentation in the embroidered fabric.

Hamed's gaze progressed from her thigh, to her bent knee, and on to the shadowed secrets between her legs. Marietta felt a stir of excitement as his eyes widened when he saw the little clamp with the crystal drop that was attached to the flesh-hood nestling within her intimate folds.

She looked deeply into his eyes. 'I wanted to please you,' she said huskily.

'You . . . do,' Hamed managed to say.

He drank in every detail of her body, but his gaze lingered on her legs and feet, as she had known they would. When he had knelt on the canalside and examined her feet in minute detail, she had detected the interest of a connoisseur. With that in mind she had gone to great trouble to make her legs, and particularly her feet, as enticing to look at as possible.

She wore a pair of gold brocade slippers, encrusted with crystal beads, which left her toes and heels bare. The slippers were arched, so that her feet were supported in exaggerated bows, her weight resting on the ball of each foot. Gold leather fastenings were wrapped tightly around her ankles and then criss-crossed all the way up her slim legs to the very tops of her thighs. She shifted position, standing so that her legs were again closed. The pale blonde of her pubic curls brushed against the topmost fastening of the leather thigh-lacing.

What Hamed could not see was that Bishi had given her a special pedicure. There were other treats in store for him, if he wished to sample them. She saw by his reaction that he would indeed wish to do more than look. He shifted uncomfortably. There was a pronounced tumescence at his groin.

A slow smile crossed her lovely face. 'My Lord is pleased with my appearance?'

'You know I am,' he said. 'You are very clever to discover what enchants me. But you must do more than look beautiful if you expect to seek my favour.'

'Your wish is my command,' she said sweetly, running her hands down over her hips and bringing them to rest on her thighs. Her splayed fingers toyed with the gold lacing. A spasm passed over Hamed's handsome face.

'Sit on the stool,' he ordered, getting off the divan in a flurry of silken robes.

She sank down, keeping her back straight and her knees together. The high-heeled slippers forced her to sit with her knees bent up at an angle. Hamed knelt before her. It gave her a thrill to look down on him. This strong, powerful warrior was willing to humble himself before her beauty. Then he glanced up and she saw her mistake. There was nothing of subservience in Hamed's face. It was clear that he was the master and she was a slave to his pleasure.

Hamed was no callow youth to be bent to her will. He was a mature and experienced man, intelligent and sophisticated. In the stronghold his word was Law. Hamed commanded great respect from his underlings. She knew that she would do well to remember that. A little tremor rippled down her spine. She wondered if she had put herself in danger by coming to him in secrecy. Only Bishi knew that she was here. What if she needed to call for help . . . ?

'Lift your foot,' Hamed ordered, startling her into obedience.

'Yes . . . My Lord.'

Marietta extended one leg towards him, her foot pointed delicately. Hamed grasped her foot and held it between his palms. His fingers traced the outline of the shoe.

'Beautiful,' he murmured. 'Such tiny feet. Each toe is perfectly shaped, each nail like a shell.'

He bent and kissed the tip of each gold-painted toenail. She saw his look of surprise as he mouthed her toes and kissed the narrow strip of foot protruding from the slipper. Bishi had perfumed her feet with sweet musk and anointed the area between each toe with a different tasting honey. Hamed's breath came a little faster as he drew the large toe into his mouth. He sucked hard, making little moaning sounds of pleasure.

Tense with fear, she held her leg out rigidly. She had not expected to enjoy the experience, but when his hot tongue began probing between her toes, licking at the honey, she found the sensation uniquely arousing. His fingers encircled her narrow ankles and slid up her calves as he moved his mouth to her bare heels. He spent a long time kissing and praising her feet, then just when her legs were beginning to ache with the strain of holding them out to him, he ordered her onto the divan.

'Make your body available to me,' he said. 'I would test this willingness you profess.'

She positioned herself on hands and knees, arching her back and pushing out her bottom. This was how he had displayed her in front of Kasim. It was a position most men found exciting; the rounded bottom-cheeks, framing that desired centre of delight, exerted an almost primitive fascination on them. She smiled inwardly thinking how much she had changed from the innocent convent girl. Kasim and Leyla had taught her well.

The little clamp attached to her flesh-hood protruded from the purse of her sex, the crystal prevented from dangling by the fleshy lips holding it tight. Hamed reached out and took hold of it, tugging it playfully, sending a warm pulse of sensation to her pleasure-bud. She could not help pressing back against his hand.

'How well trained you are,' he mused, letting go of the glittering jewel. 'But that is not what I want from you.' With a derisive little laugh he turned away.

Unsure of herself now, she watched him undress. This was not going as she had planned. She had expected that he would wish to enter her body in some way. Ah, perhaps he would prefer her tight bottom-mouth. She lay on her back and raised her legs, letting her thighs fall open. But Hamed motioned for her to sit. He had different requirements, then. She hoped she could accommodate them.

Swiftly he disrobed, until all he wore was a loose, white silk undershirt. Climbing onto the divan, he leant back against the piled cushions. His strongly erect cock jutted against the white silk. As Hamed undid his undershirt and let it fall open, Marietta saw his bronzed and muscled torso with its curling brown hair. It still gave her a shock to see the great ugly scar that marred his stomach and groin.

'Turn to face me,' he said.

Lifting her chin, he tipped her face up to his and pressed his mouth to hers. The kiss was passionate and yet tender. She sensed that in a strange way he was thanking her, but she could not understand the reason why. A moment ago he had seemed amused by her efforts at seduction.

He stared down at her face as if he would absorb every feature. There was wonderment in his eyes. What had she done to deserve such emotion? She gave a tremulous smile to hide her confusion at the strength of his reactions. She pulled away. Hamed was a disconcerting man indeed. It was safer to concentrate on his body. His mind was altogether too unfathomable, too mysterious. Leaning towards him, she ran her hand down over his stomach and closed her fingers around the stem of his phallus.

His hand reached down and enclosed her hand.

'Not that way,' he said, reaching for a curved dagger that lay on a side table. 'Wait. I would take my pleasure in my own time. Why hurry when you have taken such pains to ensnare me?'

He spoke lightly, but the dagger unnerved her. Lamplight glinted off the wickedly curved blade. The handle was of carved gold encrusted with rubies. What did he mean to do? She stiffened, feeling fear creep into her bones. She had underestimated him. Fool, she berated herself. I have insulted him by my presumption. Now he means to kill me!

Hamed saw her terror. He smiled to reassure her. 'I mean you no harm. See?'

Slowly, taking great satisfaction in the act, he slipped the razor-sharp point of the dagger under the thongs that secured the slippers to her ankles. She felt the coldness of the blade against her skin. The leather made a soft sound as the knife cut into it. As each cut thong curled away from the slipper, a tiny tremor passed over Hamed's features.

He cut all the laces until the slippers were kept on her feet only by the narrow jewelled band across her toes. Setting aside the dagger he removed each slipper in turn, sliding it free of her foot in a smooth, slow motion. The gold leather thongs still encircled each ankle like a broad metallic cuff and the criss-cross of laces encased the length of her legs as tightly as before.

'Never did I see more enticing shackles,' Hamed murmured, pressing kisses to the small diamond-shaped areas of skin between the laces.

Now that she knew he would not harm her, Marietta relaxed a fraction. In truth, the threat of danger had added spice to the situation. She could not help but respond to Hamed. His unpredictability, his air of command, earned her respect.

Slowly Hamed worked up her legs, mouthing her skin, licking and tasting. As he rubbed his cheeks against the soft oiled flesh, she felt the faintest rasp of his stubble. When he reached the joining of her thighs, he paused and darted her a mischievous glance. She tensed with expectation, waiting for him to part her thighs, realising that she wished him to do so. Indeed, it seemed that she had never wanted anything so badly.

That realisation was a shock. Somehow there had been a subtle shift between them. When she entered the room, she had imagined that *she* had been in control of the situation. Hamed had surely been captivated by her, unable to look away as she swayed towards him on her high heels. It had been her intention to make him want her. To bend him to her will.

But she had underestimated him. Plainly he did want her, but on his own terms. He was supremely confident of his power over her. She could not help but admire the way he had duped her. He was fully in control, and had been since she entered the room. Kasim had that same element of restraint, that same self-possession.

That knowledge too, made Hamed all the more desirable to her.

So now she was caught in her own trap. All she

could think of was Hamed's hot mouth on her sex. Under the pinching bite of the clamp, her pleasure-bud throbbed and grew erect, thirsting for the touch of Hamed's tongue. Her belly was a tight ball of desire. The fire which Gabriel had left unquenched, stirred into new life. She arched towards Hamed, making encouraging little movements of her hips.

'Ah no. I think not,' Hamed grinned, brushing his lips lightly across her pubic curls, so that her stomach contracted with a jolt of wanting. 'This fragrant jewel must wait for another time. It is my pleasure alone that counts this day, is it not? You came here to ingratiate yourself. And I know what I want from you.'

She smiled and nodded, though her disappointment must have shown, because he laughed richly and slapped her lightly on her buttocks. Turning her bare feet this way and that, he again admired their perfection. 'I seem to remember an area of rough skin . . . ?'

'Bishi . . . Bishi smoothed it for me. She spent a long time rubbing oil into the skin.'

'Ah. Bishi is thorough.' He pressed his mouth to her instep, licking delicately at the spot where a blue vein pulsed beneath the surface of the skin. 'Exquisite,' he breathed, biting gently at the soft pad under her heel. 'The soles are cool and like satin to the touch. And now, my dear, I want you to put them to good use.'

He positioned her so that she was sitting between his widely spread legs. 'Take your weight on your hands and lean back. Yes, that's it. Now pleasure me with those pretty feet.'

Obediently she began to caress his thighs, describing tiny circles on his golden-brown skin. The sensation of his warm flesh against her soles was pleasant. She had not realised that her feet were so sensitive. She could feel every ridge and contour of the scar. Hamed winced. She paused.

'I'm sorry. Have I hurt you?'

'It's nothing. The skin there is a little tender. Continue as you were doing.'

She resumed the stroking. The curling brown hairs at the base of his belly tickled as she brushed against them. Taking care to avoid the scar, using the lightest touch, she lifted his balls, stroking and teasing them with the tips of her toes. Hamed's belly tensed as she allowed his ball sac to rest on the tips of her toes. The weight of it was velvet-soft against her skin.

She made him wait for the touch he longed for. Slowly, so slowly, she stretched out and stroked his cock. Hamed's phallus twitched with pleasure as she worked her toes gently up and down both sides of the firm shaft. Now and then she held it firmly, gripping it with her inward curving toes, moving so that the loose foreskin worked up and down the glans.

Soon the cock-skin slid back fully and formed a creased collar for the moist, purplish glans. A tear of salty fluid gathered and overflowed from the tiny, slitted mouth. Marietta captured it with her big toe and smeared it gently around the engorged head of his member.

There was no sign of the lack of potency she knew he suffered from. His erection was stout and enduring. Indeed there seemed a danger that he might erupt at any moment. She stroked the exposed glans with the tip of her slick big toe, then rubbed against the sensitive underside of his shaft.

Hamed gave a little moan of pleasure and reached for a bottle of perfumed oil. 'Anoint your feet with this. Use your soles on the shaft,' he murmured. 'Squeeze and roll it between both feet.'

Marietta poured oil onto her soles. It smelt strongly of patchouli. Gripping the cock-shaft as he ordered, she pressed her soles firmly together and rubbed them up and down. Faster and faster she worked the oiled stem. The muscles in her thighs and stomach began to ache, but still she pleasured him. Her soles formed a slick, firm tube-shape and Hamed's member slid sweetly in and out of it. His glans was tight and so swollen that the skin looked shiny. As she continued it grew wet with his own clear moisture.

Hamed closed his eyes and let his head fall back as his hips worked back and forth in helpless arousal. His lips parted as he emitted a series of breathy grunts. As his climax came upon him his whole body tensed. He jerked and bucked as the semen burst from him. Small drops of the creamy fluid speckled Marietta's feet.

With a great sigh of contentment, Hamed fell back amongst the cushions.

'Come . . . to me,' he murmured, extending his arm and pulling Marietta into his embrace.

Marietta curled up beside him and waited until his breathing returned to normal. Her cheek lay against his bare chest. She could feel the hectic pounding of his heart and was acutely aware of the warmth and the smell of his skin. The very human quality of these things made a deep impression on her. She had not expected this intimacy. Indeed, she had expected Hamed to take what she offered, to use her in fact, and then dismiss her at once. Instead, he cradled her close, holding her as if she was more, much more, than a pleasure-slave. Now and then he leant over to kiss the top of her head, or caressed the slope of her shoulder, the curve of her hip.

It was as if they were lovers, or as if he wished to be, she thought. And she wondered about Hamed for the first time. Could it be that he was lonely, even unhappy? He had Roxelana, it was true, but that woman was a balm to no one's soul. Bishi had told her about Otsami – the Japanese woman, who Hamed admired and respected. But according to Bishi the sexual part of Hamed's and Otsami's relationship appeared to be fitful at best.

After a while Hamed shifted position, so that he was facing Marietta. He looked deeply into her eyes as if he could read her thoughts. Again she had the feeling that he was grateful for more than the fleeting pleasure she had just brought him. She smiled up at him tremulously, not knowing what he wanted from her. She had no more to give him, yet she felt that he hungered still.

'So much you bring me. With you I am renewed. Fully potent,' he breathed, in such a low voice that she caught only part of what he said. Then he seemed to recover himself. He smiled and stretched, linking his arms behind his neck.

'There is a flagon of wine on that table. Bring it here. Share a glass with me before you go back to your chamber.'

First Marietta cleaned them both with a silken cloth and perfumed water, then she poured wine into two glasses. The malmsey was the red-brown colour of garnets, thick and sweet to the taste. She sipped with relish, enjoying the experience of drinking wine after all the months of abstinence.

'Tell me about yourself,' he said. 'What were you before you came to live in Kasim's harem?'

So she told him about her homeland of Martinique. How she was of noble birth and of how her family owned sugar plantations. He listened gravely, as she described the lush vegetation and mountains of the region around their house at Pointe Royale, the smells of molasses taffy and coffee in the markets, and the bright headcloths and shawls of the native women. Hamed seemed to find her every word fascinating. It was easy to talk to him and she found herself speaking of things she had thought long

151

forgotten. Childhood memories of herself and Claudine came back. She told him how she and her friend had run wild over the huge plantation, as free spirited as the bright red and yellow flowers that grew along the edges of the cane fields.

'Where is Claudine now?'

'She lives in the harem still. Perhaps Kasim finds comfort with her, since Leyla and I . . . are here . . .' she tailed off.

With the mention of Kasim a discordant note crept into their conversation. She saw that Hamed regretted his question. He frowned as if angry with himself, then began skilfully to lead her onto safer subjects. Soon she was absorbed by the tales of his sea journeys to distant lands. His conversation was animated and interesting, much of it tinged with sharp insights and touches of humour. His maturity and experience made him more fascinating to talk to than a younger man. When he smiled his wide-set, dark eyes gleamed, almost lost in the fine wrinkles that surrounded them.

She found herself enjoying his company immensely and quite forgot to ask if she might be allowed a greater measure of freedom. She felt disappointed when he suggested that it had grown late and she should leave. Leyla was probably still with Otsami. There was nothing to look forward to in the empty chamber they shared. Besides, it was so comfortable snuggled down in the cushions next to him. Hamed was warm and solid next to her. His arm lay along her thigh, his strong warrior's hand was curved over her knee. The wine had imparted a glow to her skin and a pleasant lightness to her head.

She almost asked to stay, sensing from his slight tension, that he wished her to suggest it. But spending the night beside him would foster a dangerous intimacy. Her plans had already gone completely awry; she did not want to complicate things further.

Rather than luring him into a honeyed trap, she seemed to have stirred up new emotions within him. And if she was completely honest – within herself.

Reluctantly she stirred herself and made to leave. Before she left the room Hamed gave her a small leather casket.

'No. Do not look inside. This is for tonight.'

'Surely slaves do not receive payment?'

'You must know that you have become more than a slave. Wait until you are alone before you look in the casket. When the time is right – and I hope that you will know when it is – wear this, for me.'

With a final kiss, he let her go.

Roxelana crept up behind Bishi. Grabbing one of her arms, she bent it up behind her back. All around the chamber was evidence of Marietta's preparations. Crystal-tipped pins and perfumes lay on a side table, along with brushes and combs. Discarded garments were thrown onto a chair.

Roxelana took in everything in a single glance. 'Where is she?' she hissed through clenched teeth. 'Tell me you little wretch or I swear I'll break your arm!'

Bishi grimaced with pain. 'Where's who? I don't know what—'

'Don't play games with me. Where's Marietta? I've looked everywhere. She's not with Otsami or Gabriel.'

'I don't know. She did not say where . . .'

'Liar! Tell me at once. I shan't warn you again.' She gave Bishi's arm a vicious twist.

Bishi sobbed with pain. 'Hamed . . . She . . . she went to him.'

'But that's impossible. He gave express instructions that he was not to be disturbed.'

'It's the truth. Please you're hurting me.'

Roxelana pushed Bishi away and crossed the

chamber. On the floor was a carved wooden box, open and empty. Roxelana gave it a knowing look. A spasm of rage twisted her mouth. Kicking the box aside, she reached behind the tapestry, feeling for the niche in the wall. With a grating sound a large slab of stone swung inwards. Roxelana disappeared through the gap.

Behind her Bishi sniffled, rubbing at her aching arm.

Roxelana stormed along the secret passageway. She could not believe the audacity of the Frenchwoman. No one disobeyed an express order from Hamed. Her lips curved as she anticipated watching the punishment that Hamed would order.

Reaching Hamed's apartments she was just in time to see Marietta leave the room. Roxelana's eyes widened as she took in the details of Marietta's costume. In another moment Marietta had rounded the corridor and was lost to view.

Stunned, Roxelana stared after her. She had expected to find Hamed alone and Marietta given over to the guards. It was plain that Marietta had spent some time with Hamed. A hot rage rose within her. She lost all control. Ducking back inside the secret passageway, she took the turn which terminated in an alcove in Hamed's private room. She had never dared to enter his room by this route without invitation, but she cared nothing for the niceties of good manners at this moment.

Hamed turned in surprise when she burst into his room. He was lying on his divan, sipping a glass of wine and reading. Roxelana stopped dead, halted in her headlong rush by the look on his face. She had never seen him so angry.

'What is the meaning of this intrusion?' he said coldly.

But Roxelana was too far gone to take note of the warning signs.

'She was here. Just now. The Frenchwoman, wasn't she? But you said you wanted to be alone. You did not want anyone. Not even me . . .' Her voice faltered and to her horror she found herself near to tears.

'You forget yourself Roxelana. How dare you question my actions. Leave at once. And think yourself lucky that I do not order you thrown out!'

Roxelana took a few paces backwards. 'But you let her come to you. Why is she so special? She doesn't love you, as I do. She's only waiting for Kasim to come. You wait and see, when Kasim leaves, she'll go too—' She stopped when Hamed made a move towards her.

'Leave! Now!' he roared. 'Not another word, or by all the stars I'll give you to the field-hands for their pleasure!'

And Roxelana left, the sob that lodged in her throat almost choking her.

Chapter Eight

Kasim awoke with a start. For a moment he had heard Marietta whispering in his ear, her softly accented voice urging him to take her into his arms.

Fully awake, he realised his mistake. Claudine was curled next to him, her long red-gold hair spread out in a tangle over the pillows. As he turned towards her she opened her eyes wide and smiled at him.

'I give you good day, my Lord,' she said, in the pronounced French accent which he found so attractive.

She was warm and soft with sleep still. Stretching languorously she pushed back the bedcovers, so that her full breasts rolled into view. The nipples were small and pale coffee-brown in colour. Claudine's body was composed of a series of luscious curves. There was not a sharp edge anywhere on her. Freckles stood out on her creamy skin.

'Must you rise so early?' she purred, lifting a hand to trace the ridges of muscle on his stomach.

Kasim smiled briefly and turned his back, reaching for his clothes. Claudine was an eager bedmate. She was beautiful and extremely desirable with her honey-coloured eyes sparkling invitingly at him this morning. She was everything that most men wanted, but she was not Marietta. He had welcomed the pleasures Claudine offered during the night, drawing comfort from her softness pressed closely against him as he slept, but any desire he felt for her had dispersed in the light of day.

'Stay there for as long as you wish,' he said. 'I have things to attend to. I leave for Hamed's stronghold later this day.'

Claudine sat upright. 'You're really going? I thought it some ruse, some strategy to deceive Hamed. You are surely taking an escort at least.'

'No. I'm going alone. Hamed is a man of his word. Marietta and Leyla will return with me, after one month has passed.'

Claudine clutched at his sleeve. 'Don't do this thing. Stay here with me. It is not worth risking your life. I love Marietta like a sister and of course I pray for her safe return. But you cannnot put yourself in danger because of her. Kasim . . . please listen . . .'

Kasim shook her off in annoyance. He had confided in her because she was Marietta's kinswoman and he thought she would understand what he was about to do. It had been a comfort to tell someone the truth of his coming ordeal. Of necessity, few people knew of the real reason for his visit. The treaty had been drawn up and signed by himself and Hamed. His household were aware only that his stay in the stronghold was part of a business transaction.

Claudine tried again to dissuade him from going. When he remained impervious to her entreaties, she pressed the curve of her hip against him and wriggled invitingly.

Kasim lost all patience. 'Surely you of all people can see that there is no other way to rescue Marietta. Enough of this talk. Not one more word. Go back to the harem and leave me to prepare myself in peace.'

Claudine got slowly to her feet. Her movements

had a studied sensuality. The red-gold hair tumbled over her bare shoulders. She glanced up at him through lowered eyelids, her bottom lip pushed out mulishly. Reaching for a silk wrap she pulled it on, then turned back to him. Her mouth opened as she prepared to try and dissuade him one last time.

Kasim held up his hand. Despite himself he felt the urge to laugh at her expression. There was little of subtlety about Claudine. He slapped her shapely rump.

'Go on, get out. Now!'

Claudine gave up. She almost ran from the room. The humour faded from Kasim's face. In a few hours time he would give himself up willingly to the man who had good reason to hate him. In the pit of his stomach there was a cold sensation of foreboding.

Roxelana stood with the others in the inner courtyard as Kasim strode in through the gates. Everyone was there waiting, except Gabriel. A silence descended as Kasim stopped in the centre of the courtyard and faced Hamed. The commonfolk paused in their business to watch the unexpected entertainment. Whispers and nudges passed amongst them as they recognised Kasim Dey, Administrator of Algiers.

Kasim was alone as he had promised he would be. He was unarmed and walking with easy grace, as if he was taking a morning stroll. Roxelana felt a grudging admiration. He was either very foolish, or very brave. Whatever his attributes, there was no denying that he was extremely attractive.

He looked even better than she remembered. The first time she had seen him he had been wearing full dress-armour which, though splendid, had obscured the finer details of his body. This day he wore a high-collared silk tunic, in a deep shade of red, tucked into black figured-velvet trousers. The garments showed off his tall, spare form to perfection. A wide belt of studded black leather and knee-length leather boots completed his costume. He was bare headed. His hair, sleek and black as night, was drawn back tightly and tied with a thong at his nape. His face was hawk-like, predatory in profile.

Roxelana saw how Marietta looked at her former master. She suppressed a sneer. The Frenchwoman was a fool to display her emotions so openly. Her heart was in her eyes. Did she not have the sense to veil her emotions as Leyla was doing? Roxelana's lip curled with contempt. How naïve the Frenchwoman was.

She turned to grin at Hamed, who stood next to her, but he was intent on Marietta. His dark eyes roved over the Frenchwoman's face, moved on to Kasim, then back to Marietta. Roxelana felt pained by the tortured expression on his face. A muscle twitched in his cheek and there was a certain tension around his full mouth. If she needed further proof, she had it. Hamed was in love with the French-woman, though she doubted whether he realised the fact yet.

She clenched her fingers and chewed at the inside of her lip. Damn Marietta for existing and damn Kasim for taking up Hamed's challenge. Kasim's coming to the stronghold might well be the catalyst which forced Hamed's hand. Hamed's growing passion for the Frenchwoman would be fanned by the depth of his feelings for Kasim. How could he help using Marietta as a weapon against Kasim? And in so doing he would become embroiled ever deeper in his obsession.

Roxelana wished she did not know Hamed so well, then she could have left room for doubt. But she had sensed from the first that Hamed would be extremely reluctant to give up Marietta, despite having given his word to do so. Oh, why did he not feel that way about her? He had once. In the three years since she entered his stronghold she had never had a rival for his affections. With the coming of Marietta everything had changed. Roxelana could not understand why. She knew that she was still beautiful enough to make any man turn his head.

The arrival of Gabriel checked her thoughts. He walked purposefully out of the tower and went to stand in front of Kasim. The two men were of equal height, though beside Gabriel's heavier, well-muscled form Kasim looked almost slight of build.

Gabriel was silent, awaiting Hamed's orders. He was dressed only in a pair of tightly-fitting leather trousers, tucked into boots. A thick belt encircled his waist and his powerful chest and shoulders were bare. He carried a bundle of objects made of leather, from which thin straps trailed down and swayed in the warm breeze.

Kasim glanced at the objects Gabriel held and made some comment. For a moment a mocking smile curved his lips, then he resumed his expression of almost bored resignation. Roxelana was too far away to catch what Kasim said, but she saw a flush stain Gabriel's cheeks. She thought he would strike Kasim, but he controlled himself. Hamed made a motion with his hand and Gabriel spoke.

His voice surprised Roxelana. It was cold and strangely lacking in emotion. Where was the triumph? Perhaps Gabriel could not really believe that he had his old master in his power.

'You are Kasim Dey no longer. For the appointed time you are the pleasure-slave of Hamed. And slaves own nothing. Their bodies and minds, their pleasures and responses, are subject to the will of their master. Hamed wishes you to be attired as befits your new station. You will now disrobe. Your clothes will be given back to you on the day you leave.'

Kasim did not react beyond making a small inclination of his head. Roxelana was disappointed. She would have liked to see a show of fear, or at least trepidation. Surely Kasim could not have expected to be stripped naked in the courtyard, while everyone looked on. Hamed was being deliberately cruel by letting the commonfolk bear witness to Kasim's plight. The story of his humbling would soon spread throughout the villages. The commonfolk would carry the tale with them when they went to the souk.

Knowing this, Kasim's self-possession was amazing. He might be quaking with fury and shame inside, but no one would guess it.

Marietta's reactions more than made up for Kasim's composure. Roxelana felt deeply gratified by Marietta's look of horror. Her lips were shaped into a little 'O' of distress and her hands were clasped tightly together. She looked neither to the left nor the right, but kept her whole attention on the rigidly composed figure of her former master.

With nonchalant grace, Kasim undid his belt and dropped it to the ground. Pulling the red tunic free of his waistband, he slipped it over his head. Roxelana took a few steps closer, eagerly examining Kasim's naked upper body. Though slender, his chest and arms were corded with muscle. His skin was pale and smooth over slabs of firm muscle. Dark-brown nipples crested his pectorals.

Roxelana's tongue darted out to moisten her lips as Kasim unfastened his boots and trousers. He slipped off his underwear and soon he was naked. Standing up straight and proud, he looked Gabriel in the face. His chest rose and fell with the rhythm of his breath. Ah, he is distressed, thought Roxelana, though his eyes are defiant.

She was enjoying herself immensely. Kasim was indeed worth looking at. He reminded her of an icon she had seen in a church in Venice. The statue had been of a martyred saint. It stood in the chancel of the church, near the altar, lit by the sunlight that streamed in through a stained-glass window. The sculptor had captured those same clean lines, the whiteness of the skin, and the stark hollows and shadows of Kasim's body.

Roxelana allowed her eyes to travel slowly downwards to the ridges of muscle on Kasim's stomach and the line of silky black hair which led downwards from his navel. Her eyes lingered at his groin. Against his pale body, the sexual organs looked dark and enticing. His cock, framed by a thickly curling bush of black hair, was thick-stemmed, the head of it uncovered by skin. The ball sac was heavy and firm.

A delicious little shiver rippled down Roxelana's back as she imagined how it would feel to stroke his skin, to kiss his mouth. How delightful to take that velvety, plum-like glans into her mouth and make him shiver with delight. Roxelana loved to have power over a man, to bend him to her will, even to abuse him a little until he begged for mercy. Kasim was so restrained, so dignified, that she felt a strong urge to degrade him in every possible way.

Oh, to have Kasim all to herself. Such things she would have him do. She wondered whether Hamed would allow it, then knew all at once that he would. Did he not wish Kasim to be humiliated in every way possible? And if she took part in the preparation of the new slave, suggested new refinements, then she would feel as if she was hurting Marietta personally. What an added enticement.

She glanced briefly at Marietta and was elated to see the tears glittering in the Frenchwoman's wide blue eyes. How love made fools of women. Roxelana found the sight of Marietta's distress comforting, as if it somehow compensated her for her recent loss of status. Go on, suffer you wretch, Roxelana thought. You know what I feel now, when I look at Hamed. See how you like it.

'Bring Kasim to me,' Hamed ordered. 'Have him kneel.'

Gabriel urged Kasim forward. Kasim kneeled, his arms hanging loosely at his sides, his eyes fixed on Hamed's boots. The commonfolk watching, cheered their master and jeered at Kasim, calling out insults and suggestions for further punishment.

Hamed laughed triumphantly. 'Long have I waited for this day. It warms my heart to see my old enemy doing obeisance to me. Everyone here can see what I have reduced you to. But this is just the beginning. Oh, I shall work you until you know what it is to be submissive – pleasure-slave.'

'I expected nothing else,' Kasim said dismissively. 'Mark me well. I shall keep my part of the bargain. See that you do the same. *There* is the reason why I let you do this to me.' He glanced over his shoulder and pointed a finger at Marietta and Leyla. 'For them alone do I suffer this dishonour willingly. Yours is the shame Hamed. For cannot all see how shabbily you deal with one of your betters?'

Roxelana was impressed by the nobility of the little speech. She knew that in Kasim's position she would be crying and begging for mercy. The commonfolk moved uneasily. Some of them looked sidelong at Hamed as if they accepted the truth in Kasim's words. Kasim was an enigma indeed. Roxelana was finding him more compelling, more of a challenge, with every moment that passed.

'You speak of shame!' Hamed hissed, his cheeks flushing with anger at Kasim's presumption. 'Truly, you shall learn the meaning of the word. Bind him!'

A spasm crossed Marietta's face. 'Oh, I can't bear this,' she burst out. 'Have pity Hamed. Stop it now. I beg you.'

She took a step towards Kasim, but Leyla held her back. Marietta twisted in Leyla's embrace, almost beside herself with anguish.

'Is it not enough that you have him in your power?' she said brokenly. 'He has demonstrated his willingness to abase himself. How can you do this—'

'Silence!' Hamed's face darkened. His dark brows flew together. 'The treaty has been signed. The terms are clear. Do not speak to me of leniency. Where was the leniency when Kasim sank my treasure ships and killed my men? What mercy did he show me when he dealt me the blow from his sword—'

'But Hamed—'

'Enough,' Hamed cried. 'Be silent I say! Or by all that I hold holy, I swear you'll join Kasim.' His dark eyes bored into Marietta. Spittle flecked his lips. 'Shall I have you stripped naked and beaten while he watches? Or perhaps I'll have you beat him for my pleasure.'

A roar of approval from the commonfolk rose into the air. Their allegiance had swung back completely to Hamed. Marietta shrank back from Hamed's fury. She plainly believed that he would carry out his threat. Her shoulders slumped. She reached for Leyla's hand. Leyla placed her arm around Marietta's shoulders, murmuring words of comfort.

'Get on with it, Gabriel,' Hamed rapped, his voice flat. 'Fit Kasim with his uniform and have done.'

Some of the animation seemed to have gone out of Hamed. It was as if Marietta's outburst had unsettled him, robbing him of his moment of triumph. Roxelana saw that Gabriel too was surprised and displeased by Marietta's heated reaction. She smiled inwardly. Marietta would have some explaining to do later. Plainly, she had been less than honest with Gabriel.

Gabriel uttered a curse, and pushed Kasim hard so that he spawled headlong in the dust of the courtyard. Kasim grinned contemptuously up at Gabriel and got slowly to his feet. Streaks of dust marred his smooth, pale skin, but he made no move to brush them off.

He glared at Gabriel. 'Do your worst then – slavemaster. I care not. She's worth anything you can do to me, and more. You should know that better than anyone.'

Somehow the emphasis had changed. Everyone was aware that there was an inexplicable tension between Kasim and Gabriel. It was more, much more, than that of slave and slavemaster. Hamed too watched the exchange with a look of brooding discontent.

Roxelana's chest felt tight with loathing. That cursed Frenchwoman had somehow managed to get them all dancing to her tune. Kasim, Gabriel, Hamed; each of them in their different ways was obsessed with her. One day soon, there would be a reckoning, Roxelana swore it.

'Hold out your wrists,' Gabriel ordered. 'I'm going to repay you for all the times you forced indignities on me. Before I've finished with you, you'll weep for the love of the lash!'

He fitted stiff leather wrist-cuffs on Kasim; each cuff had a ring inset so that he could be restrained at will. Similar cuffs were fitted to his ankles and a deep collar, which dipped to a point in front, was secured around his throat.

'And now, so that you begin to realise that all your responses belong to your master . . . you will wear this,' Gabriel said, holding up a device made of padded leather fitted with straps.

Kasim could not suppress a flinch of distaste. Gabriel smiled slowly, his hands on his hips, enjoying his captive's reaction.

'But first,' he said pleasantly. 'You will assume the required position of subservience for your new master – slave.'

Gabriel pushed Kasim down onto his hands and knees, grinning when Kasim resisted.

'Now arch your back,' he ordered. 'Press your rump upwards and part your thighs. Display yourself like an obedient pleasure-slave. Your new master wants to see that rosy orifice between your buttocks.'

Kasim closed his eyes as he obeyed slowly. A deep flush coloured his face, though he pressed his lips together and made no sound.

'Is he ready for service?' Hamed asked Gabriel. 'Test him for me. Open up his body.'

Gabriel exerted pressure on the tightly-muscled globes of Kasim's buttocks, kneading and parting the firm flesh. With the toe of his boot he nudged at the soft inner flesh of Kasim's thighs.

'Spread them wider and split the crease,' he ordered crudely. 'Come now. You've ordered your own slaves to display themselves often enough. You know what's wanted.'

After an initial resistance Kasim parted his thighs even wider, so that his scrotum was fully visible between his spread legs. It was a vulnerable and yet somehow potent symbol of his maleness. Gabriel trailed the bundle of straps he held, over Kasim's rump, allowing the straps to brush lightly in the groove of his buttocks, tickling the tight little nether-mouth. He used the straps as a lash, laying two teasingly light strokes against the firm sac.

Kasim shuddered. Almost playfully, Gabriel leant down and grasped Kasim's scrotum in one hand, encircling the root of it and drawing it firmly back-wards until Kasim jumped and twitched at the contact.

Gabriel laughed and released Kasim's sac. He slipped his fingers into the exposed crevice between the parted buttocks, pulling at the dark curls that clustered there, then trailed his fingertips over and around Kasim's anus. As he jabbed a finger inside him, Kasim clenched his hips on reflex. Gabriel slapped him hard on the rump.

'Is that the way you demonstrate your willingness to please? It won't do. You obviously need some strict training. Now push back against my hand, before I lose patience and give you your first serious lashing!'

The red fingermarks stood out against the pale flesh of Kasim's rump. Roxelana watched with bated breath as Kasim took a deep breath, forcing himself to relax and open his body to Gabriel's inspection. He pressed his parted buttocks against Gabriel's hand as he was ordered to.

The lewd posture and discomfort on Kasim's face gave Roxelana an erotic thrill. She imagined plunging her fingers into Kasim's body as Gabriel was doing now. How hot and thrilling it would feel and what a wonderful feeling of power to bend such a vital, attractive man to her will. She moved her thighs together, feeling her sex growing heavy and beginning to send out that familiar sweet ache.

'He's tight,' Gabriel commented. 'His orifice will have to be trained and well-oiled before anyone can use him properly, my Lord.'

Hamed nodded. 'He's more used to using slaves than being one. We'll soon remedy that situation. On the morrow we'll fit him out with a stretching device. You will increase the thickness of the device as he becomes accustomed to wearing it. For now, buckle on the cock-restraint, then lead him away to his quarters. I'll be along shortly to see how he's settling in.'

Gabriel ordered Kasim to stand. Roxelana could see the fading, scarlet impression of Gabriel's hand marring one of Kasim's pale buttocks. How she longed to see the thin red marks bisect his muscular rump. Her palm itched to hold the switch that would inflict the marks on his skin. She doubted whether he had ever been beaten. It would be a singular delight to introduce him to the kiss of the lash.

Gabriel buckled a harness of stiff, studded leather around Kasim's waist. He tightened the buckles at the back until it fitted tightly. A thick strap hanging from the front had a large metal ring set halfway along it. Gabriel adjusted the fit and eased the ring down over Kasim's phallus and balls, then pulled the strap between his legs to enclose the root between his sac and anus. He then secured the strap to the back of the harness.

'You'll wear this harness at all times during the day, unless you ask permission for it to be removed. If you need to perform a bodily function you must beg to be allowed to do so. Every night you will clean and polish the leather. Soon you will be so accustomed to wearing the restraint that you will come to love it. It is a mark of your slavery.'

Kasim shifted his legs against the discomfort of the harness. The thick, padded strap pressed tightly into the groove of his buttocks. Gabriel laughed and made Kasim turn around in a circle, all the time flicking at his buttocks with the bunch of straps he still held. The watchers whistled and called out compliments. The effect of the stout metal ring, lodged so tightly against Kasim's body, was to thrust his cock and balls into shocking prominence. The pressure at the base of his belly caused Kasim's shaft to swell to an incipient erection.

'Not very impressive,' Gabriel said, gripping Kasim's cock-shaft and pulling at it roughly. 'You can surely do better. Come now, slave. Put on a show for your audience. Have you no pride in yourself?'

Despite his resistance, Kasim's member became fully erect, jutting up potently in front of him. Gabriel produced a small bottle of oil from his belt. He poured a few drops into his hand, rubbed it over the swollen shaft and slid up to smear oil on the glans.

Next, he produced a smaller, separate ring, with a thin chain attached to it. He slipped the ring over the cock-head, smoothing it slowly and gradually over the out-swell of flesh until it fitted tightly under the pronounced ridge of the shiny, purple glans.

Kasim looked straight ahead, his face expressionless, as Gabriel secured the chain on the cock-ring to the harness, forcing the erect stem to lie snugly against Kasim's belly. Tremors passed over the taut flesh of Kasim's stomach as Gabriel adjusted the tension of the chain. Even when not erect Kasim's cock would be held captive.

'You'll wear that ring and chain for the duration of your stay. See that you take pains to remain erect at all times when you are in company. This is a paramount rule for male slaves. You may be called upon to pleasure anyone within the stronghold, and if you fail to give satisfaction you will be punished severely. Incidentally,' Gabriel's smile was almost gentle, 'your own release will be denied you. But perhaps you expected this. Is this not a favourite punishment for your own slaves?'

As a final humiliation he clipped a stout leash to Kasim's slave collar and led him in a circle around the courtyard. When the commonfolk had had their fill of looking at Kasim, taunting and even pawing at him with their work-roughened hands, Gabriel led him close to Hamed and those of his household who watched. Kasim met Hamed's eye without flinching and it was Hamed who looked away first.

'Take him inside presently,' Hamed said. 'And give him a lesson in manners. A pleasure-slave must keep his eyes lowered when in the presence of his master. First though, you may show him to his former slaves.'

Finally, Gabriel brought Kasim to a halt in front of Marietta and Leyla.

'Well, here are those you came here for,' he said.

'See how avidly they look at you? How does it feel to have the roles reversed? You are as much on show as you forced them to be.'

Kasim did not reply. Leyla had a pained look on her face. She put out one hand in a gesture of sympathy. As she touched Kasim's bare shoulder he flinched. It was as if his fragile control was nearing breaking point. Gabriel dashed Leyla's hand away.

'You must ask permission to touch the new slave. If you ask nicely Hamed might order Kasim to pleasure you.'

Kasim looked as if he might turn on Gabriel, then he thought better of it. He recovered himself swiftly.

'Don't, my Leyla,' he whispered. 'Don't let them see that they have hurt you through me. Be strong. I am here to share your imprisonment. Let that be some comfort.'

'Oh, my Lord,' Leyla said tearfully. 'I am honoured that you abase yourself so for Marietta and me. Marietta have you no words for our Lord?'

Marietta seemed beyond speech. Slowly she shook her head. She kept her eyes lowered. Her hands were trembling visibly.

'Look your fill Marietta,' Gabriel said coldly, reaching out and grasping her chin. He yanked her head up. 'I thought this was what you wanted to see. Is this not the man who threatened you and held you against your will? Where is the triumph, the joy you take in his suffering? Tell him you hate him, as you told me. Let me hear you say it.'

Marietta twisted his grip, wrenching her chin free. She remained stubbornly silent, looking at Kasim with something like horror.

'Say it,' Gabriel ground out, his voice dangerously quiet. 'Give me this victory.'

Marietta looked him in the face. 'I . . . I cannot,' she said. 'I never wanted this. It is you who thirst for revenge, not me. I love Kasim and I am his willing subject. I'm sorry. I never meant to deceive you Gabriel. I lied when I told you that I was held against my will. But it was what you wanted to hear . . .'

The hurt on Gabriel's face was raw. He looked at her for a moment longer. She thought he looked near to tears. Then his eyes hardened, becoming cold and flat like pebbles. He whirled and strode away. Giving the leash a vicious jerk, he dragged his captive after him and disappeared inside the main building.

Roxelana sauntered up to Marietta, a cat-like smile on her small red mouth. 'Oh dear, it appears that you have offended Gabriel in some way,' she said with relish. 'Not every man here is under your spell after all, then.'

Marietta's eyes glittered dangerously. 'Do not bait me, Roxelana. Not now. I am heartily sick of your taunts, your underhand threats.' She lunged forward, reaching out for Roxelana, her fingers curled into talons. 'Let us settle our differences now!'

Roxelana sidestepped neatly, avoiding Marietta's grip. 'I welcome the day when we will fight as adversaries,' she sneered. 'But that must wait until I have visited the new slave. I have a pressing need for release. I wonder what it will be like to have Kasim pleasure me.'

She glanced at Hamed for his permission. Hamed nodded curtly, his face stark with contained emotion. 'Go to him, Roxelana. Show him what is required of my slaves.'

Roxelana smiled slowly and let out her breath on a low sigh. 'It will be my pleasure to obey you, my Lord.'

Marietta looked at Roxelana with horror. 'You cannot mean to do this. Kasim needs time to adjust to his new position. He is unused to this treatment. Have you no pity?'

'None,' Roxelana said happily. 'You should know that by now! It is useless to plead for clemency. The way you've behaved this day, you ought to be ordered to watch Kasim's ordeal as a punishment!' She flashed another glance at Hamed. 'Is that not so, my Lord?'

Hamed fixed Marietta with a level glance. 'It is true,' he said softly. 'I've allowed you much leeway. You are too wilful, and not mindful of your position here. You reach too high, too soon. I think you need a lesson in obedience.'

Marietta gaped at Hamed in incomprehension. 'But I don't understand. I've done nothing wrong . . .'

Roxelana snorted with derision. 'You think not? Playing one man off against the other . . .' Well pleased with herself, her kitten face glowing with satisfaction, she flounced into the stronghold, her mocking laughter trailing behind her.

Marietta lay back in the marble tub as Bishi bathed her and laid out a clean costume.

It was an hour since the gathering in the courtyard. Hamed's threat hung over her, making her feel nervous and jumpy. She had expected him to order her to go directly to a place of punishment, but he had dismissed her along with everyone else. His voice sounding tired, he had said: 'Bathe and change. You will attend me after my usual rest. Await my orders.'

The stronghold was quiet at this hour. The heat of the sun shut out behind wooden shutters and diffused by the ornate iron screens at the windows. Over the canal the heat-haze shimmered above the oily dark water. Most people, the commonfolk included, took a rest during the heat of the afternoon.

Marietta sat up fully, feeling the cool perfumed water slip over her skin like silk. She reached out to a side table, where Hamed's gift, the small leather casket, lay. Taking out the ring, she slipped it onto her thumb; it was too big to fit any of her fingers.

172

The cabochon ruby gleamed as it caught the light. The ornate setting was of gold, twisted into a complex design of flowers and foliage. Why had he given her his own ring? Whatever the reason it seemed that he regretted their moment of closeness. Perhaps she had hurt him without meaning to. Was she ever cursed to bring unhappiness to those men who enjoyed her favours?

She slipped the ring off and replaced it in its box. Hamed had been charming and animated that night in his chamber. She thought he liked her for herself, as well as for her body. But in the courtyard, just now, he had been remote and cold. As he followed Gabriel and Kasim into the tower, his shoulders had been slumped.

She felt a stab of pity for him. The taste of victory was apparently not to his liking. She could have told him that it was better not to dwell on past slights. Gabriel too had been twisted by his desire for revenge. The only positive way was forward. She had believed that all of her life. If she had not, she would have been unable to adjust to a new life in a foreign land.

She felt moved to go to Hamed, to explain how she had coped with emotional turmoil. But she sensed that he was not in the mood to listen to platitudes. There was something else troubling him, beside Kasim. For some reason Hamed's eyes seemed haunted, bleak, when he looked at her. He spoke of giving her lessons in obedience and had even allowed himself to be swayed by that vixen Roxelana's words.

But what had she done wrong? Marietta could not fathom him.

The cool, silky water lapped against her skin. She took up the pad made of vegetable fibre and began to scrub at her limbs.

It saddened her to know that she had hurt Gabriel all over again. It had been inevitable that he would find out the truth, but she had not meant for the disclosure to be so stark, so public. It was plain that he had been devastated when she told him that she loved Kasim. But Kasim had needed desperately to be told that. His anguished face, flushed darkly along his high cheekbones, had tugged at some place deep inside her. She had been rewarded by the warmth that flared in the depths of his black eyes.

She sighed. Everything was so complicated. She was full of fear for Kasim. Was he even now being forced to pleasure Roxelana? The Saints only knew what she was forcing him to do. She felt sorrow and rage at the thought of it. Tears pricked her eyes. She clenched her hands tight, crushing the fibre washing-pad into a shapeless mass.

How would Kasim cope with the humiliation of being brought so low? Uppermost in her mind was concern for him. But a larger part of her being was bound by self-disgust. She knew that she envied Roxelana's power over Kasim's helplessness, even while she detested her. For had she not also been strongly aroused by the sight of Kasim as Gabriel displayed him to Hamed?

The vision of Kasim's taut buttocks, splayed obscenely so that Gabriel could penetrate his anus, sent a shock of sensation to her pubis even now. She saw again the strongly erect phallus, so desirable, so familiar – and now with its shiny, purple glans imprisoned by the ring. How sweetly it pressed against Kasim's flat belly, secured by the thin chain to the belt at his waist. And how horribly compelling was the darkness of the leather harness against the taut, muscled whiteness of Kasim's body.

When Gabriel brought him close, she had smelt the clean sweat of Kasim's body, mixed with the evocative smell of leather. She had wanted to reach out to Kasim, to hold him, and stroke him. To comfort him in his distress. And if she was completely honest, to use him – as Roxelana was doing at this very moment.

Marietta gave a little moan of anger and frustration and sank down in the perfumed water, so that her face was covered and her hair stranded in the water like pale seaweed.

While Bishi was tightening the lacing of her violet leather corset, Hamed walked into the chamber.

For a while he said nothing, only seating himself and watching as Bishi completed Marietta's dress. The corset had been specially made for her. It was curved at the top, shaped to fit under the swell of each of Marietta's breasts. A little cuff supported them, while leaving them bare. A wide strip of boned velvet ran down the centre of the corset, separating and forming her breasts into two high cones.

Marietta felt a surge of pure sensual pleasure as Bishi drew in the back lacing tightly. Her body from chest to hip was held in a wickedly constricting grip. As she breathed, the top part of her lungs swelled, pushing her breasts up and out even more provocatively. Never had she worn such a strict, merciless garment. She smoothed her hands down over the shiny, violet leather, her fingers playing over the intricate seaming. The corset was long at the front, dipping low, so that it just brushed the top of Marietta's pubic curls.

Bishi picked up the short, transparent skirt, which matched the corset and held it out for Marietta to step into it.

'Leave her skirt off this time,' Hamed ordered, his voice a little hoarse. 'Her sex is to be displayed prominently. Put these on her. The nipples first.'

He handed Bishi two pairs of exquisitely wrought silver clamps, each with a large amethyst droplet attached to the chain.

Bishi teased Marietta's nipples until they gathered

into hard pink nubs, then she attached the smaller pair of clamps. The pinching caress sent little rushes of sensation through Marietta's imprisoned flesh. As the large amethyst drops swayed back and forth the pressure on her nipples was increased.

'They feel good. Yes?' Bishi grinned.

Marietta opened her mouth to agree that they did, but saw the scowl on Hamed's face. She decided that it was better to remain silent.

'Now the labial clamps. Attach them firmly . . . to the inner lips,' he said softly.

'My Lord? They are a little heavy—' Bishi began, but Hamed held up his hand.

'The inner lips, ' he insisted. 'I want Marietta to be very aware of her hot little sex. And I want it to be decorated most beautifully. She is to be presented to my new pleasure-slave and I want her senses bejewelled as well as her body.'

Marietta's blood quickened as she absorbed his words. He was taking her to Kasim? She parted her legs eagerly, so that Bishi could attach the labial clamps. The sooner Hamed had finished decking her with baubles, the sooner she would see Kasim again. Oh, Kasim. She could hardly contain her fear and excitement.

Bishi's expert fingers brushed the scant fleece away from the plump sex-lips, smoothing and pulling at the tender pink frills as she took hold of them until they were distended and protruding a little from the split-plum shape of her vulva. Her knuckles brushed against Marietta's flesh-hood, awakening the hungry pleasure-bud within it.

Hamed watched Bishi's every move closely. His dark-brown eyes flickered to Marietta's face, watching for signs of enjoyment as she allowed Bishi to handle her. His eyes gleamed at the little indrawn breath which she could not suppress. As she felt the coldness of the clamps and their pinching bite, when

Bishi secured them firmly, Marietta chewed at her bottom lip.

'You will come to relish the unfamiliar heaviness and the almost painful heat,' Hamed promised. 'It mirrors closely the feel of a woman's engorged sex organs. Soon you will find yourself permanently aroused and you will beg me to give you release.'

Marietta glared defiance at him. She would never beg, she vowed. Kasim had chastised her more forcibly than Hamed, and she had not begged him to pleasure her for a long time. She remembered the little gold cage of mesh, which Kasim had forced her to wear over her sex for weeks, during her training. How she had burned and simmered for the pleasure he denied her. She smiled inwardly. How well she had been trained. Compared to Kasim, Hamed was a novice at the art of domination.

Despite her denials, she had to admit that wearing the new labial clamps was an unsettling experience. The silver ornaments were indeed heavier than she was used to and the weight of them on her delicate inner folds made her whole mound ache and burn. The ornate chains hung down to mid-thigh and the amethyst drops brushed against her inner thighs as she moved, tickling and scratching the sensitive skin.

'So, we are ready for the next step. If you please Marietta,' Hamed said, indicating that she should lie down on the divan and part her thighs.

She did as he ordered. He produced a little glass vial of violet-coloured powder.

'Some oil Bishi. Just a few drops,' he said.

Tipping some into the palm of his hands he anointed Marietta's pubic curls, tweaking and stroking the springy curls until they glistened wetly. Then he sprinkled a little of the glittery powder onto the hair, working it into the roots with his fingers. The violet powder shimmered in the late afternoon sunlight that spread dusty bars of light across the divan where she lay.

'Excellent,' Hamed said, making little sounds of admiration in his throat.

Marietta lifted her arms on his order and he dusted violet powder on the pale hair that frosted her armpits. As his warm fingers massaged the oil and violet glitter onto the hair, she smelt the subtle perfume of it, orris root and attar of roses.

'There,' he said with satisfaction and a certain pride. 'Almost finished. One thing more. I want Kasim to see how supremely beautiful I expect my slaves to be. Stay as you are and spread your sex-lips for me.'

Avoiding his eyes, Marietta did as he told her. Her fingers pressed the outer lips of her sex open. She felt the welcome submission flood her, as it always did, when asked to perform this act. It was hateful, so intimate, and so arousing to spread herself open completely to the gaze of a master or mistress.

Putting a drop of oil on her flesh-hood he smoothed it back until the erect little nub slipped free. Marietta squirmed under his fingers. Her bud began to pulse and grow hot. In the base of her belly was an answering sensation. The heavy clamps pulled her inner lips wide open as the weight of them carried them sideways to lie along the line of her inner thighs. She felt mortified that her vagina was pulled slightly open and her flesh-tube revealed to his gaze. Surely he could see deep inside, to the most intimate recesses of her body.

Hamed took no notice of the moistly gaping orifice. His fingers were steady as he worked the little flesh-hood back and forth until her pleasure-bud stood out stiffly erect. She gave a little murmur of shame and delight. Hamed grasped her clitoris tightly between finger and thumb and began working a tiny, ame-thyst-studded ring over the morsel of flesh.

Marietta bit back a cry as the cold metal was forced bit by bit over her engorged button. It seemed that all sensation was gathered into the pinched and throbbing region between her flesh-lips.

'Finished,' Hamed announced, wiping his fingers free of oil and coloured powder.

When Hamed bade her stand, Marietta stood with her legs a little apart, unwilling to close them together on the burning discomfort of the nub-ring. But Hamed knew what she was doing.

'Close your legs. I want the purse of your sex to settle around the ring and clamps. By the time you display yourself for Kasim, the whole of your sex will be wet and engorged. You could not control your responses if you wanted to. How delectable Kasim will find you. And how unattainable.'

Marietta closed her eyes briefly, a hot flush rising in her neck and heating her face. So she was to be the instrument of torture for Kasim. He was to see her displayed before him, aroused and ready for the touch of a lover and completely unattainable to him.

It was unbearable, degrading – and oh, so beguiling a thought.

Chapter Nine

Marietta had some difficulty in walking as she followed Hamed. The heavy labial clamps swayed with her every movement, exerting a downward pull on her tender flesh, and the little nub-ring pinched ever more cruelly with each step she took.

Hamed must have realised that she was in some discomfort, but he urged her to take long strides. She could only think that he took pleasure in thinking of her imprisoned vulva, the slick, wet flesh moving against the unyielding metal objects.

Once he stopped and turned to her. Reaching out, he gripped the nipple-clamps, pulling at them until the erect little flesh-cones were stretched and distended.

She gasped and writhed under his touch, her eyes filling at the smarting pain in her breasts. Hamed smiled slowly and loosened the clamps. He cupped her chin.

'I can see your pleasure even through your tears. Does not the heat and pain thread you through and through?'

Though she denied it silently, it was true. And it was all the more horrible that he knew it. She hung her head and would not reply to his taunts. He lifted her chin, pressing his fingertip into the hollow beneath it. She had no choice but to look into his face.

'What a superb little pleasure-slave you are,' he murmured. 'I think I'll keep you – for ever.'

'But you cannot . . . You promised . . .'

At her look of horror he smiled again and began to move off along the corridor. Marietta stumbled after him in her high-heeled, backless slippers, biting her lip against the pain it caused her to keep up with him. He seemed to be setting a quicker pace now, so that her discomfort worsened.

Between her legs the metal restraints grew warm and slick with her juices.

Soon they came to a part of the stronghold which she did not recognise. The walls here were rough and in a bad state of disrepair. Rush lights flared from wall sconces, sending long black shadows to climb the walls. The lintels over the stone doorways were of stained and blackened wood. She gained an impression of great age. There was a smell of dust and decay.

Hamed paused and ushered her into a small room, gloomy and with a low ceiling. It was also lit by the flickering light of rush candles. In the room there was a selection of heavy wooden furniture; two chairs, a table, and a low wooden chest with a curious sort of hurdle attached to the lid. All of the furniture was dark with the patina of age. A low wooden frame in the centre of the room served as a bed. A thin, dark mattress and cushions, thrown onto the floor in an untidy heap, were the only concessions to comfort.

Marietta's eyes took a moment to adjust to the fitful light. She heard Roxelana's laugh before she saw her, then, a moment later, she caught sight of Kasim. He was spread face down on the bed. His wrists and ankles had been secured to rings set in the wooden bed frame. The muscles of his back were bunched against the pain his tormentor was inflicting. He still wore the leather harness. She saw the thick strap that bisected his buttocks. It was dark with his sweat. The taut flesh of his rump glowed a deep rich red.

Roxelana stood over Kasim, a pliable switch with a notched tip in her hands. Her red hair was scraped up into a bun. She wore a tightly-fitting leather tunic and matching trousers, tucked into high boots. Over the tunic she wore a stout leather corset which fastened with straps at her waist and hip. She turned at their approach, her grin fading as she saw Marietta standing behind Hamed.

'You are working the prisoner well, Roxelana. Do not stop on my account,' Hamed said.

'Kasim!' Marietta breathed, making a little sound of distress.

He turned his head to one side. She saw that his loose, dark hair was damp with sweat. Strands of it stuck to his face.

'Marietta? Is that you? Have they harmed you?'

'Silence!' Roxelana grated, landing another lash on his straining buttocks. 'Slaves must ask permission to speak!'

Kasim groaned and writhed as she lashed his spread thighs with the switch. Through gritted teeth, he whispered: 'Come to gloat over me, have you, Hamed?'

Hamed did not at first reply. He placed his hand on one of Kasim's simmering buttocks, assessing the heat in the sorely abused flesh.

'That's enough for now Roxelana. Anoint him with soothing oil then let him up.'

'But I've only just begun—'

'Free him. I have other plans for him.'

Roxelana's little red mouth pursed with displeasure, but she did as she was bid. Smoothing back a few strands of her fiery red hair, she poured oil onto Kasim's buttocks and rubbed it into his skin, making no effort to be gentle. Kasim flinched away from her hand, wincing as she chafed at his sore skin. When she had finished she unclipped the fastenings of Kasim's wrists.

'Secure his hands to the belt at the small of his back,' Hamed ordered.

Roxelana did so, then she unfastened Kasim's ankles. Pushing him roughly off the bed, she forced him to his knees in front of Hamed. Marietta saw that his cock was semi-erect and dark against his pale skin.

'The leg stretcher also?' Roxelana asked.

Hamed grinned. 'Certainly. I want this slave to remember what he is at all times. The feeling of having his thighs forced apart, will emphasise the fact that he has no control over his own body. He will wish to close them and find it all the more humiliating that he must of necessity keep them apart.'

A rigid bar was fixed to Kasim's ankle cuffs, so that he was forced to kneel with his thighs held wide apart. Though his face was smudged by pain and his hair hung to his shoulders in a sweaty tangle, Kasim glared defiantly up at Hamed.

Roxelana picked up the switch and slapped it against her leather-clad thigh. Marietta watched her in mute fascination. Roxelana was dressed as a female guard. She looked harsh and pitiless in the tightly-fitting black leather. The corset gave her neat figure a look of severity, which was menacing and yet compelling. Her mouth was set in a hard line.

Roxelana pressed the switch against Kasim's mouth.

'Kiss it,' she ordered.

Kasim turned his head away. Roxelana smiled

nastily and said; 'No matter. The lash loves you despite your scorn!'

She played the notched tip lightly back and forth along Kasim's cock-stem, flicking it so that the front and then the back of the switch sent stinging little blows up and down the shaft.

'Let's keep you rigid for your master. That's it, flex the muscle at the base of your stem. I want you strongly erect and rearing upright.'

With his dark eyes glowing and a deep flush of shame creeping across his high cheekbones, Kasim complied. The stout fleshy stem became rigid as Roxelana stroked and tormented it. Soon his glans was swollen and tight, flaring delectably around the imprisonment of his cock-ring.

'Better. Much better,' Roxelana murmured, adjusting the little chain that connected the head of his phallus to the belt at Kasim's waist. He grimaced at the tightening pull of the chain, his potently erect member jumping and twitching against the extra pressure.

Hamed gave a satisfied grunt. He reached out and lifted a lock of the night-black hair, letting the waves trickle over his fingers. Kasim tried to pull his head away, but Hamed meshed his fingers in his hair and forced Kasim to look up at him.

'How is it,' he mused softly, 'that you remain so full of pride?' With his other hand he smoothed the hair back from Kasim's forehead and ran the pad of his thumb across Kasim's hard, shapely mouth. 'Your poise is not diminished. It is even enhanced by your torment. Curious, is that not so Marietta?'

Marietta dared not answer for the emotion clogging her throat. She was ashamed that a rush of excitement came over her from just looking at Kasim. His troubled beauty called out to her. How beguiling, how strange was the mixture of tenderness for his plight and the violence of the attraction she felt for him at this moment.

She could smell his sweat, the hot leather smell of the harness, and the animal scent of his hair. She took a halting step forward, then checked her movement, expecting Hamed to order her to stop. But he only laughed softly.

'Go closer if you wish. I want you to admire my new pleasure-slave. And *he* may gaze on *your* beauty all he wishes, but he will not be allowed to ease his desire for you.'

Hamed now addressed Kasim. 'I wonder if you approve of the way I dress my female slaves. See how the corset hugs Marietta's creamy flesh so tightly? How it constricts and shapes her form? Notice how the nipple-clamps compress her jutting teats? You desire this female slave with a penetrating and visible intensity do you not, Kasim? Even now your cock weeps with moisture.'

'Marietta,' Kasim murmured, his voice deep with longing, 'looks exquisite. But she looks that way naked and unadorned as I have often seen her.'

He raised his eyes to look at her. They blazed with emotion. Despite his posture of supplication, Marietta felt the knowledge that he was her master vibrate into her very soul. Nothing could change what he was, what he meant to her.

A fire seemed to flare into life within her at the sound of his voice. The strongly rearing shaft, the teardrop of clear moisture, which seeped from the little mouth, was all for her. She wished with all her heart that Kasim could sink his hard flesh inside her.

Perhaps Hamed would order Kasim to pleasure her while he watched. Hamed though, looked displeased. He had gone to a great deal of trouble to make her look beautiful, after the fashion he favoured, and Kasim said he found her just as beautiful naked; as nature made her. Marietta hid a smile.

Beside Marietta, Roxelana gave a snort of displeasure.

'You are too kind, my Lord,' she said to Hamed. 'Is this truly punishment? All these soft words and longing looks you allow them to exchange? And where is Kasim's gratitude? He should be thanking you for bringing Marietta to view him in his chamber!'

'True enough. We'll have to teach him to be grateful. Marietta sit on the bed. Allow Kasim to admire your jewelled flesh.'

Marietta moved across the room, her high heels clicking on the cracked and worn tiles. She sat down with her knees pressed demurely together. Violet ribbons criss-crossed her calves, gleaming softly in the light from the rush candles.

The ghost of a smile passed across Kasim's face. Marietta knew the source of his humour. How many times had he ordered her to display herself in the position of subservience? In his presence, in the harem, she would have been required to kneel, with her shoulders pressed back and her arms linked in the small of her back. Always her thighs must be parted to display her sex and the pale fleece which crowned it.

Her present posture was so unusual that it prompted them both to share the private joke.

Unaware of the moment Marietta shared with Kasim, Hamed rapped out an order.

'Roxelana bring one of those flares over here. I want Kasim to see every detail of what is denied him.'

Roxelana hurried to obey. She was obviously excited by the prospect of taunting them both. The yellow light threw jagged patterns across Marietta's body. As she lay back, propped up by her bent arms, and parted her legs, the violet powder glimmered on her pubic curls.

'Move close Kasim. Position yourself between her knees,' Hamed ordered.

Roxelana nudged Kasim with the toe of her pointed leather slipper as he crossed the room with difficulty.

'Hurry up,' she spat.

'Lift your feet Marietta. Place the heels of your shoes on the bed,' Hamed said.

Marietta did as he asked, the muscles of her feet and calves tensing as the spiked heels dug into the soft mattress.

'Slide your buttocks to the very edge of the bed. I want your sex presented as openly as possible. Good. Now bear down and push out your bottom-mouth.'

Marietta felt her stomach curl with shame as she obeyed Hamed. But, despite her reticence, the familiar feeling of willing submission began to surface. It seemed that she could not help her body's responses.

Kasim watched closely as the heavy labial clamps were revealed in their entirety. The way they hung down, swaying slightly in space as she balanced her bottom on the very edge of the mattress, caused her inner flesh-lips to be elongated a little and drawn together.

'No. No. That won't do,' Hamed said. 'Lie back and draw up your knees, but prop up your upper body with cushions. Reveal your open womanhood. And I want you to see Kasim's face as he admires you.'

Marietta did as he asked. And in this position the labial clamps slipped one to each side, lying along the indentation where each thigh met each buttock. The amethysts glittered in the flame-light. As before, her inner lips were pulled open to reveal the moistness of her hungry vagina.

'Ah yes. Much better,' Hamed said. 'See, Kasim, how her sex is decorated? Look closely. Have you not yearned to gaze on this choice little morsel?'

Kasim could not resist, despite Hamed's taunts and Roxelana's derisive laughter. He let out his breath on a sigh of longing and bent his neck, studying the moist, rosy flesh which he had not laid eyes on for many weeks.

Marietta felt her clitoris begin to pulse at the eagerness on his face. His eyes widened as the little ring on her bud was revealed to his gaze. She knew that she was wet, her sex had been made plump and ready for pleasure by the pinching grip of the exquisite jewellery.

'Tell me now that Marietta's fleshpot is not more beautiful than you have ever seen it!' Hamed said with triumph. 'Speak the truth and you will have your reward.'

Kasim's voice was hoarse when he answered. 'Truly I have never admired it more.'

'And you want to lick and suck at it? To breathe in her fragrant musk, don't you? Answer me now! Let me hear you say it.'

'I want to do all those things. As you well know. But you torment me by asking. Now you will tell me that I am forbidden these potent pleasures.' Kasim's voice was bitter, his eyes as hard and dark as obsidian.

'On the contrary,' Hamed said smoothly. 'Beg a little and who knows what you might accomplish.'

Roxelana laughed richly and placed her hands on her leather-clad hips. She stood with her legs parted and her shoulders pulled back.

'Truly, you are cruel to promise the impossible, my Master,' she purred at Hamed.

Kasim flashed a look at Hamed to see if he was serious. Hamed's handsome face was expressionless. Kasim closed his eyes briefly. A muscle in his face twitched. Then his voice came, dark and low. 'Please . . .' he said, then louder, more insistently. 'Please.'

Marietta felt a dart of heat go straight to her womb

at the longing in Kasim's voice. She had never thought to hear him utter that word. His lips moved imperceptibly closer. She saw the tip of his tongue protruding. How eager he was for the taste of her.

'Wait!' Hamed snapped. 'You will pleasure Marietta's greedy little sex, because she has been obedient and she deserves the release she craves. But you will not be allowed the luxury of touching her flesh. Instead you will pleasure her with . . . this.'

He thrust a feather between Kasim's lips. 'Hold it in your teeth and bend close. That's it, tickle her sex. And you may enjoy the rich scent of her arousal, although you are forbidden to taste it.'

Marietta moaned in frustration and disappointment. She longed for the feel of Kasim's mouth, the lash of his hot tongue. How cruel Hamed was to deny them both in this way. Then she felt the soft caress of the feather as it worked along the moist inner surfaces of her spread sex. The feel of it was delicious as it circled her imprisoned bud.

Kasim's breath was hot on her intimate flesh as he moved his head back and forth. The feather soon grew damp with her moisture and slipped more seductively around the folds and grooves of her vulva. Now and then the little, brush-like tip of the feather entered her vagina, tickling at the slick flesh-walls.

Kasim described circles, round and round her clitoris, tickling the swollen end of it until she thought she would go mad with the subtle pressure. The pinching grip of the nub-ring contrasted deliciously with the soft stroking of the feather. The feeling of bearing down, of pushing out her vagina for this stimulation became stronger.

She found herself moving her hips, thrusting towards his face as, now, the naughty wet feather tip worked its way down the groove of her bottom and licked at the puckered mouth that also pushed out obscenely to welcome it. Oh, how wanton she felt. And how glad she was that Kasim, her beloved master, was the instrument of her pleasure.

The feather tip flicked over her anus, tickling the few blonde curls that framed it. She sank down further onto the feather, tensing and opening the tight little orifice, longing for the thrill of penetration. Kasim pressed the flexible tip firmly against her anus, exerting a gentle pressure until it slipped a short way inside her. He rotated it until she felt she would cry out against the subtle, ticklish pleasure of it.

Kasim made a sound deep in his throat and she knew that he drew a singular pleasure from seeing her writhe under him. If he could not taste her and make love to her with his mouth this was the next best thing.

Now the feather was withdrawn and applied to her bud again, flicking over and over it, until the familiar pooling of pleasure began deep within her belly. She was near now and Kasim sensed it. Patiently he applied the feather tip, circling her engorged bud which throbbed and burned inside the ring.

'Oh, my love. My Master,' she whispered as the heavy pulsings spread and broke over her.

'Silence,' Hamed said, but Marietta was beyond caring what she said or did.

She thrust her hips forward, bucking uncontrollably. Her womb contracted and her vagina leaked honey moisture onto the base of the feather. She was as wet as a dewy rose and as fragrant. She was glad that Kasim could view her pleasure so minutely and smell her musky heat. Glad too that she had spoken of her love for him. It would be some comfort for him in the long, unfulfilled nights to come.

Then she felt a new sensation and almost cried out as she realised what it was. Kasim had abandoned all caution and pressed his lips to her sex. She felt his mouth cover her soaking folds as he ground into her in an achingly erotic kiss. For a second she felt his teeth as he closed them over her bud. There was a pulling sensation, a moment of discomfort, then she was free.

Kasim had stolen the bud-ring.

Kasim drew back from her and spat the tiny ring onto the floor. With a tiny, bell-like noise it bounced over the tiles to become lost in the shadows. Marietta felt a ripple of fear. Surely Hamed would punish Kasim severely for that act of defiance. But it was not Hamed who reacted first.

With a cry of rage, Roxelana kicked out at Kasim. The pointed toe of her leather boot caught him under the ribs. She hit him across the shoulders with the switch – hard enough to make him cry out with pain. Hampered by his bonds and the leg stretcher he was knocked off balance.

'You wretch! You'll pay for your disobedience many times over.'

Kasim grinned up at her. 'It was worth it. Do your worst. I care not.'

Using the switch like a goad, Roxelana urged Kasim towards the sturdy wooden chest.

'Get up Marietta,' Hamed ordered, his lip curling with fury. 'We'll leave this wicked slave in good hands. Follow me. I have work for you to do.'

Marietta only had time to see that Kasim was kneeling with his back to the chest and Roxelana was securing his arms to the wooden hurdle that topped it. His ribs were visible under his skin as his back was forced into a bow-shape by his tight bonds. Though he struggled and cursed, Roxelana had her way.

Then Hamed hustled Marietta out of the door and half dragged her along the corridor and back to his apartments.

* * *

Kasim suppressed a groan as Roxelana forced his elbows over the wooden bar and secured them firmly with leather straps.

The wood pressed uncomfortably into his shoulder-blades. He was leaning back slightly, his sore rump pressed firmly against the wooden chest, his knees forced wide apart by the leg stretchers he still wore.

He felt vulnerable and a little afraid. In this position his cock and balls were displayed prominently. Pleasuring Marietta with the feather had made him so hard it hurt. It had been a torture to press so closely to her sex and not be able to plunge himself inside her. The cock-ring bit into his engorged glans, making him ache and throb with repressed pleasure. His sac, tight and hard, hung between his parted thighs, open to Roxelana's gaze and whatever new torments she might dream up.

His earlier bravado faded fast, but he wouldn't let the sharp-faced vixen know that. He knew she would beat him and he felt a sort of welcome thrill at that knowledge. It had been worth anything to taste Marietta again. He ran his tongue around the inside of his mouth, savouring the last faint traces of her sweet musk.

Roxelana stood in front of him, hands on her hips, feet planted squarely. In her shiny, black leather outfit, she was like Sita, the captain of his female harem-guard. There was that same innate cruelty, the enjoyment of dominance over others. He knew that Roxelana would show him no mercy. His buttocks still simmered from the previous beating. That last position, pressed face downwards on the bed, had not been so bad. He had been able to hide his face and stifle his moans.

This time it would be worse. Much worse.

As if she had guessed his thoughts, Roxelana raised her arm and placed a first stinging blow across his chest, followed by another and another. Between the strokes, she concentrated on flicking his nipples with the notched tip of the switch, until they stood out erectly and glowed a deep, poppy red.

Kasim tried not to make a sound as she placed the strokes down the sides of his straining ribcage. He held his moans caged behind his teeth as she beat him with less force on his stomach. Then she placed the strokes higher up again, laying them across the bulge of his pectorals. His silence seemed to anger her. She gave a grunt and concentrated on his abused nipples in earnest.

Though the strokes were less hard, they were as intense. It was the stinging heat; the relentless, moist stroking of the notched tip; and the exquisite soreness, which grew and grew until he thought he couldn't bear it any more, that almost brought a cry from him. He might have remained silent, but Roxelana leant forward and pinched the reddened tips viciously.

She changed her grip when he uttered the first gasping moan. Her little red mouth curved with satisfaction. Then her fingertips played gently over his singing flesh. Up and down his ribcage they went, then dipped to his taut stomach, drawing little rushes of bruised feeling from every one of the red marks that stood out starkly against his white skin.

'So you have a breaking point,' she grinned. 'You cry out with pleasure-pain now. They all do. But don't think I've done yet. I'll have you sobbing and begging me to stop before I finish with you.'

Kasim tossed back the sopping black curls that hung in his eyes and flashed her a look of pure venom. Roxelana smiled back at him. Her cruel mouth was pursed and her green eyes were hot with desire.

'Then again . . . perhaps I'll have you first. Hamed has forbidden it. But who's to tell him? Besides, he's busy. No doubt he's about to bury his flesh inside Marietta. You worked her well. Our master was so inflamed by her reactions that he couldn't wait to get at her!'

She grabbed a handful of his hair and lifted his head so that she could stare into his face.

'Ah. I see that that thought pains you more than this beating.' She made a little sound of disgust. 'She's got all of you dancing on her leash. What fools men are. Can't you see that she's playing you all off, one against the other. It's a game to her, no more.'

'Marietta's not like that,' Kasim said quietly.

'No? Did you know that she went to Hamed of her own free will and seduced him? Gabriel too?'

'You lie!'

Roxelana smiled nastily. 'I was there. I saw how she pleasured Hamed without being ordered to. Ask her why he gave her his ring, if you don't believe me. But she's not so clever. Hamed, Gabriel too, have seen her true colours. She's feckless and manipulative. And she'll pay dearly for it. Hamed's not fool enough to be duped by such a woman.'

Kasim tried to push away the images that came into his mind. Marietta and Hamed. Marietta and Gabriel. He'd expected nothing less. She was a pleasure-slave and they would take advantage of her unique beauty. But to go to either of them freely? To offer them – her love? It was unthinkable. Her love was for him alone. Was that not the reason why he had abased himself? Surely this was not all for nothing.

His eyes pricked and he hung his head so that Roxelana would not see how much she had wounded him.

'Another lick of the lash I think, before I have you pleasure me,' she said pleasantly. 'You'll plunge into me when I order it. Oh, I'll milk you of your juices, just see if I don't.'

When she began to flick the switch back and forth across his cock-stem he did not react. Even when she grasped his sac and closed her fingers tightly around it, he did not flinch.

The desire, which Marietta had prompted, burned in him still, but it seemed to have sunk away and become a sullen ache. He thought of Gabriel and Marietta making love and was inflamed by the image he conjured, even while jealousy ate at him. Roxelana revelled in his distress. It was as if she found his mental distress more compelling than his physical discomfort.

'Keep that cock firm and ready and you'll get your reward,' she hissed, as she laid thin, red lines neatly across his spread thighs. 'I'll take what Marietta wanted from you and think of her while I drain you dry!'

She taunted and goaded him while she continued to beat him. He felt sore and hot from his chest to his knees. It seemed that the feeling on his skin became concentrated. He felt an echo of his torment in his mind. As if all of him, body and soul, was a riot of pain.

And then he found that something strange began to happen. His resistance receded. He began to welcome each stroke of the switch, each new star-burst of pain. As Roxelana moved on to concentrate on a new area of his chest, stomach, or thighs, the last pain faded to be replaced by warmth and a sort of concentration of sensation; as if all his nerve ends were coming more fully to life than ever before.

It was terrifying, this feeling of acceptance, this giving up of the will to resist. He did not hate Roxelana any longer. Every stroke she laid on his sore flesh was like a gift. If she had stopped now, he might have begged her to continue. He clenched his teeth together, hard. Any sound he made would be an entreaty, and that he would never allow.

Was this what it meant to be truly a slave? Did Marietta and Leyla feel this eagerness, this almost overwhelming flooding of gratefulness and submissive lust?

He felt as if he stood outside himself, watching. This new craving was building and building. Something gathered in the pit of his belly. In the centre of the pain there was a jewel-like promise – dark and clear cut. Kasim reached out for it. And felt himself tip over into a bottomless abyss of pleasure in pain.

'Oh, you wretch!' Roxelana screamed, as his seed jetted into the air and splashed onto her hand. 'You did that on purpose to deny me my pleasure!'

Kasim hardly heard her. His hips worked back and forth. He twisted and groaned under the renewed onslaught of the switch. The savage strokes on his cock-stem coaxed from him the continuing ripples of sweet, spiked release.

His sac had become as firm as a stone as the fluid rose into his shaft and burst free from his tortured glans. The restraints prolonged his pleasure past the time he would have believed possible. Tremors ran up his thighs. Shaking, half fainting, he endured the intense paroxysms.

The afterglow of pleasure did not fade for a long time. He caught his breath, as slowly, so slowly, the pressure faded. There was a buzzing sound in his ears. A final drop of semen dripped down his still erect penis.

Roxelana flicked it away with the switch. Her face was twisted with frustration.

'I'll beat you until you weep. Then you'll use your tongue on me. I won't be denied, I tell you. You'll learn that or continue to suffer – slave!'

Somewhere inside Kasim's head he was aware that he screamed; 'No! No!'

But it was not Roxelana's threat that prompted his heated denial. It was himself that he fought. For how could he reconcile himself to the knowledge that he had found ecstasy in surrender, in the negation of his will? He who was so restrained, so careful to keep his responses and desires on a short rein.

Oh, that he, the master, should have been made to understand the delights of being a slave. It was unbearable. Yet he acknowledged the justice of his training. It was right that he should know how Marietta felt when he chastised her. How could he have remained ignorant of the potent pleasures of submission for so long?

A sob lodged in his throat.

He had been made truly a slave – by his own capitulation. He knew with complete certainty that nothing could ever be the same for him again.

Chapter Ten

*H*amed drew the cool, perfumed tobacco deeply into his lungs. The ornate *narghile* bubbled gently as he drew on its flexible pipe. He half-closed his eyes, the better to admire the two perfect near-naked bodies of Marietta and Leyla.

The two women lay sprawled amongst silken cushions. Bishi had prepared them with her usual eye for detail. Marietta wore only black satin slippers, secured by wide, black ribbons which encircled her ankles. The ribbons were tied in a large bow which rested just above her exposed heel. Leyla wore a matching pair of slippers, but hers were white.

Leyla moved her hand down over the curve of Marietta's hip, then up over the indentation of her waist to cup one of her breasts. Bending her head, she began suckling, closing her full red mouth on the pertly jutting nipple.

The way they caressed each other, their languid movements and their eyes, which were drowsy with passion, soothed rather than aroused Hamed. He had ordered Gabriel to prepare the evening's entertainment, but for some reason he found he was not enjoying the spectacle. Marietta and Leyla seemed absorbed in each other. He might not have existed.

He felt lethargic and depressed. Some element was missing from the entertainment. He knew suddenly what it was.

'Bring Kasim here,' he ordered and had the satisfaction of seeing Marietta's hand halt on its path across Leyla's rounded thigh.

'Continue,' he said, none too gently. 'Let not the anticipated presence of your old master hinder your pleasure. Give your sighs, your passionate whispers, to me.'

The expression on both their faces tore at him. What he wouldn't give to have a woman care about him like that. There was devotion as well as love for Kasim in the two sets of eyes which regarded him so coolly. Only Otsami looked at him like that and their relationship was hardly one of consuming passion.

He wanted to shock Marietta and Leyla suddenly. To see their eyes brimming with tears, their lips trembling with distress as he ordered Kasim to perform ever more erotic and submissive acts. For in bringing their master low, he also struck at Marietta's and Leyla's happiness. He felt cruel satisfaction at the thought of their sufferings.

Marietta in particular deserved it. She had given him hope, then snatched it away again. He had thought himself too old to be ensnared by any woman, however beautiful. Yet he trembled at the sound of her name. Just the sight of her made him feel weak. He despised himself for feeling that way, but he could not help it.

He had even begun to consider new possibilities. Maybe he should take a wife. The idea appealed to him. But the sight of Marietta's face when she saw Kasim standing in the courtyard, dashed all his hopes. There was no doubt where her true affections lay. Marietta had been playing with Hamed, trying

199

to influence him by weaving a sensual spell around him.

Part of Hamed understood that. What other course was open to her? She had only her beauty and her wits with which to fight him. He was, after all, her adversary. In her situation he would have done the same thing. She had been softening him up, hoping that he would be lenient when she pleaded for Kasim.

He understood, even sympathised. But he felt a bone-deep disappointment. It was a classic situation. An ageing man had been duped by a beautiful young woman. He had let himself fall under her spell because he wanted to.

Now he felt hurt and foolish and he wanted revenge.

He laid aside the flexible tobacco pipe, curling it around the brass bowl of the *narghile*. He stroked his chin with one strong, calloused finger. Knowing how Gabriel hated Kasim, he was sure that his slavemaster would take the opportunity to put Kasim through his paces.

A slow smile spread across his face. How better to punish Marietta than to force her to watch while Gabriel worked a new slave.

Hamed stood up and clapped his hands.

Gabriel hurried to fetch Kasim. Hamed was in a strange mood this night. He had never seen his master so melancholy. Perhaps he could devise a special entertainment to please him.

As he neared the old quarter of the stronghold, Gabriel recalled how his first master, Selim the jewel merchant, had broken him to the servitude of pleasure. Selim had been a good teacher. His methods were harsh but never overly cruel. Gabriel would use those same methods on Kasim. He judged that Kasim was about ready to begin the next level of training. According to Roxelana, he had responded to the regular beatings with a quite extraordinary eagerness.

'It's as if he secretly yearned to be beaten. Perhaps no one ever dared lay hands on him before,' she told Gabriel.

'Perhaps Kasim knows more than he expected to about becoming a slave,' Gabriel replied grimly. 'He is about to learn a lot more.'

Privately Gabriel almost envied Kasim. There was so much that was new to him, so many spiked pleasures to discover. And it was to be Gabriel's delight to initiate Kasim.

When he entered the mean little room, Kasim was asleep on the bed. He was naked, except for a thin strap around his waist, and he was tethered by his wrists and ankles to the bed posts. He lay on his back, his slim, strongly muscled limbs relaxed. One leg was bent at the knee. It sagged to one side, opening out the area of his lower belly. The pale tendons under the paler skin of his groin, were prominent in the fitful light.

Gabriel's eyes was drawn by the thick silky curls that surrounded Kasim's cock, which was erect even in sleep. It lay to one side of the hard belly. The shaft was firm and enticing and the glans, free as it was from any skin-covering, looked as soft as brushed silk.

Gabriel stood looking down at the sleeping man for a moment. Though he fought to deny it, he saw that there was something noble, even beautiful about Kasim. Despite his reservations, he had always been drawn to this man. There was a quality of leadership, something that inspired devotion, about him. Gabriel knew how cold and severe Kasim appeared to those who did not know him well. But he knew also what passion was caged within that strong, spare frame. The more Kasim wanted someone, the more he resisted giving in to his baser urges. If anything, that was his fatal weakness.

The black and gold shadows, provided by the rush lights, highlighted the hollows and planes of Kasim's body. His skin was pale and unblemished except for the striation of whip marks across his chest and stomach. There was a strip of darker skin at his neck, where the sun had tanned the exposed flesh above his tunic neckline.

Kasim was so deeply asleep that he did not sense Gabriel's presence in the chamber. He muttered something in his sleep and half turned onto his side. One arm was bent behind his head, forming a pillow for his cheek. The night-black curls tumbled over the bent arm. Against them Kasim's profile was as clear-cut as a Greek statue.

The muscles moved under his skin as Kasim buried his cheek against the flesh of his inner arm. A patch of dark hair was visible in his shadowed armpit. He breathed deeply, looking as relaxed and innocent as a child, his ribs rising and falling in gentle rhythm.

The leather body-harness hung on the wall. It gleamed from a fresh application of polish. Gabriel smiled. Kasim must have requested that Roxelana remove the harness before he slept. What had she made him do to earn that privilege?

At the images that sprang to his mind, a pressure built in Gabriel's groin.

Marietta stood in the small chamber next to the room where Gabriel stood looking down on the sleeping Kasim.

'See how eager my slavemaster looks?' Hamed whispered, close to her ear. 'How will he wake Kasim do you think? With the lash – or with a kiss? Look at Gabriel's face. He is torn by both desire and thoughts of revenge. And you, my dear, are at the centre of this dilemma. Does not that thought shame you?'

Marietta clenched her hands together so tightly that the nails bit into her palms. She knew it was true that both Gabriel and Kasim loved and wanted her. But it was not her fault. She had not tried to make this thing happen. It was just the way things were. The knowledge that they both suffered tormented her. She wished there was some way to resolve the problem.

Oh, why did jealousy and hatred have to get in the way? She had never wanted anyone to be hurt on her account. It seemed natural and right for her to love two men. Perhaps her French blood made her more able to accept that fact. For now, she could not deny her feelings for either of them. Kasim was embedded in her heart as firmly as an arrow-tip and somehow Gabriel had worked his spell on her too.

She needed the jewel-dark presence of Kasim beside her for always and Gabriel, who blazed like the sun, owned a larger part of her than she had cared to admit. For a while Kasim had eclipsed all thoughts of anyone else. But her feelings for Gabriel had been only sleeping. Meeting the blond slave again had forced a shift in her perceptions.

Might it be possible for all of them to live together in harmony? She thought of that often while she lay curled next to Leyla in the dark hours before dawn. She could accept the fact of loving more than one person. Why could not Gabriel and Kasim reconcile themselves to it too?

Instinctively, she knew the answer. Women found those things easier. Leyla and herself were devoted friends and lovers. Neither of them felt the need to compete with each other for Kasim's affections. It did not matter that each shared pleasures with him. Each was content with the place they occupied in his heart.

It could have been the same with Kasim, Gabriel,

and herself. But Kasim and Gabriel struck sparks from one another. Partly it was their stubborn male pride. Each one of them needed to feel that they alone were first in her affections. But it was also the fact that their feelings towards each other were unresolved. The solution was so simple. If only they would seek it.

Oh, how she hated them being enemies. She did not think she could bear to watch as Gabriel misused Kasim.

It was cruel of Hamed to bring her here to this tiny room. His strong hands held her captive and she had no choice but to look through the space between the bricks into the room beyond.

The stonework was cold against her naked flesh. Hamed pressed her close to it, so that the rough edges dug into her. His breath was hot against the back of her neck. She felt his arousal, his hard thighs warm against her buttocks. The musty smell of the little room clogged her nostrils. She struggled in Hamed's grip, but he was immovable.

'Watch,' Hamed hissed. 'See what a good slave Kasim has become. Gabriel will test his obedience and, if he is not prompt in doing as he is ordered, Gabriel will beat him.'

Marietta shut out Hamed's voice. Her whole attention became centred on the two figures visible through the narrow space. She shivered, partly from the chill in the room, but also with trepidation. She did not want to watch, but now she could not look away.

Kasim sighed gently and moved in his sleep. How peaceful he looked.

How vulnerable and how achingly desirable.

A sigh, which escaped Kasim's lips, seemed to penetrate right through Gabriel.

He felt the stirring of desire. It was sudden and

unexpected. Kasim was completely at his mercy, yet somehow he still seemed defiant, vital in all his splendid male beauty.

Roxelana had followed Hamed's orders to the letter and Gabriel knew that an ivory phallus was buried deep within Kasim's anus, stetching and easing the tight opening. The only visible sign of the object, in the position in which he lay, was the thin strap which ran between his legs and connected to the waist strap, at both back and front.

It must be degrading for Kasim to have to wear the strapped-on device, both night and day, knowing that he could not work the phallus free of his body. Worse still was knowing that he was being trained as an instrument of pleasure. Surely the thought of being ordered to submit for any and everyone's gratification must haunt his days and nights. Gabriel found the thought pleasing.

Kasim knew how Gabriel had felt now. As a pleasure-slave Gabriel had been taught how to lose the emphasis of self; the importance of the individual. No one but the master's or mistress's wishes mattered.

Gabriel had learnt his lessons well. And in them he had found a unique freedom. Did Kasim begin to savour the humiliation, Gabriel wondered. Had he also embraced that special freedom; the freedom that came with the giving up of his will, the denial of all choice? Gabriel would test the depths of these new and subtle emotions.

The little orifice between Kasim's buttocks was surely ready to be plundered. The size of the ivory phallus had been increased daily, until now it was the length and circumference of an average male organ. How enticing it would be to remove the phallus, oil the puckered little mouth, and ease himself into Kasim's hot – perhaps willing – interior.

For a moment longer Gabriel hesitated. It would be

205

too cruel to wake the prisoner from sleep with such an act. He was not a natural sadist. Then he recalled the time when Kasim had pressed him face down onto the velvet bedcover in his private apartments and plundered his body without the least gentleness. How Gabriel had burned for release that time, his cock straining and weeping salty moisture as Kasim slammed into him.

But Kasim had taken his pleasure and left Gabriel sobbing with outrage, his body aroused and left wanting.

Well, Gabriel was his slave no longer and Kasim was there for the taking. Slowly Gabriel's hands strayed to his belt. He opened the front of his leather trousers and released his strongly erect member.

Watching, Marietta held her breath. The sight of Gabriel's erect organ sent a shiver of mingled horror and lust down her spine. She wanted to turn away, but conversely she wanted to watch Gabriel force Kasim to pleasure him. Even – she forced herself to admit – to join in with what was to happen. Her tongue snaked out to moisten her mouth. She remembered the taste of Gabriel, musk and lemongrass. And the texture of Kasim's skin, so smooth and cool against her lips.

Moving swiftly now, Gabriel grasped Kasim around the waist and tossed him fully onto his stomach. Half awake, Kasim cursed and struggled, but Gabriel had the advantage of his greater strength and Kasim was hampered by his bonds.

Kasim's struggles excited Gabriel further. The way the naked limbs strained against him as Kasim fought to escape, was intoxicating. He could smell Kasim's cleanly scrubbed skin and the spice of fear on his breath as they thrashed together on the bed.

'I . . . could beat . . . you into submission. But I prefer it like this,' Gabriel grated. 'I like to feel you fighting me. It is no use, of course.'

He grabbed the leather waist-strap and jerked on it, hard. Kasim swore as the leather cut into him before the belt parted with a snapping sound. Reaching between Kasim's buttocks, Gabriel took hold of the end of the phallus. He jerked the object free and tossed it onto the floor.

'Now. Are you ready to be used – slave? Show me how willing you have become.'

Gabriel laughed as Kasim grunted in outrage and struggled harder.

'You call this submission?' he sneered. 'Come on slave. Split your crease for me!'

Gabriel kneeled between Kasim's thighs. His cock nudged at the taut buttocks of the man spread out beneath him. Though Kasim's struggles did not lessen, Gabriel sensed an erotic tension in him. Perhaps he had anticipated this assault, even longed for it. Kasim had been kept without sexual easement for many days. Something he was not used to.

'I'll use you, as you used me, remember?' Gabriel said, pressing with all his weight onto Kasim's back and hips to hold him still. He clawed at the tightly clenched buttocks, dragging them open to expose the unwilling little mouth.

'How does it feel to be helpless, eh? To know that your body can be used for another's pleasure, whether you wish it or not?'

'Damn you!' Kasim spat.

Gabriel used his knees to force Kasim's thighs apart. Then with a cry of triumph he pressed the head of his cock to the well-trained anus. It was oiled and ready. There was only a little resistance before he slipped inside. The sensation of the puckered flesh-ring as it scraped the head of his phallus was wonderful. The grip on his cock-stem was hot, smooth, and delicious.

Gabriel thrust strongly while Kasim moaned and twisted under him.

'That's it – slave. Work that body for me,' Gabriel said through clenched teeth.

Little groans escaped Kasim and his bound hands clenched into fists, but he had stopped resisting so much.

Gabriel was lost in pleasure. This was the man who had betrayed him. Yet, even while he wreaked revenge on his unwilling flesh, he felt an odd tenderness towards him. He squeezed his eyes shut as he pushed himself into Kasim. The sensation of the tight flesh-ring around the base of his stem was exquisite.

In the little side room Marietta pressed her fingers to her mouth. Tears glittered in her wide eyes. This was too much. Kasim was hating everything Gabriel did to him. She could not watch any more. She wanted to run through the door, to throw herself on Gabriel's back and drag him off Kasim.

She almost cried out, but Hamed sensed what she was about. He pressed his large hand to her mouth and though she bit at his fingers, almost sobbing in her frustration, he did not remove it.

Then something about Gabriel's attitude communicated itself to Marietta. There was a subtle shift in the way he held Kasim down. His hands became almost gentle, wondering. Gabriel lifted his head and the flickering rush light brought his expression into clear view. Marietta froze. She saw the troubled grey eyes grow soft and introspective as the bitterness there began to fade. Gabriel's well-shaped mouth started to tremble.

Marietta stopped struggling against Hamed. A strange feeling rose within her. There was no violence now in the way that Gabriel took his pleasure. Kasim too had quietened. He seemed to have stopped struggling altogether. There was a moment of intense silence, like the calm before a storm.

And she began to hope . . .

Suddenly Gabriel was ashamed of taunting Kasim.

There was no nobilty in taunting a caged animal, only shame for the tormentor. He reached out and stroked Kasim's muscular back. The hurt inside him, nurtured for so long, fragmented, gave way.

'Why did you betray me?' Gabriel found himself asking.

'I . . . did not,' Kasim grunted, twisting his flushed face to one side.

'Liar!' Gabriel said, tangling his hand in the loose black hair and jerking Kasim's head back. 'Liar,' he said again, but the word came out like an endearment.

He plunged against Kasim's firm, pale buttocks, feeling his balls brush against the velvet skin of Kasim's sac. Kasim loosed a strangled groan. Gabriel grinned inwardly. There was no doubt that Kasim was enjoying being forced. He lost all control and began bucking and sweating under Gabriel, rubbing the head of his straining cock against the thin mattress.

Kasim murmured something so low that Gabriel could not hear it. He bent forward and, to his astonishment, realised that Kasim was mouthing his name, over and over, in such a way that it sounded like a prayer.

Gabriel was shaken to his core. He drew his shaft almost all the way out of Kasim's anus and began to rim the little mouth with slow tenderness. He no longer wanted to hurt and degrade Kasim, he wanted to pleasure him, to see his narrow, saturnine face take on an expression of pure enjoyment.

Kasim moaned softly as Gabriel concentrated on varying his strokes. Now and then he would lunge forward, slowly filling Kasim with his hard flesh. Sometimes he drew his member free and rubbed the swollen cock-head up and down the damp cleft of Kasim's buttocks.

But though his body was held in thrall by Kasim's

male beauty, Gabriel's mind ran free. For the first time, he wondered if he had been mistaken about Kasim's part in his imprisonment. Surely Kasim did not hate him. He could feel the way Kasim pressed himself back against him, the way he allowed Gabriel the use of his body. Kasim wanted Gabriel. And Gabriel was glad of it.

Suddenly Gabriel was tired of carrying the weight of revenge. There had always been a powerful attraction between Kasim and himself. Loving Marietta, as they both did, had only served to complicate that fact. He leant forward, so that he lay pressed to Kasim, skin to skin, connected closely by belly and chest to Kasim's rump and back.

Holding in his desire with a supreme effort he ceased to move. He mouthed the back of Kasim's neck, feeling the soft dark curls against his cheek. Flicking out his tongue, he tasted the salt on Kasim's skin. 'Tell me the truth, now. And have done,' he ordered gruffly. 'Do it now and we'll never speak of it again. I care not what you did to me. Only admit it and I'll give you the release you crave. You had me thrown into gaol and then sold. Tell me why.'

He waited. He realised only then how much he had longed to hear Kasim explain his actions. Tears pricked behind his eyelids, his inheld breath hurt him as he willed Kasim to speak.

'I swear by all that I hold holy, that I did not betray you,' Kasim said slowly and clearly. 'How could I when I desire you as much as I do Marietta. I gave you the freedom I promised. I detect Sita's hand in the betrayal you speak of. It seems that we were both betrayed.'

Gabriel took a moment to absorb the significance of Kasim's words. Instinctively he knew he spoke the truth. Sita. Of course. How blind he had been. Then he realised that it did not matter. All that had ever mattered was that Kasim had not wanted him. He had withdrawn his attentions. Cast him out from the only place he had ever wanted to be. Which was at the side of Kasim and Marietta, serving and loving them both.

'But why . . . why did you let me go?' Gabriel's voice shook with passion. 'You could have asked me to stay. I would have. Gladly.'

'I know that. I was afraid. I did not want to share Marietta. Even with you.' Kasim turned his head and gave a wry grin. 'That was my mistake. I did not think that it was possible to have everything I wanted. Both of you in fact. You and she would have drawn away from me. I could not bear that. Now I see that perhaps it would not have been that way.'

Could this be the Kasim he knew speaking so candidly? For a moment longer Gabriel held on to the hate, then suddenly it had gone. It was as if a cloud of dark matter was expelled along with his breath.

Gabriel gave a great groan and pulled Kasim onto his side, so that he lay cupped against Gabriel's bent form. All at once he believed him completely. Kasim desired him, even loved him a little. Gabriel cradled the hard muscled body close against his chest. His fingertips nipped at the erect male nipples, pinching and squeezing them until Kasim squirmed and strained back against the cock-stem that pierced him so completely.

'Please. Oh, please . . .' Kasim murmured, and Gabriel was lost.

As he began to move again inside Kasim, slowly at first, he reached down and closed his fingers around Kasim's aching hardness. Moving his hand up and down he collared the glans, feeling it swell and throb against his palm.

Kasim gasped as the squeezing fingers milked him, and he began to work his hips, responding to the leashed violence of Gabriel's passion. Gabriel's hand worked up and down as he pumped Kasim's cock.

Their bodies slipped against each other, sweat-slick and hot, as they coupled with hungry and desperate passion.

The heat within Gabriel gathered and erupted. He cried out as he emptied himself into Kasim. At that same moment he felt the warm spurting of Kasim's seed. Kasim rose up against him, almost sobbing out his relief. They remained locked together, Gabriel's heart thudding against Kasim's back, until their breathing quietened.

Tenderly now, Gabriel eased himself free and positioned himself so that he lay facing Kasim. He stroked the red weals on Kasim's pale flesh and encircled the bonds at his wrists.

'You do realise that I am still the slavemaster to Hamed and I owe him my loyalty? He has been a good friend to me. For the appointed time I follow Hamed's orders.'

'I understand,' Kasim said coolly. 'Do what you must. It is *kismet*.'

'I will do Hamed's bidding. But I cannot find it in my heart to be cruel to you, Master.'

Lifting his hands, Gabriel cupped the narrow, hard face and gazed into eyes that looked as black as night. When he spoke there was a catch in his voice: 'And after you leave this place. I shall come too?'

Kasim nodded, his hard mouth creasing at the corners in a smile. His hands came up to cover Gabriel's.

'It will not be easy, but we shall make a new beginning. Now. Tell me now what happened to you to make you hate me,' Kasim said evenly. 'Sita took you. What then?'

'I will tell you later. It matters not. Only this matters now . . .'

Bending forward Gabriel claimed Kasim's mouth. Kasim responded with fierce passion, sucking at Gabriel's tongue and nibbling at the tender skin of his lips. As Gabriel tasted Kasim, he seemed to absorb his very essence. The prolonged kiss became the most intimate of acts, sealing their relationship. Somehow it was more binding than the joining of their two bodies had been.

Kasim's breathy moan of passion vibrated down his throat. And for Gabriel, some of the ache of loneliness disappeared for ever.

Marietta pressed her forehead against the damp stonework and drew in a shuddering breath. In the next room Gabriel and Kasim were sharing a loving embrace.

The impossible had happened. She could hardly believe it. Her hopes and dreams had a chance of coming true now.

Behind her Hamed was rigid with anger. His fingers held her with a hurting grip, but she did not care. She felt weak with happiness and a raging desire.

Watching Gabriel make love to Kasim – for that's what the chastisement had become – she had experienced a stab of wanting, so powerful that her knees almost buckled. Her sex throbbed and burned. She felt the gathered wetness there. Every tiny movement caused the surfaces of her sex-lips to rub slickly together.

When Hamed thrust his hand roughly between her thighs she tried to draw away, not wanting him to know how powerfully she had reacted to the scene in the next chamber. Her arousal was hers alone this time, not something for a slave to give to a master for his pleasure. But it was too late.

'As I thought,' Hamed said with pain and fury in his voice. 'You're wet for them. You desire both Gabriel and Kasim, don't you? And now I know what their true feelings are for each other! Gabriel professes to be my slavemaster, ha! You're traitors all of you.

'Well I care not. I'll deal with you all later. But first, you, Marietta, pleasure me. You're ready enough.'

Marietta froze. She felt too emotionally fragile to respond to Hamed. Even pretence was beyond her. Her heart and blood cried out for the satisfaction offered by the two men she loved. It was impossible for her to share any part of that with someone else. Surely Hamed would respond if she explained. He was intelligent, open to reason.

'Hamed. Please. I . . . I do not wish it. Not now . . . I beg you to allow me to refuse you.'

'You refuse?' Hamed sounded incredulous. 'You forget yourself. A pleasure-slave's function is to obey. That is all.'

Without preamble, he freed his cock and grasped her roughly around the waist. Nudging her thighs open with his knee he bent her over and began jabbing his staff between her spread buttocks. His breath was hot and urgent on the back of her neck. In his eagerness he was clumsy.

Marietta closed her eyes. The tears squeezed through her lashes and trickled down her cheeks. The expected intrusion was hateful to her. For the first time she experienced deep revulsion at being forced to submit.

She tensed, ready for the thrust of the hard male flesh, but it did not come. For a while longer Hamed butted against her, using his hand to try and insert his rapidly dwindling member. At last he realised it was useless to persist. She felt how small and soft he had become and was grateful that the threat was past.

'Your failure is my blessing, my Lord,' she whispered softly.

With a strangled sob, Hamed pushed her away. Turning away he adjusted his clothes. When he turned back to her, she saw that he was trembling

with repressed emotion. She dared not meet his eyes.
He grasped her wrist and dragged her from the room.

'Where . . . where are you taking me . . . ?' she
gasped, alarmed by his attitude.

'To the place where all treacherous and disobedient
slaves go. To the place of correction.'

It was useless to resist him, he was too strong. She
allowed him to lead her down the corridor and
through a low archway. The light there was dim and
it felt wet underfoot. Her heart beat fast, but she
comforted herself with the thought that there were
only two weeks left before Hamed would set his
captives free. Just a few days more and then . . . a
new beginning.

Nothing Hamed did would alter that fact. The
place of correction could not be so bad. She had once
been exhibited in the souk, displayed naked and
beaten on the platform of public punishment, and
she had survived that. There could be nothing worse
to face at Hamed's hands. A dismissive little laugh
rose in her throat, but at Hamed's next words it died
away.

'Hurry now Marietta. For Roxelana awaits you and
she is eager for your company. I have to leave my
stronghold on business, but you'll be in safe hands
until I return.'

She had never seen him so angry, or so hurt. A
chill spread through her. Hamed was one thing.
Roxelana was quite another.

Chapter Eleven

Marietta wept and twisted under the bite of the broad leather strap. Padded manacles held her captive. She pressed herself to the hard stone wall in an effort to escape, but Roxelana jerked her forward. The strap cracked against her sore buttocks again and again. Marietta moaned as each new explosion rioted through her.

But though Roxelana beat her steadily, the blows were designed only to punish, never to damage. The broadness of the strap ensured that Marietta's skin stung and grew sore, but it would not be unduly marked. Marietta pressed her thighs together as the edge of the strap scraped across her pubic fleece, but her tormentor dragged her legs apart and secured her ankles to rings set into the wall. As the strap slapped at her inside thighs, Marietta cried out more loudly. She was afraid that Roxelana would beat her sexual mound and that fear made the sweat break out on her skin.

Tears poured down Marietta's flushed cheeks. Every inch of her skin seemed to be glowing. Soon she would beg Roxelana to stop and the thought that she was near to breaking was more unbearable than the pain. She swallowed the pleas that rose to her lips as she realised that the intervals between each new lick of the strap were growing longer.

Perhaps Roxelana tired. The blows were slowing. They came intermittently now, drawing little flares of pain from her abused flesh. Roxelana's green eyes glittered as she teased Marietta with the lash, playing it almost gently across her thighs and her simmering buttocks. Moving close, she pressed the flat side of the strap against Marietta's parted sex-lips, grinning with satisfaction when she saw the wetness that darkened the leather.

'Even at such a time your hot little sex awakes,' she mocked. 'It would be a pity to neglect such a hungry morsel.'

Marietta tried to twist away from the eager fingers which slipped between the lips of her vulva and pinched at the tender flesh. Her bud pulsed as if it had become the heart of her body. Though she hated the intrusive fingers and winced at each touch of her sore flesh, she felt the familiar building of pleasure.

Deep in her belly a fire awoke and would not be quenched. Not even when Roxelana beat her buttocks in time with the strokes of her fingers. Marietta bucked against the cold stone, pressing into it with her hip, feeling it scrape against her thigh. Words of denial rose up in her, as the familiar feeling of submission flooded her. She sank down onto the slippery fingers, feeling them enter her body and begin to work in and out.

'No. No,' she breathed, fighting herself as her sore and heated buttocks seemed to find an echo in the delicious throbbing that spread through her sex.

Oh, it was hateful to moan and writhe with pleasure while Roxelana stared intently into her face, searching for and relishing every flicker that crossed it Though her cheeks burned with shame, she felt her climax approaching. Every muscle in her body tensed. Impossible to stop the outrush of sensation.

She choked on a scream as she came. It felt as if her whole body exploded in a white-hot spasm of pleasure. Every inch of her abused skin resonated to the heavy, pulsing rhythm in her womb. She bent her head and sobbed with the delicious anguish of it.

'I hate you,' she hissed under her breath.

Roxelana grinned. 'I know. That's what makes you so enticing.' She withdrew her fingers and laid the strap aside.

'Rest now,' she said in a curious tone that was almost gentle. 'There will be more of this in the days to come. Much more. I'll awaken your flesh to many delights of pleasure and pain. And you will be glad to do my bidding.'

Marietta lifted her head and glared her defiance. 'Never will I do anything for you . . . willingly. Hamed will come for me soon. Or he'll send Gabriel.'

Roxelana laughed. 'Hamed has forgotten you. And no one but me knows that you are here.'

Days passed and no one came to fetch Marietta.

A chill draught blew under the ill-fitting wooden door. A tiny window, glazed with thick, greenish glass, let in a small amount of diffused light.

Marietta sat on a wooden platform, covered with straw. Huddling under the one thin blanket Roxelana allowed her, her feet curled under her for warmth. The white satin slippers, once so exquisite, were scuffed and stained, the toes torn where she had scraped them against the floor as Roxelana beat her. Apart from the ruined shoes, she was naked.

There was a bucket in one corner of the room and a flask of clean water on a solid wooden block which was placed up against one wall. Manacles of lined and padded leather hung from rings set into the wall and the block. There was no furniture, no light, nothing to divert the prisoner from the knowledge that this was a place of correction.

Roxelana had made it clear that Marietta must beg for any and every concession to her comfort.

This, Marietta refused to do. Time after time she bit back her pleas. Roxelana could force her to obey her, force her to feel pleasure, but she could not make her collude in her own mistreatment.

Each day was the same. She lost track of time and began to fear that she would end her days in the awful place. Surely Hamed had forgiven her disobedience by now. Why did he not come for her? Why did Gabriel not come? Perhaps it was true that no one knew she was there.

As she moved, the blanket brushed against her sore skin. Her buttocks felt warm and tingly from the most recent beating. She winced. Roxelana was more pitiless than any man. She had never been beaten so thoroughly or so often. Roxelana was an expert with a whip or a leather paddle. She knew just when to stop before the pain became unbearable, or there was danger of any lasting damage.

After every beating Marietta's skin was anointed with soothing oil, so that the tenderness, the sting, faded quickly to be replaced by a horribly beguiling warmth. Every movement seemed to send little shards of sensation to her nerve ends. Sensations which mirrored closely the feeling of sexual arousal.

It was then that Roxelana would coax the pleasure from Marietta's body. Sometimes she brought an ivory phallus to insert in whatever orifice she favoured that day. Other times she used her tongue or fingers to bring Marietta to a shattering climax. Marietta was filled with self-loathing at the way she responded. She tried to hold back, but her well-trained flesh betrayed her. Always there would come that eagerness, that tingle of welcome, for any master or mistress who sought to chastise her.

Even the uncaring caress of the blanket on her sore skin sent stealthy fingers of lust to her groin. She pushed her feelings away, practising suppressing them for when Roxelana was near. One glimmer of weakness, one moan of pleasure, and Roxelana exploited it to the full. Marietta recalled Roxelana's parting words.

'Ask me nicely and I'll bring you some fresh fruit to eat,' she purred. 'That wouldn't be so difficult to do. Come now. Ask me. Let me see that pretty mouth shape itself around an entreaty.'

Marietta glared at her tormentor. She knew from bitter experience that things were not that simple. Roxelana desired more than pretty words before she bestowed any favours. She wanted Marietta to crawl on her knees, to offer her sexual services freely. And Marietta did not intend to give her that satisfaction.

'Keep your fruit,' she spat. 'Just let me out of this place!'

'Please yourself,' Roxelana shrugged. 'But you'll do anything I ask before long. They all do.' Laying aside the thin riding crop, which had added new marks to the striations covering Marietta's buttocks, she left the room.

'Please Otsami. You must help me rescue Marietta.'

Otsami looked down at Leyla who was sprawled across the futon, wearing a silk kimono which hung open to reveal her nakedness. She reached out a tiny, slender hand and drew her fingers lightly across the rich swell of Leyla's breasts. She never tired of looking at them, stroking them, tasting their sweetness. She loved their hugeness and the large wine-red nipples. Women of her own country did not have breasts like that.

'And why,' she said in her sing-song voice, 'must I help you?'

220

'Because I love Marietta. And Kasim and Gabriel love her too. Do you want us all to be unhappy?'

Otsami considered this as she continued to caress the creamy underswell of Leyla's breasts. She saw with satisfaction that Leyla's long black eyes were taking on the glazed look which she had begun to recognise.

'No,' she said. 'But I want to be happy also. This Marietta has many lovers. If I help you, you will go away. And I shall be alone. More alone than before . . . before this.'

She slid herself onto the futon beside Leyla and kissed the side of her full red mouth. Leyla turned to her and gathered Otsami into her arms. Holding her close, she kissed her deeply, her lips opening to suck at the delicate pink tongue.

Leyla pressed on Otsami's shoulders and held her at arm's length.

'But you need not be alone, sweet lady. Come with us. Kasim will welcome you to his house. He is rich and has many women.'

A smile creased Otsami's longish, oval face. Her slanting black eyes were bright as jet.

'Oh, Leyla. I did not think you would ask.'

Leyla reached for the small lacquered box which lay beside the bed. Opening it she took out two small metal balls, the size of quail's eggs. Handing one to Otsami, she smiled.

'How could I leave you behind when you have given me such gifts as these?'

'Then allow me,' Otsami said, moving forward with swift grace and taking the little balls from Leyla's hands.

She pressed Leyla back onto the futon and ran her hands down over the lush white body. The kimono fell away and lay on the futon like the bright folds of a butterfly's wings. Leyla linked her arms behind her head and let her thighs fall open. Otsami's tiny white

221

hands slipped over Leyla's belly and down to the parted mound of her sex.

Otsami marvelled every time she touched the deep-red folds. Everything about Leyla's body was so – luxuriant. The feel of her intimate flesh, so silky and fragrant. Gently she parted the plump flesh-lips, loving their engorged firmness, and slipped the two little metal balls inside Leyla's vagina.

'So much better for a lover to insert the *rinnotama*,' she murmured. 'Sit up a little and rock back and forth as I pleasure you.'

Leyla did so. The *rinnotama* moved inside her, making a gentle, muted clicking sound as they rolled about. She began to breathe more deeply as Otsami's delicate fingers moved in circles around her hooded bud.

Otsami's small, pink tongue licked her own lips as she stroked and rubbed at Leyla's flesh-hood. Ah, how strongly erect her little pleasure-bud is as it slips free of its covering. So firm and jutting against my finger, she thought. It is almost like a man's *henoko*. I shall take it into my mouth and suck it soon and then Leyla shall plunge the little flesh-stem inside me.

Leyla's head fell back, exposing the white column of her neck as her hips began to work back and forth. Little moans escaped her as the metal balls rolled and clicked inside her. Moisture seeped out of her and gathered like honey around Otsami's delicate fingers. 'Say you'll come with us . . . when . . . we leave . . .' she murmured. 'Oh, Otsami. Sweet Otsami . . .'

Otsami reached two fingers deeply inside Leyla's vagina, rotating the metal balls while the tension in Leyla's pelvis built to a crescendo.

Gabriel listened to the sighs coming from behind the paper partition.

He smiled to himself. Leyla had done it. She had persuaded Otsami to help them escape. By the whis-

222

pers and the passionate sounds, he knew that the victory had been an easy one. Leyla and Otsami were well-suited, with much in common. He was happy for them. It had troubled him that Marietta had been the centre of so much attention recently. Leyla was too gentle, too loyal, to comment or react. But he had wondered if she felt hurt or left out.

Now with Otsami for a friend and lover, there would be no problem.

The generosity of women never failed to amaze him. Was it possible that Kasim and himself could find the inner peace of a similar contentment? He did not know, but he was willing to try. There was no choice really.

The months alone, when he had thought himself betrayed, had been the most miserable of his life. His judgement had been impaired by his grief, otherwise he would have seen what Kasim pointed out.

It had been Sita all along who had misused him. Sita, the female guard, who was eaten up with jealousy and envy. She had let Gabriel think that Kasim had ordered his arrest and his sale in the slave market. Well, one day there would be a reckoning. But that wasn't important at the moment.

First they must free Marietta, then they must get away from the stronghold. All else would become resolved in the fullness of time.

A spasm crossed his remarkable face. How truly painful and pleasurable it was to love. Sometimes the pain almost broke him in two.

But how much worse was the void, when all emotion was distilled into hate.

The door opened with a creaking sound. Marietta blinked against the flare of light as Roxelana reappeared holding a lantern aloft. In the other hand she carried a bucket. Hanging the lantern on a wall hook, Roxelana advanced towards the platform.

223

'Sleep well?' she said conversationally. 'Up you get. It's time for your bath. I'm going to be your bath attendant. Aren't you lucky?'

Marietta did not reply. She pushed the cover aside and sat up warily. There was a high spot of colour on each of Roxelana's cheeks. Her pretty cat-face was animated and eager. From bitter experience, Marietta knew that Roxelana was at her most unpredictable when in a good temper.

'Hurry up now. Stand over there on the wooden block.'

Marietta hastened to obey. Roxelana was quite capable of flinging the contents of the bucket over her if she refused to co-operate. She climbed onto the block, which was large enough for her to lie full-length, and stood facing Roxelana. What new torment did she plan? Marietta had been taken daily to a small bathing place over the past few days. Why the change in routine?

'Put your hands in the manacles,' Roxelana said. She secured Marietta's wrists to two rings set low down in the wall. Marietta would be able to sit or lie down, while remaining restrained.

The padded leather cuffs were not uncomfortable, but the usual feeling of swimming helplessness at being held captive flooded her through and through. There was spiked pleasure in this feelng, a willingness to submit. Oh, Kasim you taught me too well. It is so hard to resist. She tried not to let Roxelana know this. But perhaps she did know it.

Roxelana's little red mouth was pursed in a half-smile. She reached out a hand as if she would stroke the soft flesh of Marietta's thigh: 'So beautiful . . .' but the touch did not connect. Swiftly Roxelana turned the movement in another direction, swooping her hand up to pat her tumble of red curls.

Marietta could not look at her. Inside her a little pulse began to beat treacherously.

224

Roxelana rested the bucket on the wooden block. She dipped her hand inside and withdrew a dripping sponge.

'Sit down,' she ordered. 'Lean back on your elbows and let your knees fall apart. Relax. I want you to enjoy this. I'm going to.' She smiled, showing her little white teeth.

Slowly Marietta did as she was bid. She tried to conceal her tension, but she was afraid. What price would Roxelana exact for giving her this treat? She forced herself to relax. What did it matter what her tormentor's motives were? She would take what was offered and be glad of it. The touch of warm, perfumed water was always a delight.

In a swift, smooth motion Roxelana squeezed water over Marietta's shoulder. Marietta let out a gasp of shock. The water was icy. Roxelana laughed and plunged the sponge back into the bucket. Deliberately pausing before she squeezed the water out, she trickled the cold water all over Marietta's neck, shoulders, and back.

Marietta shivered uncontrollably. Icy runnels ran down her breasts. Gooseflesh rose on her skin and her nipples shrank to hard pink points. She twisted and turned trying to avoid the deluge, but Roxelana flicked and splashed the cold water over every part of her.

'Enjoying your bath? Part your legs,' she ordered curtly. 'You'll find that a delicious warmth follows the cold. Soon you'll be panting for my ministrations. Stretch open wider. Do I have to secure your legs as well?'

Reluctantly, Marietta parted her thighs. When Marietta's sex lay open to her view, Roxelana picked up a spongeful of water and trickled it onto Marietta's parted flesh-lips. The water's icy caress made her intimate flesh tighten and ache. Marietta's teeth began to chatter as a sudden keen draught played over her chilled skin.

Roxelana was enjoying herself so much that she did not notice the door of the little room opening. Marietta saw two shadows slip inside the room and advance on Roxelana. She recognised Gabriel and Leyla. Her eyes widened with surprise and relief.

Then everything happened at once.

Leyla threw a sack over Roxelana's head and pushed her off balance. Roxelana fell against the wooden block. Marietta kicked out hard. Her feet connected with the bucket and the rest of the contents poured over Roxelana.

Roxelana screamed with rage as the water soaked her clothes. She rolled onto the floor, twisting and turning as she tried to dislodge the sack. Gabriel kneeled on the struggling woman, while Leyla wound a length of rope around the sack, trussing Roxelana up neatly. Quickly, they freed Marietta's wrists. Gabriel began to rub at her chilled skin with the blanket.

After a few moments the warmth came flooding back into Marietta's body. She smiled up at Gabriel gratefully. The feel of his strong hands and his muscular bulk was reassuring. She really was going to escape.

'Here. Put this on,' he said, placing a thick woollen cloak around Marietta's shoulders.

'I thought I'd have to stay here for ever . . .' Marietta began.

Gabriel kissed the top of her head. 'Forgive us for taking so long to get here. No one knew where you were. Leyla asked Otsami for help. She was only too willing.'

'We must hurry,' Leyla said, smiling briefly at them both. 'There'll be time to talk later. But first . . .'

Picking up a flexible switch which lay on the floor next to Roxelana, Leyla began to strike her with it.

Roxelana cursed and sobbed, her cries muffled by the thick sack. Leyla brought the switch down again and again, each stroke connecting with a crisp snapping sound.

'Take that! And that! You vixen. This one's for me. And this is for Marietta!' Leyla's long dark eyes looked fierce and pitiless.

Gabriel and Marietta watched without speaking as Leyla beat Roxelana unmercifully. Roxelana twitched and howled under the onslaught. After a while she began to whimper. Leyla appeared to be unmoved. She raised the switch for another blow. Marietta put a hand on her friend's arm and took the switch from her hand gently.

'That's enough,' she said evenly. 'Any more and you'll be as bad as she is. You don't want to kill her.'

Leyla nodded, her long dark eyes unfathomable in the light from the lantern. 'No. I don't. I just want her to know how it feels.'

'I think you made your point,' Gabriel said grinning. 'Come then. Shall we go?'

'Where to?' Marietta asked.

'To freedom,' Gabriel said.

'But where . . . ? How . . . ?'

Gabriel laughed and led her towards the door. 'So many questions. I'll tell you on the way.'

'We'll be caught. The risk is too great. Hamed—'

'Hamed has left the stronghold. No one knows when he will return.' Gabriel squeezed Marietta's waist. 'Be brave for just a little longer. This nightmare is almost over.'

As Leyla passed Roxelana, she raised her voice. 'We're going far away. To a place of safety. Farewell vixen!'

As they neared Otsami's apartment Gabriel melted into the shadows and was gone.

'He'll meet us later, never fear. Come,' Leyla ushered Marietta onwards.

Otsami welcomed them at the entrance to her apartments and ushered them inside.

'All is ready. Come with me Marietta. I have clothes for you and hot food.'

Marietta sipped at a dish of tea, grateful for the comforting warmth of the porcelain against her palms. After the austerity of the last few days the peaceful atmosphere of the surroundings was like balm to her soul. Otsami helped her into a kimono and covered her pale hair with a scarf, then she came and sat at the low lacquer table with Marietta.

'With your hair covered, you will be mistaken for one of my attendants when we leave,' Otsami explained.

Marietta ate hungrily from the tiny dishes of food that were laid out before her. She turned to Otsami. 'Thank you for helping me,' she said. 'But you put yourself at risk by coming with us. How will you return in safety?'

Otsami smiled shyly. 'I am happy to help my friend Leyla,' she said in her soft, sing-song voice. 'I . . . I shall not return. Hamed has changed, he is not the man I once knew. I have changed too.'

Marietta did not question her further, though she sensed that there was something left unsaid. She watched Otsami move around the room with smooth shuffling steps. The Japanese woman picked up a large book and stroked it lovingly, then she folded it in a square of silk and put it with the rest of her belongings. Her jet black hair hung in a straight curtain down her back. It swept back into two wing-shapes from either side of her longish, oval, white face.

Marietta was struck by Otsami's serenity. Her movements were slow and graceful. She did not seem alarmed or upset about the prospect of leaving the stronghold for good. Marietta was anxious to get away. At any moment they might be discovered. Where was Gabriel and Kasim? Had they escaped already? Before she could ask, Leyla appeared. She too was dressed in a kimono.

Otsami walked around her, smiling. 'You look charming. Both of you make beautiful *geiko*. Come then. It is time. Keep close behind me. Take tiny steps and do not hurry. Otherwise your walk will betray you.'

They crossed the courtyard and reached a small side gate without incident. It was as they were passing along a main corridor that they were challenged. Marietta felt her heart miss a beat, but Otsami reached calmly inside her robes and produced a small leather case. Marietta recognised the gift Hamed had given her.

'I have Hamed's express authority to leave,' Otsami said, producing Hamed's cabochon ruby ring. 'He orders me and my attendants to join him.'

For an instant longer the guard hesitated, then he waved them on. It was almost too easy. Hamed's ring was the key that opened all other doors. Marietta smiled inwardly. How ironic that his gift had given them their freedom. In less time than Marietta would have believed possible, they stood outside the main building.

Shadows detached themselves from the night and Marietta saw two hooded figures mounted on horses waiting nearby. One of them, tall and spare of build, beckoned. She went towards the figure without hesitation. All her senses were alert to his particular presence. She did not need to see his face to know him. At once she was lifted up and placed in his strong male arms.

'Kasim,' she breathed, absorbing his touch and his familiar, clean smell in one instant.

He did not speak. Only brushing the top of her

head lightly with his lips before wheeling the horse around and cantering off into the darkness. She just had time to catch a glimpse of the other horseman. He too was tall, a little broader than Kasim and completely at ease in the saddle. As he turned his head she saw a strand of blonde hair that fell free of the hooded cloak.

Gabriel. So he was escaping with them. She felt a fierce joy race through her. Leyla mounted up behind Gabriel and Otsami seated herself on the packhorse. The little cavalcade moved off, keeping a gentle pace. Soon Marietta and Kasim were far ahead.

The cool air whipped against Marietta's face. One arm held her close in an iron grip. The horse plunged through the night. Hoofbeats drummed in her ears. She pressed herself against Kasim's warm muscled chest. His hard thighs moved against her buttocks, making her catch her breath as her sore skin awoke at the contact. The warmth and nearness of him was powerfully erotic.

She longed to touch him, to feel his cool skin against her own. For a while she resisted. He threw back his hood and his dark hair streamed out behind him. She saw the clean line of his jaw, his straight nose, and his cruelly sensual mouth. And now the need to reach out to him became unbearable. She slid her hand inside his hooded robe and up over the planes of his chest. There was a gap in his tunic at the neckline. She pressed her fingertips to the hollow of his throat where a pulse throbbed warmly.

Kasim reacted as if she had plunged a knife into him. He made a sound in his throat and reached up to cup the back of her skull in one long slender hand. Turning her face up to him, he swooped down and claimed her mouth in a demanding kiss.

She leant into him as he plundered her mouth. His other arm pressed into the small of her back with almost hurtful strength. She felt as if she was drowning in the warm taste of him. Only the pressure of his knees and thighs guided the horse. She swayed into him, balancing her body to the rhythm of him as he moved in time with the horse. She seemed to feel every muscle, every sinew, of his rigidly held form.

She was breathless and weak when he let her go.

'My Lord,' she murmured against his mouth. Then, emboldened by his response, she whispered, 'I have need of you. Urgently.'

'And I you,' he said gruffly. 'It has been too long.'

Exerting pressure with his knees, Kasim reined in the horse. Nearby was a copse of cypress trees. Waiting for the others to catch them up, he called for them to go on. Marietta felt like laughing aloud at their recklessness. What if they were being followed? What must Gabriel and Leyla think? It was obvious why she and Kasim had stopped. But she did not care. All she could think of was Kasim and the desire that was like a note of music vibrating right through her.

Kasim dismounted first, then helped her down carefully. As she slid down his body, she felt his hardness dig into her belly. The kimono felt strange; the slender tube-shape, hampering her movements so she almost fell. Kasim steadied her, his strong arms holding her close as if he was afraid she might slip free and escape him.

Shaking with need, Marietta leant against a tree as Kasim tore at the kimono. The unfamiliar folds hampered his eagerness. She laughed huskily when he lost patience with the sash and cursed under his breath.

'Do it this way,' she breathed, pulling the garment above her ankles.

He slid the kimono up her body. She wore nothing under the garment and trembled as his hands touched her bare thighs then skimmed over the curve of her hips. Soon she stood naked from the waist down, the silken fabric bunched up around her waist.

Glancing down at her skin, pearl-pale in the moonlight, he caught his breath. His eyes skimmed over the curves of her body, the pouting belly, the lightly shadowed pubis.

'My own Marietta,' he said. 'I have missed your golden presence almost as much as your incomparable body.'

The wind moved in the trees as Kasim knelt before her. She felt his hands move on her thighs, then his warm mouth questing, searching for the hungry and aching heart of her. His loose black hair brushed against her skin. She tensed her belly and pushed towards him. At the first hot contact of his tongue, she cried out. A spasm of wanting seemed to twist her womb.

'It's been so long . . . so long . . .' she murmured. 'Kasim. My life. My love.'

It did not matter that he was too eager, too starved, for gentleness. He stabbed his tongue into her, licking at the juicy little orifice that hungered for the thrust of his hard male flesh. She felt the scrape of his dark stubble as he burrowed into her, the bristles teasing little hot scrapings against her skin. The tip of his tongue pressed against her flesh-hood, imprisoning the bud that ticked beneath the tender folds.

Marietta meshed her fingers in his hair and pulled him closer, grinding her hips, rubbing her soaking vulva against his mouth and chin. Kasim's arms encircled her hips as he ground into her with his lips and tongue. He seemed to revel in the taste and feel of her. Her wanton gyrations drew a moan from him. But he stopped when he sensed that she was near to climaxing.

Standing, he claimed her mouth again. 'I want you to melt with me inside you, my treasure. All the time I was in Hamed's power, I dreamt of doing . . . this.'

In one swift movement he grasped her hips and lifted her onto him. She felt his cock-stem slip inside her. The swollen glans was wonderfully big as it eased inside her tight entrance. She braced her back against the tree as Kasim began to thrust strongly.

'Forgive me. My need is great,' he whispered hoarsely as he plunged into her, holding her close up against his pubis.

She felt his mouth on her neck as he kissed her. He nibbled at her ear lobe, then traced a burning path along her jawline, tasting her skin as if he would imprint her forever on his senses. All the time he moved strongly inside her. She loved his passion. The way she had the power to make him lose control. Was this the same Kasim? The restrained and cold master who chastised her so thoroughly?

This loss of control, was another side of the man she adored. And she loved every facet of him. His dark and secretive desire to hurt her into pleasure; the way he demanded her complete subjugation to his needs; and, conversely the melting submission he was capable of. Would his time spent in Hamed's stronghold bring ever new dimensions to his enigmatic personality?

The scent of him surrounded her. She smelt the night in his hair. The smoky musk of his body and the flatter, animal scent of his arousal. She bucked against him, grinding her erect clitoris against his shaft, but her pleasure eluded her.

He could not hold back much longer and she wanted to come with his hard flesh filling her, working into her with almost hurting force. Slipping a hand between their bodies she pinched the tip of her flesh-lips together, rubbing her bud in a circular motion.

'Yes. Oh, yes. Take your pleasure,' Kasim whispered against her mouth. 'Let me feel you break. Milk me with your sweet inner muscles.'

His words tipped her over. With a muffled groan, she came. Her vagina convulsed around his shaft, forcing his semen into her. As he cried out and spasmed she dug her heels into the small of his back, pressing her sex so closely to his pubis that they seemed forged of one flesh.

His hands cupped her face as he kissed her, murmuring endearments. After-tremors shook him now and then. He held her gently, supported by his bent thighs. He was hard still and he did not withdraw. Soon he began to move again, slowly and without the frantic need of the first coupling.

She moved with him, matching his pace as their pleasure built. Arching her neck, she raised her chin and the headcloth slipped free. Her pale curls tumbled down around them, veiling them against the night's blackness.

Kasim buried his face in the tangled curls, breathing in her clean scent as his pleasure built and crested for the second time. While Marietta hungered still, he drew free and fell to his knees before her. His face was warm against her thighs.

Again she felt his tongue, but this time he pleasured her with long slow licks. Marietta climaxed against his hot mouth almost at once. The spasms were deeper, slower this time; less intense, but they went on and on. She felt the bearing down, that, for her, often followed such intense pleasure. Her sex pulsed and gave up Kasim's seed in a warm flood. Kasim placed a final kiss on her still throbbing bud, then released her pubis for an instant.

Before she had time to encompass the loss of his touch, she felt him lapping their mingled juices from her spread thighs. The gesture was so intensely intimate that it brought tears to her eyes. When he stood up and gathered her to his chest, she sighed and trembled in his embrace, too moved, too lost, for words.

If he hadn't held her she would have sunk to the ground on boneless legs.

She saw that he understood. He laughed and she saw the white flash of his teeth.

'No time to rest, my treasure. We must away before a search is mounted. I should not have tarried. But you are irresistible. Worth everything I own. Worth everything I've had to do.'

At the memory of the public stripping, the harness he'd been forced to wear, she could have wept. How he had humbled himself.

'Oh, Kasim. Am I worth so much to you?' she whispered.

'Never doubt it again,' he said, kissing her briefly.

He stood up and clothed himself. Marietta adjusted her kimono, then took his outstretched hand. They mounted the horse. This time she sat behind him. Kasim urged the horse forward and they galloped away into the night.

With her arms around his waist and her cheek pressed to his broad back, Marietta felt perfectly content. In her happiness she found space to pity Hamed. Nothing had turned out as he'd imagined it. When he returned he would find the stronghold almost empty. There would be only the taste of ashes to welcome him.

Who would comfort the ex-pirate? Roxelana was plainly his favourite no longer and Otsami had deserted him. Then she remembered Bishi. The little servant-girl loved him with simple purity.

Somehow Marietta knew that there was hope for Hamed. And she was glad of it.

Then, into her happiness, there crept a shadow. The matter of Kasim and Gabriel was unresolved. They had formed a truce, of sorts, she had seen them embracing as lovers through the spy-hole, but could they agree to live together?

Oh, if only they would be content to love each

other and love her in turn. Then her world would be perfect. But perfection, she thought, was too much to hope for.

Kasim's back was warm beneath her cheek and the steady rhythm of the horse's movement was soothing. She closed her eyes. It had been an exhausting few days and the thought of returning to the harem was becoming even more beguiling by the second.

Her eyes drooped. She felt satiated in body and mind. All she wanted to do was sleep the clock around. When she woke she would tackle the one thing that nagged at her. Now that she was sure of her feelings for both men, the solution could not be so difficult.

She would worry about Gabriel later.

At this precise moment, she had all she wanted. Kasim. Always, always Kasim, first.

LOOK OUT FOR THE ALL-NEW BLACK LACE BOOKS – AVAILABLE NOW!

All books priced £6.99 in the UK. Please note publication dates apply to the UK only. For other territories, please contact your retailer.

MIXED SIGNALS
Anna Clare
ISBN 0 352 33889 X

Adele Western knows what it's like to be an outsider. As a teenager she was teased mercilessly by the sixth-form girls for the size of her lips. Now twenty-six, we follow the ups and downs of her life and loves. There's the cultured restaurateur Paul, whose relationship with his working-class boyfriend raises eyebrows, not least because he is still having sex with his ex-wife. There's former chart-topper Suki, whose career has nosedived and who is venturing on a lesbian affair. Underlying everyone's story is a tale of ambiguous sexuality, and Adele is caught up in some very saucy antics. **The sexy *tour de force* of wild, colourful characters makes this a hugely enjoyable novel of modern sexual dilemmas.**

WICKED WORDS 10
Various
ISBN 0 352 33893 8

Wicked Words collections are the hottest anthologies of women's erotic writing to be found anywhere in the world. This is an editor's choice of the best stories from over five years of this immensely popular series. With settings and scenarios to suit all tastes, this is fun erotica at the cutting edge from the UK and USA. Combining humour, warmth and attitude with imaginative writing, these stories sizzle with horny action. **A scorching collection of wild fantasies.**

Coming in August

SWITCHING HANDS
Alaine Hood
ISBN O 352 33896 2

When Melanie Paxton takes over as manager of a vintage clothing shop, she makes the bold decision to add a selection of sex toys and fetish merchandise to her inventory. Sales skyrocket, and so does Mel's popularity, as she teases sexy secrets out of the town's residents. It seems she can do no wrong, until the gossip starts – about her wild past and her experimental sexuality. However, she finds an unlikely – and very hunky – ally called Nathan who works in the history museum next door. **This characterful story about a sassy sexpert and an antiquities scholar is bound to get pulses racing!**

PACKING HEAT
Karina Moore
ISBN O 352 33356 1

When spoilt and pretty Californian Nadine has her allowance stopped by her rich Uncle Willem, she becomes desperate to maintain her expensive lifestyle. She joins forces with her lover, Mark, and together they conspire to steal a vast sum of cash from a flashy businessman and pin the blame on their target's girlfriend. The deed done, the sexual stakes rise as they make their escape. Naturally, their getaway doesn't go entirely to plan, and they are pursued across the desert and into the casinos of Las Vegas, where a showdown is inevitable. The clock is ticking for Nadine, Mark and the guys who are chasing them – but a Ferrari-driving blonde temptress is about to play them all for suckers. **Fast cars and even faster women in this modern pulp fiction classic.**

THE BLACK LACE SEXY QUIZ BOOK
Maddie Saxon
ISBN 0 352 33884 9
£6.99

- What sexual personality type are you?
- Have you ever faked it because that was easier than explaining what you wanted?
- What kind of fantasy figures turn you on – and does your partner know?
- What sexual signals are you giving out right now?

Today's image-conscious dating scene is a tough call. Our sexual expectations are cranked up to the max, and the sexes seem to have become highly critical of each other in terms of appearance and performance in the bedroom. But even though guys have ditched their nasty Y-fronts and girls are more babe-licious than ever, a huge number of us are still being let down sexually. Sex therapist Maddie Saxon thinks this is because we are finding it harder to relax and let our true sexual selves shine through.

The Black Lace Sexy Quiz Book will help you negotiate the minefield of modern relationships. Through a series of fun, revealing quizzes, you will be able to rate your sexual needs honestly and get what you really want from your partner. The quizzes will get you thinking about and discussing your desires in ways you haven't previously considered. Unlock the mysteries of your sexual psyche in this fun, revealing quiz book designed with today's sex-savvy girl in mind.

Black Lace Booklist

Information is correct at time of printing. To avoid disappointment
check availability before ordering. Go to www.blacklace-books.co.uk.
All books are priced £6.99 unless another price is given.

BLACK LACE BOOKS WITH A CONTEMPORARY SETTING

☐ SHAMELESS Stella Black	ISBN 0 352 33485 1	£5.99
☐ INTENSE BLUE Lyn Wood	ISBN 0 352 33496 7	£5.99
☐ A SPORTING CHANCE Susie Raymond	ISBN 0 352 33501 7	£5.99
☐ TAKING LIBERTIES Susie Raymond	ISBN 0 352 33357 X	£5.99
☐ A SCANDALOUS AFFAIR Holly Graham	ISBN 0 352 33523 8	£5.99
☐ THE NAKED FLAME Crystalle Valentino	ISBN 0 352 33528 9	£5.99
☐ ON THE EDGE Laura Hamilton	ISBN 0 352 33534 3	£5.99
☐ LURED BY LUST Tania Picarda	ISBN 0 352 33533 5	£5.99
☐ THE HOTTEST PLACE Tabitha Flyte	ISBN 0 352 33536 X	£5.99
☐ THE NINETY DAYS OF GENEVIEVE Lucinda Carrington	ISBN 0 352 33070 8	£5.99
☐ DREAMING SPIRES Juliet Hastings	ISBN 0 352 33584 X	
☐ THE TRANSFORMATION Natasha Rostova	ISBN 0 352 33311 1	
☐ SIN.NET Helena Ravenscroft	ISBN 0 352 33598 X	
☐ TWO WEEKS IN TANGIER Annabel Lee	ISBN 0 352 33599 8	
☐ HIGHLAND FLING Jane Justine	ISBN 0 352 33616 1	
☐ PLAYING HARD Tina Troy	ISBN 0 352 33617 X	
☐ SYMPHONY X Jasmine Stone	ISBN 0 352 33629 3	
☐ SUMMER FEVER Anna Ricci	ISBN 0 352 33625 0	
☐ CONTINUUM Portia Da Costa	ISBN 0 352 33120 8	
☐ OPENING ACTS Suki Cunningham	ISBN 0 352 33630 7	
☐ FULL STEAM AHEAD Tabitha Flyte	ISBN 0 352 33637 4	
☐ A SECRET PLACE Ella Broussard	ISBN 0 352 33307 3	
☐ GAME FOR ANYTHING Lyn Wood	ISBN 0 352 33639 0	
☐ CHEAP TRICK Astrid Fox	ISBN 0 352 33640 4	
☐ THE GIFT OF SHAME Sara Hope-Walker	ISBN 0 352 32935 1	
☐ COMING UP ROSES Crystalle Valentino	ISBN 0 352 33658 7	
☐ GOING TOO FAR Laura Hamilton	ISBN 0 352 33657 9	

BLACK LACE BOOKS WITH AN HISTORICAL SETTING

BLACK LACE ANTHOLOGIES

BLACK LACE NON-FICTION

To find out the latest information about Black Lace titles, check out the website: www.blacklace-books.co.uk or send for a booklist with complete synopses by writing to:

Black Lace Booklist, Virgin Books Ltd
Thames Wharf Studios
Rainville Road
London W6 9HA

Please include an SAE of decent size. Please note only British stamps are valid.

Our privacy policy
We will not disclose information you supply us to any other parties. We will not disclose any information which identifies you personally to any person without your express consent.

From time to time we may send out information about Black Lace books and special offers. Please tick here if you do _not_ wish to receive Black Lace information. ❑

Please send me the books I have ticked above.

Name ....

Address ....

....

....

....

Post Code ....

Send to: Virgin Books Cash Sales, Thames Wharf Studios, Rainville Road, London W6 9HA.

US customers: for prices and details of how to order books for delivery by mail, call 1-800-343-4499.

Please enclose a cheque or postal order, made payable to Virgin Books Ltd, to the value of the books you have ordered plus postage and packing costs as follows:

UK and BFPO – £1.00 for the first book, 50p for each subsequent book.

Overseas (including Republic of Ireland) – £2.00 for the first book, £1.00 for each subsequent book.

If you would prefer to pay by VISA, ACCESS/MASTERCARD, DINERS CLUB, AMEX or SWITCH, please write your card number and expiry date here:

....

Signature ....

Please allow up to 28 days for delivery.